I wa
touch
revea
food.

in annoyance. I picked up the tray and threw it on the ground with a low growl of warning.

Food does not go in the nest! I shouted at him in my mind.

"*Kari.*" Fury poured off of him in a palpable wave that upset my inner wolf. But I didn't back down. He'd tried to soil my space with *fish* and—I sniffed—*beef.*

I glowered at him, not at all caring that the food was now decorating the floor. Better the carpet than my sheets.

"You will *eat,*" he demanded.

I snorted. This had nothing to do with me eating and everything to do with him disrespecting our nest.

"I mean it," he said, his tone ice cold and his purr long gone. "I'm done with this self-harm bullshit."

He wanted to talk about harm? He tried to put *food* in my *nest.* "You're a terrible Alpha." He should know better than to destroy such a cherished space. *My space.* Something I'd never had before. Maybe that was part of his game—this desire to make me feel at home only to remind me that I wasn't home, or safe, and entirely under his control.

My heart skipped a beat.

Yes.

That had been the point of this lesson. He'd allowed me to feel a few days of comfort just to rip it away by—

"A *terrible* Alpha?" His ire spiked across my senses, quieting my inner turmoil for a second.

Did I call him that? I couldn't remember. I was too focused on my nest and the situation and… *Why am I acting like this?* I'd never been territorial before. And I knew better than to consider this bed mine, let alone to make a nest.

"I've bathed you, fed you, purred for you, offered you warmth and protection, and you think I'm a *terrible Alpha?*" His voice rose to a roar of sound that had me shrinking inside the nest and calling to my wolf on instinct alone. Fur sprouted across my skin, shifting me into my animal state faster than I'd anticipated.

Because of the nourishment, I realized.

Already I was feeling stronger, and Alpha Sven had barely given me much more than comfort and food.

A furious growl followed my transformation, the Alpha angrier than I'd ever seen him. "You will shift back right now," he commanded. "Or so help me, Kari, you will *not* like the consequences."

X-CLAN SERIES

Andorra Sector
X-Clan: The Experiment
Winter's Arrow
Bariloche Sector
Hunted

V-Clan Wolves
Blood Sector

BARILOCHE SECTOR

X-Clan Series

To: Becca
#BBBS
Lovely to meet you!

USA TODAY BESTSELLING AUTHOR
LEXI C. FOSS

This is a work of fiction. Names, characters, places, and incidents are either the product of the author's imagination or are used fictitiously, and any resemblance to actual persons, living or dead, business establishments, events, or locales is entirely coincidental.

Bariloche Sector

Editing by: Outthink Editing, LLC

Proofreading by: Katie Schmahl & Jean Bachen

Cover Design: Jay R. Villalobos with Covers by Juan

Cover Photography: CJC Photography

Cover Models: Kristen & Mason

Published by: Ninja Newt Publishing, LLC

Print Edition

ISBN: 978-1-954183-80-3

To Fur Assistant Zoey, your cuddles and support helped me survive this book <3

Special thank you to Bethany, Katie, and Jean, for making this deadline possible. And to Louise and Diane, thank you for keeping me above water and for being my much-needed life support <3

BARILOCHE SECTOR

X-CLAN SERIES, BOOK 4

BARILOCHE SECTOR

Music Playlist

Animals - Architects
Dead Butterflies - Architects
Dying Is Absolutely Safe - Architects
Flight without Feathers - Architects
Haunting - Halsey
Heaven's a Lie - Lacuna Coil
Immortalized - Hidden Citizens
Lithium - Evanescence
Little Wonder - Architects
Purify - Lacuna Coil
Stay Alive - Hidden Citizens
Wicked Game - Three Days Grace
World of Shame - Ego Likeness
Wrong Side of Heaven - Five Finger Death Punch

BARILOCHE SECTOR

AN X-CLAN NOVEL

Life is a series of prisons.
And in the end, there's only death.

Kari Zamora

My father enslaved me. Ruined me. Sold me. Left me to
suffer.
Until *he* rescued me.

Alpha Sven Mickelson of Norse Sector claims to be my
savior, to want me to live, and vows to protect me. But I
know Alphas can't be trusted. All he wants is my mating
bond. To own me. To make me his.

No one cares what I want. I'm just a doll. A being to be
used and depraved.

So maybe I'll use this Alpha instead.
Or maybe he'll become the Alpha I've always craved.

Sven Mickelson

My destiny is to lead. To own. To possess. I'm an Alpha of
significant birthright, and I'm ready to claim what's mine.
Except she continues to deny me.

Omega Kari is broken. Destroyed. A female shredded apart by those she trusted most. And I'm the only one who can piece her back together. If she lets me.

I sense the fighter lurking beneath her fur, and I'm daring her to come out to play. Because when she does, I'll finally be able to stake my claim.

So go on, then, little wolf.
Give me your pain.
And together, we'll burn Bariloche Sector to the ground.

Note: This is a standalone shifter romance with Omegaverse and dystopian elements. Please review the author's note inside for content warnings, as this story contains depressing material.

A NOTE FROM LEXI

This book might be one of the hardest I've ever written. It wasn't the story that I struggled with so much as Kari's voice. She's so incredibly broken. She took me to such a dark place, perhaps the darkest I've ever visited within my own mind. It was a depressing experience, but it blossomed into a tale of beauty and strength.

That said, I feel it's important to warn readers that this book is emotionally distressing. Kari is at the heart of her depression when her story begins, and it bleeds off the pages. She's suicidal, shattered, and hopeless. If you're struggling with sad feelings or easily swayed by depressive material, I would reconsider reading this book. Or start at Part II, where her healing journey begins.

This is a story of growth and strength and power. But for Kari to become the wolf she needs to be, she has to overcome her past.

While other books in this series contain underlying themes of dubious consent, this one focuses on the nurturing aspects of a healing relationship. There are strong elements of non-consent from Kari's past, but this book focuses more on her present and future.

As such, Sven is a different kind of Alpha. He's thoughtful and meticulous, and while he pushes Kari in his own way, he's more respectful about it than other Alphas in this world. He's what Kari needs, even if she doesn't want to admit it.

This story broke my heart. But the end was worth the pain.

I hope you enjoy the final installment of the X-Clan series. And hopefully, we will meet again when I introduce the V-Clan sectors of this world.

Hugs,
Lexi

Content disclaimer: This book contains depressive material, including suicidal thoughts, scenes of self-harm, and strong sensations of hopelessness. This book may not be suitable for readers who are triggered by depressive content.

A WARNING FROM KARI

My world is a nightmare.

I'm a sterile Omega female because my father didn't want me to take a mate. So he turned me into a shell of a being, used solely for male pleasure and dark deeds.

Alphas took me.

They abused me.

They broke me.

I no longer know how to trust or how to live.

My story is cruel. It's twisted. It's not for the faint of heart.

Happy-ever-afters don't exist in this universe. Only pain and suffering and power exchange.

Maybe one day I'll escape it all.

But today isn't that day.

Tomorrow likely won't be either.

Sven Mickelson promises to help me. I don't believe him. I know what he really wants—an obedient little Omega willing to take his knot. He won't give me a choice. He'll take me because he can.

Alphas are all the same.

They're dark, soulless beings with the single-minded desire to procreate.

My father ensured that would never happen.

So now all I am is a fuck sleeve.

I learned my place long ago.

Nothing ever changes.

Because this universe isn't kind; it's savage.

Alphas are dominant and lead. Betas work for them to maintain productive societies. And Omegas are the prized jewels, the rare beings Alphas take as mates to help continue the X-Clan race.

But that's not my story.

I'm an Omega with a broken womb. There's only one fate for me. And it's certainly not one of devotion or love.

You've been warned.

PART
I

SCANDINAVIAN SECTORS

CHAPTER ONE

KARI

WINTER SECTOR

One more night. That's it. Survive this and I'll be... I trailed off on the thought, unsure of how to define my future state. My life rested in Alpha Enrique's hands. I wouldn't be free. There would still be pain. But it couldn't be worse than Bariloche Sector.

The sensors buzzing against my erogenous zones suggested otherwise. They served as a blatant reminder of my purpose in this world.

A pleasure sleeve for Alphas.

They didn't care about my well-being or enjoyment. Only theirs. Always theirs.

Howls reverberated around my cage, sending shivers of cruelty down my spine. My stomach churned. My thighs clenched. And my slick permeated the air.

The vibrations increased, forcing my arousal and sending lightning through my veins. It burned. It throbbed and pulsated. It *hurt*.

One more night, I repeated to myself, willing my mind to relax. *I can handle—*

A fierce growl rose above the others, causing all the hairs along my arms to stand at attention. Blood splattered along the ground as the Alphas brawled. They all had one objective in mind—*knotting me.*

They would take turns. One after another. Until I was a broken mess on the floor.

These sensual stimulators had intensified my state to a point of near estrus, inspiring all the Alphas around me to go into a rut.

Who would break through the barrier first?

Would he be so lost to the violence that I might actually die this time?

Would there be two of them trying to get inside me at once?

I shuddered, recalling the vivid image of my sister being nearly knotted to death just last week. Her mate had been killed, leaving her a pile of bones and flesh with only one purpose—to take a knot.

My eyes fell closed.

Are you alive? I wondered for the thousandth time this week. *Or did peace finally find you?*

I often wondered what death would be like. Quiet. Soft. Gentle. An oblivion of darkness. The ultimate escape.

No, my inner wolf snarled, sending a jolt down my spine and drawing me back to the present. My legs shook with need, my body begging these Alphas to take what belonged to them, to make me whole.

It was a false promise. No matter how hard they tried, I would forever be dissatisfied because of what *he* had done to me.

A knot only created more agony.

Not that the Alphas ever noticed. They gained their release, which was all that ever mattered to them.

A roar of sound had me curling into a tight ball, the violent dance coming to an end.

I didn't even bother to look at who had won. Nor did I

listen to the female Alpha addressing the contestants to discuss whatever came next.

I already knew.

They would take turns in order of strongest to weakest, ensuring the best Alphas in the room had me while I was still conscious.

It worked well for me in the end. The strongest were always the cruelest. And they tended to knock me out first.

Sweet oblivion would be mine soon. I just had to endure. Survive. Wait.

The electricity humming over my skin continued to taunt my reactions to life, ensuring my body provided smooth entry for whoever took me first.

My nipples beaded in false evidence of interest.

All programmed responses to my body's inherent preconditioning. Omegas were born to accept the knot, to be the lowest of society, to serve as slaves who were fucked and used to an Alpha's content.

Betas stood by and did nothing, choosing instead to maintain societal standards by doing whatever the hell they did every day.

And Alphas ruled.

Well, not all Alphas. Only the strongest. The others were warriors who protected the king among them.

Although, from what little I'd seen of Winter Sector, it seemed this colony was mostly Betas. Which explained why Alpha Enrique had been recruited to join Alpha Vanessa's ranks. She needed a Second, someone to protect her back and serve at her beck and call.

The Alpha of Bariloche Sector had told me I was to be Alpha Enrique's gift for his service. He'd told me to be a good Omega and do whatever was asked of me. In return, he might one day tell me the fate of my sister.

It was all a lie.

I'd learned long ago never to rely on an Alpha's word.

But Alpha Enrique did give me hope. He wasn't like the others. He was always… kinder. Supportive. Curious, even. He never lost himself to the hallucinogenic rages of the others. He'd held me while I'd cried.

A whirring of energy put my instincts on full alert as the glass around my cage began to rise.

It's time, I thought numbly, trying and failing to close my eyes.

The Alphas surrounding me roared with violent intent, their instincts to claim taking hold of reason and sending them all toward me.

One cut through the masses, his blue eyes that of a wolf with icy determination. He destroyed everyone in his path, the rage etched into his features causing my heart to skip several beats.

He's going to rip me apart, I realized, noting his massive size and feral growls. It was a thought that had crossed my mind several times before, but something about this Alpha made it all the more real.

He exuded a dominance that I felt deep within my soul, causing my wolf to whimper with the compulsion to submit immediately to his needs and allow him to do whatever he desired.

The other males tried to reach me first, but their bones snapped beneath his wrath and the growls of another.

I squeezed my legs together, both in need and in fear.

There wasn't just one male coming for me, but two.

And from what I could read of their approach, they were equal in strength and stature.

If they both enter me at once… I trailed off, unable to fathom the experience. It would be unlike any of my history and would destroy me before I even had a chance to breathe.

Alpha Enrique's snarl met my ears, his fury over the mounting situation evident. *He knows I'm going to die.* I tried to shift my attention to him, to tell him with my eyes that I accepted my fate, but strong hands wrapped around my waist before I could summon the strength to move.

My wolf immediately went limp, surrendering herself to the much stronger Alpha. He had me in his clutches now. There was nothing I could do but try to survive it.

I couldn't tell which one held me, and I fought not to care. His heat wrapped around my clammy skin, making me moan as the vibrations continued to force my interest.

He tucked my head against his chest, then sprinted through the crowd, looking for a safe spot to mount his prey.

I closed my eyes, willing myself to find a secret place inside my mind that allowed me to escape the horrors that I knew were coming.

Only, icy air met my hot flesh what felt like half a beat later, drawing my eyelids upward once more.

He intends to knot me outside? In the snow?

I whined a little at the concept, not liking at all how that would feel. He'd probably leave me for dead afterward.

And what happened to the second Alpha? I wondered deliriously.

I could hear the howls and growls echoing behind us as this Alpha ran, but he was too fast for them. Too strong. Too *dominant.*

He eventually slowed his pace, leaving me to shake in his arms with a convoluted mixture of dread and anticipation.

I needed him inside me.

And yet, I knew his knot might kill me, too.

It was a dizzying combination of desires that stirred a

mewling sound from my lips.

"Shh," he hushed, the sound odd to my ears and accompanied by a low growl that stirred another of those moans from my throat.

He cradled me with one arm, holding me against his upper body, while his opposite palm roamed over me with interest. His fingers immediately touched my sensitive parts, stroking me like the prize he probably thought me to be.

The rumble in his chest intensified, his irritation palpable.

Something about my situation irked him. Was I not wet enough? Did he expect me to beg? To cry out with need? What did he—

The buzzing against my slick flesh ceased, stirring a shocked sigh from deep within. It was so sudden and unexpected that it prompted black dots to dance before my eyes.

Then the stimulators on my breasts disappeared, followed by the one placed deep inside my wet channel.

He yanked it out, like it was in the way.

A jolt ricocheted through me at an alarming rate, stealing my vision.

"Don't worry. I've got you, little wolf," the Alpha told me softly, his words reverberating through my mind.

I wasn't sure if they were real.

Or if I'd made them up.

Regardless, I could only say one thing back to him. *Yes, you have me. And that's exactly what I'm afraid of.*

I couldn't tell if I'd voiced it out loud or not.

Likely the latter.

Because, by the time I even considered the thought, I'd already fallen into my coveted oblivion. A sea of darkness. My favorite state of being—unconsciousness.

CHAPTER TWO

KARI

Scandinavian Airspace

Reality jarred me back to life with a crackle and pop inside my ears. My inner animal stirred in confusion, the air around us foreign and reeking of fish.

Where am I?

Wind roared outside the tin can walls, barely drowning out the two male voices nearby.

Am I alive?

Something soft and warm encircled my shoulders, but I was strapped down with a belt buckle across my hips.

An Alpha said something before glancing back at me with dark, lethal eyes. I blinked at him, not having caught whatever he'd said. Satisfaction glimmered in his expression as he refocused on his blond-haired companion.

They were seated in two executive-style chairs, surrounded by electronics and gadgets. A sprawling window of sky sat before them, the starry night highlighted by the moon overhead.

Flying, I finally determined. *We're flying.*

I'd just taken my first plane ride recently, having been transported from Bariloche Sector to Winter Sector. The Alpha of Bariloche Sector had forced me to turn into a wolf before locking me inside a cage and leaving me in a cargo hold for what had felt like days.

These Alphas had instead wrapped me in a blanket… and strapped me into a chair similar to their own.

I studied them, wondering where they intended to take me.

They were alike in stature and size, their dominance a palpable air around them that confirmed these two had been the ones I'd feared in my cage.

But from what I could tell, they hadn't really touched me yet. Only removed the sensors, swathed me in soft fabric, and buckled me into a chair. My arms and wrists were free, as were my legs. And the belt at my hip wasn't locked, just a snap I could easily undo myself.

I frowned. *What's going on?*

I peered out the window beside me, noting the dark sky. There weren't any answers lurking beyond the glass.

My nose twitched as I searched out the scents, noting the fishy stench and metallic undertones.

I scanned the space for a moment, sensing someone else back here with me. Someone familiar.

Snow.

Enrique's betrothed.

Her scent radiated from the cargo area near the back of the plane. Did they have her locked up in a box or something? Similar to how I'd been taken to Winter Sector?

My frown deepened. *Why would they take Snow?* She was a Beta princess and therefore revered. Did they intend to hold her for ransom?

Or maybe she wasn't here at all and her scent was just in my head.

I'd only met the female in passing when Alpha Vanessa had flaunted me as a gift for Alpha Enrique. The Beta princess hadn't reacted, but I imagined she wasn't thrilled by the idea of her betrothed receiving an Omega as a present. My existence could only be used for one purpose —satisfaction. Because Betas couldn't take the Alpha knot. At least not without risk.

Minutes passed by in silence as the two Alphas at the front of the plane relaxed.

I waited for one of them to make a move, knowing full well they wouldn't just keep me in this small area and not use me to their hearts' content.

But those minutes lengthened until the plane began to descend through the sky.

It was still dark, indicating we hadn't gone very far or for very long. Maybe an hour flight in total? I couldn't really say, nor did I care. I was more interested in where we were going. The ocean took up the view from one side of the plane as we landed. A small village area appeared on the other side, with modernized buildings in the distance.

Lots of snow, just like Winter Sector.

Norse Sector, I guessed, aware of the various X-Clan sectors throughout the world. My mother had taught them to me as a young girl, telling me where to go should I ever escape Bariloche Sector. Norse Sector had been on her list, but who knew if I could trust that old information? I also didn't even know if I'd estimated my location correctly.

The two Alphas spoke to each other in low tones, their words vibrating through the small space.

I tried not to listen to them, preferring my thoughts to their debate. But it was hard not to pick up on the nuance of their conversation. *Me.* The blond wanted to know if the dark-haired one intended to fight him for me.

"You wouldn't win," the dark-haired one said flatly.

"I know," the other replied without missing a beat, surprising me. Alphas rarely conceded so easily. And looking between them, I wasn't so sure either of them was right. They seemed pretty evenly matched to me.

"So why are you challenging me?" the one with lethal black eyes demanded.

"I'm not. I just want to know if I need to prepare to issue the challenge."

"What the hell is wrong with you?"

The blond merely stared the other male down. "Answer me, Kazek. Are you going to fight me for her?"

Testosterone radiated around the plane, calling to my inner wolf. She longed to submit and fulfill the ache between my thighs. The sensors had left me unsatisfied. But at least they weren't still buzzing all over my body.

"You always were a cocky son of a bitch," the one called Kazek muttered.

The other Alpha didn't reply, just continued to stare at him.

"Shit, you've got it bad, man. You don't even know the girl." Alpha Kazek paused. "Your funeral, Mickelson. I won't challenge you for her. However, others likely will."

Mickelson, I repeated to myself, recognizing the last name. *Alpha Ludvig Mickelson of Norse Sector.* He'd definitely been on my mother's list as an Alpha worth trusting.

But in my experience, there were no Alphas worth trusting. Not in this new world, or in my life.

The two males continued talking, but I stopped listening, instead thinking of my mother and sister.

The former had died over a decade ago at my father's hands. She'd refused to satisfy one of his generals. And she'd paid the ultimate price... after my father had made her watch his generals play with my already broken sister.

My jaw clenched at the memory, my heart aching with the loss.

She's in a better place, I reminded myself, the mantra one

I'd repeated several times over the years. *She's not hurting anymore.*

"Do you want the girl or not?" Alpha Kazek snapped, his tone sending a tremor down my spine. Angry Alphas always unnerved me. When their tempers flared, I usually paid the price in the form of physical brutality.

"She's mine," Alpha Mickelson replied, his tone stirring another shiver within me.

Strong wolf. Dominant male. Worthy mate. My inner animal practically purred in expectation. But the human part of me knew better than to evaluate him in such a manner.

I would never take a mate.

That wasn't my purpose in this world.

Alpha Kazek snarled something before finishing with, "You want her, then you fight the Alpha of Norse Sector for her. I won't do it for you."

His words gave me pause.

Wait… I thought Alpha Mickelson was the Alpha of Norse Sector?

I didn't have time to fully consider the question because the blond Alpha was already coming for me. My limbs shook with anticipation and fear, knowing what would come next.

His big hand found the buckle at my waist faster than I could blink, and he scooped me right up into his burly arms like I weighed nothing. A soft whine escaped my throat from the contact, my body innately reacting to the pain to come.

He responded with a rumble from his chest, the sound making me flinch. It wasn't a growl so much as a soft reverberation.

A sound of annoyance, maybe?

Except, no, that wasn't quite right.

It… it actually felt kind of nice. The hum continued

from his chest, stroking over me and my senses and causing my wolf to settle immediately inside me.

I barely even noticed him carrying me off the plane, my mind and animal too focused on the soothing rhythm coming from his chest.

A purr, I thought, wanting to nuzzle into him. *He's… he's purring.*

My mother had told me about this once, had said it was a sound only Alphas could make. She'd been so dreamy when she'd spoken about it, saying it had been one of the few moments she'd ever truly felt at peace.

Savi had mentioned it, too. Her Alpha mate had occasionally purred for her.

But no Alpha had ever purred for me before.

"What's your name, little wolf?" the Alpha asked with that rumble in his voice.

I swallowed. "Ka-Kari." It came out on a choke of sound, my voice cracking as though I'd just spent several days screaming.

Maybe I had.

My body wasn't mine to control. I reacted as instructed, did everything the Alphas told me, all in hopes to gain a few moments of silence alone.

"Kari," he repeated, his low voice over my name like a sensual caress. "I'm Sven."

Not Ludvig Mickelson, then. Maybe a brother? Or a son?

"Welcome to Norse Sector," he continued. "You'll be safe here."

Safe? I nearly snorted. I wasn't *safe* anywhere.

His purr intensified as though he sensed my doubt, his hold tightening around me as he carried me with ease past the village-style area—which I now suspected was part of the airport—and down a path toward the taller buildings I'd seen from the plane.

16

Soft light illuminated our path, the snow elegantly shoveled off the sidewalk and into piles beneath giant trees. The vegetation was different from that of my home, not that I'd spent much time outside. I'd only ever shifted into my wolf when an Alpha had demanded it. Sometimes they'd preferred to rut in animal form.

My stomach twisted with the thought, wondering how this Alpha would choose to mount me.

He responded by purring even louder, the vibration soaking into my skin and demanding I relax. It was almost enchanting. And slightly… annoying… because I knew it was all a false method of coaxing me into a more pliant state to fuck me.

"Shh," he hushed. "I'm not going to hurt you, Kari."

This time my snort escaped my mouth before I could swallow it.

He paused midstep to peer down at me with a pair of hypnotically blue eyes. His blond hair fell over his forehead, forcing him to shake his head to knock the locks backward. Only, the strand fell over his face once more, giving him an almost boyish appeal.

Except there was nothing *boyish* about him.

He was all hard masculine lines, chiseled jaw, and perfect cheekbones. Beautiful, really. But most Alphas were. Although, this one had a hint of wolf to him, too. I could see his animal staring out at me, assessing my appearance and appropriateness as a mate.

His inner beast would soon scoff at the notion, realizing I was too broken to ever accept his knot indefinitely.

I couldn't provide him with an heir. I couldn't even go into estrus.

"When I say something, I mean it," he said, capturing my gaze. "I will not hurt you, Kari. I vow it."

I knew better than to believe him. So I just looked away. He could try the honorable card all he wanted. He could even pretend to be nice to me. I'd enjoy it for what it was—a distraction until the real him came out to play.

"All right," he murmured. "I'll prove it with actions, then."

I wasn't sure what he meant by that.

However, his rumbling purr distracted me from trying to figure it out.

He resumed his pace, and I rested against his chest, absorbing the sound and wondering if it would follow me into my dreams later. I could use a peaceful night of sleep. Perhaps he would rumble for me after he fucked me tonight.

I closed my eyes, allowing myself to be lulled for a few seconds more.

If anything, I would use this memory to survive whatever lay ahead.

Because I'd seen this Alpha in action; I knew violence and murder lurked within his soul. It was only a matter of time before he used me as an outlet.

After all, that was my purpose in this life. Why would he be any different?

CHAPTER THREE

SVEN

Norse Sector

Kari curled into me, her petite form wearing more scars than any Omega should ever possess. Not that the marks were visible. No. These were internal wounds, ones I saw etched into her pale blue irises and forever darkening her black pupils.

This female had suffered in a way no woman ever should. And especially not an Omega. They were too rare to torture, even one in her condition.

Sterile, Alpha Vanessa had said. *Kari is sterile.*

It was why she'd been relegated to the service class, her existence only useful for one act.

While that might be true, that didn't mean she deserved to live inside a cage and be used to inspire ruts and violence and whatever else had been done to her.

Bariloche Sector had sent her to Alpha Enrique as a wedding gift.

How charming.

Yet, rather than use her as intended, Alpha Vanessa had stripped the Omega and forced her arousal with a bunch of sensual toys.

Fucking bitch, I seethed. Kari would have been ripped apart by those volatile and inept Alphas in attendance.

Which I suspected had been the entire point. The infamous Queen of Mirrors was known for her bloody proclivities. She'd probably wanted to watch Omega Kari suffer before Alpha Enrique finished the job.

And he would have, too. Even though he'd probably been the only other Alpha in the room who'd had enough strength—both mentally and physically—to help the girl. He would have been lost to the rut after watching everyone play.

I shook my head, annoyed all over again.

Kari stirred in my arms, her wolf reacting to my agitation.

I hushed her and strengthened my purr once more. It was a sound reserved for mates. Yet it came so naturally to me now, my wolf content and pleased with the female in my arms. He didn't care that she was supposedly sterile. He wanted her anyway. And so did I.

It was a feeling I'd never experienced before. Some might assume it was just an Alpha reacting to the potent presence of an Omega, but Kari wasn't the first Omega of my acquaintance.

As I was the son of a powerful Alpha, several sector leaders had reached out with offers to arrange a mating for alliance purposes. But none of the Omegas I'd met had ever spoken to my wolf.

At least, not until I'd seen the petite little blonde in the glass cage. And when her scent had hit me? I knew I had to have her.

She wasn't meant to be a servant in Norse Sector. She was meant to be mine. I felt the truth of it deep within my soul. And my wolf wholeheartedly agreed.

Sterile, I thought again, frowning. *If she's sterile, then why am I reacting so strongly to her?*

Because this wasn't just about knotting her. I wanted to save her to keep her as mine.

An asinine reaction, honestly. I didn't know her. But her natural perfume served as a beacon to my inner animal.

Even as we entered the heart of Norse Sector, where the pack scents warmed the air, all I could smell was the female in my arms.

"Sven," Joel said as I approached the central building amid the corporate corridor. He stood outside at his usual post, the Enforcer one of my least favorite on the staff.

"Joel," I returned, pausing as he blocked my entry.

"What have you got there?"

I merely looked at him. Kari's scent provided a sufficient answer. He knew I held an Omega, and I wasn't about to explain why.

"Where'd you find her?" he added before inhaling deeply. His nostrils flared with interest, stirring a growl from my wolf.

Kari stiffened in response, making me instantly regret the warning sound I'd released. I reignited my purr for her, which had Joel's eyebrows rising in surprise.

Yeah, you and me both, buddy, I thought. But I didn't give him the satisfaction of that reply out loud, instead telling him, "I don't have time to chat. Open the door and tell Alpha Ludvig to meet me in the guest suite."

"You want me to give him an order?" Joel sounded incredulous.

"No. I want you to give him *my* order," I countered. "Is that a problem?"

Joel's teeth gnashed together as he roughly opened the door. "Not at all," he muttered through his clenched jaw. As I moved by him, he grumbled, "Cocky fucker."

"With good reason," I tossed back at him without a glance. "Have a good night."

I couldn't help the sarcastic twinge in my tone. He was my superior in age but my inferior as far as the wolf hierarchy went. Not because of my father's leadership role, either. But because I'd fought and challenged my way up the ranks. The only two above me—other than my dad— were Kaz and Alana.

I didn't challenge them out of respect.

But that didn't mean I couldn't beat them.

I readjusted Kari in my arms as I called the elevator down with a swipe of my thumb. She didn't make a sound or any attempt to move as we entered.

After keying in the special code that would allow us to ascend, I shifted her in my arms again and repeated, "I'm not going to hurt you."

She didn't scoff this time. I decided that was an improvement.

"You're no longer a slave," I added for good measure, my thumb brushing the raw skin around her throat. It had taken some effort to remove her collar, and the damage around her neck suggested it hadn't been taken off in a very long time. It was likely programmed to shift with her, therefore functioning as a tracker of sorts. That was why we'd destroyed it.

And also because it was just wrong to collar such an exquisite creature.

Her hand lifted tentatively to her throat, her eyes widening upon feeling her skin. "Why…?"

"Because you're no longer a slave," I said again as the doors opened into the penthouse of this building.

The long corridor ahead of us had a door at each end, both leading to a protected space of sorts that was meant for guests who needed a little added security. Only those with security codes could access this floor. It also meant Kari wouldn't be able to leave, but the spacious apartments and outdoor living space should satisfy her while I worked out all the particulars with my father.

I stepped into the hallway and went left, then used my watch to open the door.

Kari didn't take in her surroundings at all, her focus on her neck. I caught the slight tremble in her fingertips as she continued to touch the base of her throat.

"Does it hurt?" I asked her.

"It always hurts," she whispered.

I glanced at her throat. "Your neck?"

"Everything." It came out so soft that a human probably would have missed the reply. But my wolf ears had picked it up, along with the broken way she'd said it.

"Are you hungry?" I started toward the kitchen area inside as I voiced the question.

She didn't reply.

"Kari? Are you hungry?" I tried again. I wasn't sure how stocked the pantry and fridge were since this guest area was rarely used. I would likely need to go grab her some supplies and bring them back.

She slowly shook her head.

"Thirsty?" I offered.

This time she started to shake her head but ended up nodding.

Balancing her with one arm, I opened the fridge with my opposite hand and found a pack of water bottles inside with little else. "Here," I said, retrieving a bottle and handing it to her.

Small fingers twisted off the cap before tipping the contents toward her full lips. She didn't look at me while she did it, instead choosing to focus on the wall. After a few sips, she stopped. But she clutched the water like a lifeline, so I didn't try to take it away from her. Instead, I carried her through the living area to the bedroom and showed her how to access the outdoor area.

"In case you want to stretch out your wolf," I explained before turning back into the room. "The bathroom through there should have everything you need. I'll see what I can do about finding you some clothes as well."

"Why?"

"For your comfort," I replied.

"Oh."

I walked her over to the bed and set her on the mattress. Her eyes rounded, her pulse skipping a beat as she began to squirm. It took me a moment to understand the cause of her sudden terror, and I nearly growled in response. "I'm not going to fuck you, Kari. Not like this, anyway."

Oh, I fully intended to take her. But not in this state.

While her sweet slick definitely appealed to my wolf, the undercurrent of fear destroyed the mood. I wanted her to be pliant and aroused. Not terrified and sensitive from erotic sensors.

"I don't… I don't…" She swallowed, her gaze falling to the floor. "I don't understand."

I ran my fingers through my hair and considered her situation. She'd gone from being forcibly stimulated in a glass cage to a rather lavish bedroom in the span of a few hours. I could understand some of her confusion, given what Vanessa had clearly intended to accomplish with that initial stunt of dangling a sensually excited Omega in front of a crowd of hungry Alphas.

Kari had expected to be fought over and fucked.

And I'd taken her straight to a bedroom upon arrival.

So her mind had gone directly to her purpose, and now she didn't understand my annoyance.

I crouched to the ground before her, placing my palms on the mattress on either side of her dangling legs. She sat up a little straighter, alertness flaring in her gaze as I purposely forced her to stare down at me rather than up.

"Norse Sector isn't like Winter Sector or Bariloche Sector," I promised her. "You're not a slave here. You're…" I couldn't find the right word. My wolf said *mine*, while my brain wanted to call her a *guest*. But neither was truly right. "Well, we'll figure out what you are. But you belong here now."

A buzzing on my wrist kept me from saying anything more. With a rotation of my arm, I pulled up the message from my father and stood once more.

"I need to meet with Alpha Ludvig to inform him of your sector transfer," I told her softly, using my dad's name and title out of habit. I almost always referred to him in that manner around others. Kaz was one of the few exceptions to that rule, mostly because he felt like family to me more than a usual packmate.

"Try to wash up and get some rest," I suggested. "I'll be back to check on you in a bit. And I'll bring food, too."

She didn't reply, so I glanced down to where she still clutched the water bottle like a lifeline.

"No one will enter these rooms except me. And maybe Alpha Ludvig, depending on what he needs. Very few have the access codes. You're safe here, Kari."

Her expression told me she didn't believe that for a second.

I sighed and shook my head. "You'll see I'm right," I promised her. "Go take a shower and sleep. I'll be back soon."

She didn't reply.

Rather than stand around and wait, I left, deciding again to prove myself through actions instead of words. I couldn't even pretend to know everything she'd been through, but I had a pretty reasonable idea for some of it.

The Alpha of Bariloche Sector wasn't known for his kindness.

And that collar around her neck just proved that point further.

With a low growl, I stepped into the hall to find my father waiting for me beside the elevator. "I smell an unmated Omega and an overabundance of fish," he said by way of greeting. "Why?"

CHAPTER FOUR

KARI

My wolf whined inside me as a new presence lingered nearby. *Alpha. Superior. Dominant.*

I could feel him more than see him, his presence a beacon that demanded submission.

Sven had said no one would enter these rooms aside from him and Alpha Ludvig. Which meant the latter had arrived. But he wasn't in the room. Otherwise, I would be able to hear him clearly. Instead, all I picked up on were the low rumble of voices.

I took another sip of the water, pacing myself in case Sven had lied and decided to come back to knot me. I'd learned long ago that it was best to suffer through sex on an empty stomach. Whenever I ate first, I ended up losing the contents of my insides on the Alpha, and that never ended well.

The low murmurs continued, their tenors suggesting they hadn't moved.

I set the bottle down and wrapped the blanket tighter around myself before standing. A peek out the bedroom door confirmed they weren't inside the apartment space. So I crept forward toward the main door to see if I could hear them any better.

Maybe they would reveal their plans for me.

Sven had said I wasn't a slave. He'd also said he didn't intend to fuck me in my current state—whatever that meant—and that we would figure out my place here.

But never once had he asked if I wanted to be here. Or bothered explaining why he'd taken me away from Winter Sector. He'd just kept telling me I was safe.

I nearly laughed.

An Omega was *never* safe around an Alpha.

As I approached the door, their voices became clearer to my wolf hearing. If I were more nourished and a stronger shifter, I probably could have discerned their words from the other room. Alas, I had to press my ear to the door to really make out what they were saying.

"… some glorified pet?" the deeper voice asked.

"That's not what—"

"I heard what you said, Sven. She's an unmated sterile Omega that you want for yourself. That's not how this works, and you know it."

"I won her. Therefore, she's mine."

"Correction. She's *mine*," the deep voice replied in a lethally soft voice. "Everything you do reflects back on Norse Sector. And that includes engaging in brawls with other Alphas over an Omega slave."

Silence fell, sending a chill down my spine.

"It was the right thing to do," Sven said after a beat. "I won't apologize for it."

"This isn't about right and wrong, but about how your decisions impact the sector as a whole. If what you've told me about the situation is true, then yes, you won her fair and square. But she is not yours, Sven. She belongs to Norse Sector now. And she will be available for all the Alphas as a result."

My stomach twisted, my future flashing before my eyes.

Sven had said I wasn't a slave here. I hadn't exactly

believed him, but removing my collar had been a nice touch.

"She's not ready for that," Sven said in an equally dominant tone. "She's malnourished, exhausted, and terrified. I know you can smell it as well as I can. She needs to eat and sleep. She also needs to be examined to determine if she's even really sterile."

"And you want to be the one to oversee that process." It wasn't a question but a statement.

"I won her. Therefore, it should be my responsibility to properly prepare her for Norse Sector."

I almost snorted. Of course he would be the one to offer to feed me and "examine" me himself. I knew what that meant. He would knot me before the others. Get his fill of me and pass me on to his friends.

All Alphas were the same.

They only cared about their knot. Their pleasure. Their *need*.

It was never about Omegas or what we wanted. We were just here to bend over and take it.

I didn't bother listening to the rest of their conversation. I'd overheard what I needed to know.

Sven Mickelson was just like every other Alpha I'd ever met. He'd won me in a violent game and taken me to his home sector. Away from Alpha Enrique—the only male wolf of my acquaintance who had ever given a damn about my desires.

Now what? I wondered. I was in a place I didn't know, one my mother had claimed was different, with Alpha males who wanted to turn me into a slave of their own sort.

Yeah, he had removed my collar. But that didn't mean anything if he intended to just keep me in this glorified prison for the Alphas of Norse Sector to use.

My teeth ground together as I ventured back to the bedroom.

He lied to me. I wasn't sure why that surprised me. Or maybe *surprised* wasn't the right term. It… it… well, it hurt for some reason. Maybe because he'd awakened a small glimmer of hope—a glimmer my mother had inserted into my thoughts as a young girl.

She'd always said there were decent Alphas out there.

For just a few minutes, I'd nearly believed her.

Alpha Sven had been almost tender with me. But his true colors had shown out in the hallway. He considered me his property because he'd *won* me.

And now he planned to prepare me for the Alphas of Norse Sector.

No doubt by pretending to be kind and considerate. Just to rip it all away when his need to rut came along.

Well, I wouldn't make it easy for him. He'd taken away my one escape by removing me from that cage. I was supposed to only suffer through a final night. Then Alpha Enrique was going to help me.

He was the only Alpha who ever kept his word.

Now I had no way to reach him because Alpha Sven had stolen me. He'd ruined everything.

I hated him.

I refused to obey him.

And I would start by not eating.

Or bathing.

I dropped my blanket and looked down. Actually, I'd take it one step further.

I would no longer be human.

My wolf happily obliged my call, our freedom to shift at will a unique experience. The collar had always controlled me. Without it, I could finally bond with my animal side the way a shifter should.

Alpha Sven had unknowingly provided me with the opportunity.

Now I'd repay him by using it against him.

You want me healthy enough to take your knot? Good fucking luck.

I was done being a pleasure sleeve.

I wanted the right to choose. And at this point, I chose starvation… and death.

My wolf growled in disapproval.

It's better this way, I argued.

She snorted out loud, reminding me that I'd shifted. On my own. Without someone demanding it.

Huh.

It had been so natural I'd barely felt it. Usually, changing hurt, almost as though my bones were being forced the wrong way. But this had been akin to standing up.

I spun around, reveling in the feel of being free. My fur fluffed out as static electricity stroked along my spine. I wanted to run. To frolic. To play. But there was nowhere for me to go other than that outside area.

I trotted over to the door Sven had shown me and nosed my way outside. Then I skipped to the end of the grass-coated patio area in less than a minute.

Well, that's disappointing.

It just led to another door, which opened into a room like the one I'd just vacated. A peek out the bedroom door revealed a similar living area as well. So it was really two suites tied together by the hallway with the elevator and the outdoor patio.

I went back outside and looked up at the tree branches overhead. They were attached to live trees with roots in the soil and grass below, and they mostly blocked the sky above. Glass windows stretched high over the balcony walls completed the enclosure, allowing me to see the ocean and the moon beyond without risking any attempt at jumping off the platform to the waves below. Considering I was at least twenty stories in the air, I could understand that safety measure.

Well, this definitely beat my cage in Bariloche Sector. But I knew better than to become accustomed to this luxurious prison cell.

Once Alpha Sven realized that I had no desire to adhere to his commands, he'd throw me in a box.

Just like my father had.

My wolf whined a little at the thought. So I distracted her by giving up the reins to her animalistic senses.

Go sniff.

Go roam.

Go explore.

And maybe I could even coax her into destroying a few things along the way. Like the pillows inside.

You can't trick me, Alpha Sven. I know your kind. So I'm going to try something new and not submit. You have nothing to hold over my head to force my compliance. So what do I have to lose?

CHAPTER FIVE

SVEN

Kari had been asleep when I'd first tried to bring her food earlier. She'd torn up the couch cushions to make her version of a bed. I'd considered picking her up and taking her to a real mattress to curl up on, but she'd looked so cute sleeping in her tight, furry ball that I hadn't wanted to disturb her.

Still, we would have to talk about the mess she'd made. That couch wasn't cheap, and my dad wouldn't be pleased to learn it had been destroyed by an Omega in wolf mode.

I'd probably be put in charge of cleaning it all up since she was my responsibility. But seeing her in her animal form made it all worth it. She had soft-looking blonde fur that matched her natural hair color. Which was interesting to me because my fur was dark brown mixed with streaks of white and therefore not at all like my chin-length ash-blond hair.

Hmm, I wondered if her eyes were blue or if they changed in wolf form.

When I opened the door to her suite this time, it was the first thing I discovered.

Blue.

I almost smiled. Until I realized the state of the room. "What the hell?" I breathed.

She'd destroyed more than the couch this time. The wood table had been reduced to sticks. The cushion fluff decorated various parts of the room. There were pillows gutted everywhere. Books reduced to paper shreds. Two overturned shelves. A smashed television. And an array of shattered dishes.

The Omega had thrown a tantrum.

She sat smugly in the middle, giving me a look that begged me to retaliate. *What now, Alpha?* her glittering irises asked.

I wasn't even sure what to say.

"Why?" I demanded. "Why did you destroy the room?"

She huffed in response, the sound unapologetic and borderline annoyed.

I narrowed my gaze, trying to figure out what the hell this little wolf was thinking. A quick check of the kitchen showed that she hadn't tried to eat anything. So I wandered to the bedroom—and found the sheets in tatters on the ground—and continued to the bathroom.

The shower smelled clean with no signs of someone recently using shampoo or soap. Which implied she hadn't bathed either.

Just turned into a pretty blonde wolf and destroyed this half of the penthouse.

I didn't bother to check the other side. This would already require significant cleanup. "Those were really nice sheets," I informed her as I reentered the living space. She hadn't moved from her spot, her expression still smug. "Most Omegas would have loved using those to nest."

She bared her teeth at me, growling low in her throat.

"That's cute," I returned. "Want me to growl, too?"

She snorted as though to say, *Do your worst, Alpha.*

Clearly, she wanted a reaction from me. Some sort of

reprimand. Or maybe she was punishing me for leaving by throwing this colossal fit.

Well, I wasn't one for games.

I'd helped her out of a bad situation, and this was how she repaid me? By pissing all over my hospitality?

"Shift," I told her. "Now."

She lay down instead, her eyes drifting away from mine in subtle submission. I started to growl, only a faint shiver down her spine held me in check.

It hurt to force a submissive wolf to shift when she didn't want to, and it seemed Kari wasn't in the mood to be human today. Perhaps she was still healing. Of course, that didn't explain the state of the room. But I couldn't even pretend to understand what it was like to be in her situation.

Alphas were meant to take care of weaker pack members, not exploit them.

Sighing, I crouched before her. "I promised not to hurt you, Kari," I said as softly as I could. "And I'm going to keep that promise."

Her ears twitched, but she didn't react in any way. Yet I suspected this was some sort of test on her part, a way to see how far she could push me before I unleashed on her.

Some Alphas lacked patience.

I wasn't one of those Alphas.

Reaching forward, I gently stroked my fingers over her perky ear, the gesture meant to soothe. However, her fur flicked with uncertainty, her trepidation a potent scent that had me retracting my touch and standing once more.

If she was determined to remain in wolf form, I'd allow it for now. So long as she ate something.

I wandered to the kitchen in search of something animal appropriate and found a bowl for water, then grabbed a plate to put a raw steak on it.

35

She didn't move, her body stiff on the floor as she waited for whatever I intended to do. The poor girl reminded me of an abused pet, her stance ever vigilant as she anticipated the worst in everyone around her.

It would take time to gain her trust—something I was unfortunately short on since my father wanted to introduce her to the pack. He didn't plan to pass her around so much as offer her the opportunity to find an appropriate protector.

Omegas required sex, just like Alphas. The innate needs created a purposeful relationship where Alphas could knot and expel aggression in a fulfilling manner, and in return, the Omega felt safe and gratified.

However, I wanted more than that.

I desired a mate, and while biology might claim that to be an impossibility with Kari, my wolf felt otherwise.

Hence the shortened timeline—not only did I need to prepare her to meet the pack, but I also needed her ready to agree to be mine.

Fortunately, I adored challenges of all kinds. And this one would be the most rewarding of them all.

"I'm going to give you another day to acclimate to your new surroundings," I said as I returned to the living area. "But I expect you to eat while I'm gone." I set the bowl and plate in front of her. "A shower is also recommended." I glanced around the room. "And maybe try not to destroy anything else. This is already going to be a bitch to clean." Not to mention, expensive to replace.

She didn't look at me, but those ears twitched again, confirming she'd heard and followed everything I'd said.

"Twenty-four hours," I added as I started toward the door. "And I mean it, Kari. I expect you to eat. You won't like the consequences if you don't."

I'd promised not to hurt her, and I wouldn't, but I also wouldn't tolerate self-harm. Of which, not eating qualified.

"If you don't like the raw meat, then shift back. There are a lot of options in the fridge." I gestured to the kitchen.

She didn't acknowledge me.

Rather than repeat myself, I left.

She had twenty-four hours to show improvement.

If she didn't, I'd show her how a real Alpha reacted in this situation. I suspected she wouldn't enjoy it. But she'd survive. And she'd thank me for it later.

CHAPTER SIX

SVEN

I STUDIED the raw steak in the snow, well aware of where it'd come from—the high outdoor balcony above that belonged to a certain guest suite.

Lars sniffed the meat, his furry head cocking to the side as he picked up the traces of Omega from the teeth indents on the top.

He lifted his big black snout up and pinned me with a pair of curious brown eyes.

"She's a new addition," I said in a low voice. "Alpha Ludvig intends to introduce her in a few weeks."

Or days, I thought in annoyance.

When I'd reported on Kari's state to him yesterday, he hadn't shown me any leniency, stating I needed to prepare her before the pack caught wind of her scent.

Which she wasn't exactly helping me out with by tossing her fucking food off the balcony.

She probably thought it went into the ocean, as she wouldn't have been able to see the small strip of land from her vantage point. It would just look like all water from the glass windows lining the outdoor patio walls. She'd clearly found one of the ventilation slats to toss her food out through.

Normally, we left those vents closed to protect the

enclosure from snow drifts. However, I'd left them open because I thought she'd appreciate the fresh air.

I'd have to rectify that during my next visit. Assuming I even remembered it. All I could really focus on was my desire to tie her down and teach her a lesson in respect.

Disobedient little Omega. I warned you, little one, and you tossed my single demand out the literal window.

Lars grunted, drawing my gaze back to him. He could probably pick up on my mounting aggression.

There was one thing I despised—disrespect. As a young Alpha, I experienced it regularly. But there was a reason I'd moved up through the ranks. And Kari was about to find out why the wolves of Norse Sector considered me almost as superior as Kaz and Alana, despite my age.

"Don't tell the others," I said to Lars, my quiet tone authoritative. As I was a higher-ranking member of the pack, he'd adhere to my demand. Still, I felt it necessary to explain why. Subordinates were more willing to comply when provided with a worthwhile reason to act. "She's not ready to meet anyone yet." At his continued stare, I added, "She's from Bariloche Sector."

He visibly flinched, his wolf releasing a low growl.

"Yeah, my feelings exactly." Bariloche Sector was notorious for mistreating Omegas. But no one ever did anything about it because we all had our own problems to handle.

Like keeping the Infected off our turf.

X-Clan wolves were immune to the zombie virus, but that didn't keep the infected humans from trying to bite us anyway. We were warm-blooded and food in their dead minds.

I'd grown up with this life, the pandemic having taken

place almost eighty years before my birth. But others like Kaz often spoke of life pre-infection.

Was Kari from that time period? I wondered, glancing up at the building. *How old is she?*

Perhaps I'd ask her.

After I made her tell me why she'd thrown a perfectly good steak off the fucking balcony.

Oh, you'd better have eaten something else. Anything else, I thought, my teeth grinding together in frustration. Maybe leaving her for another day had been the wrong move. However, it'd seemed like she'd needed space.

I shook my head.

Well, you've had your space, little wolf. Almost thirty-six hours of it. Because I'd been roped into helping my mother with a task earlier that had taken a lot longer than expected.

Which meant Kari had been here for two days now.

And if my suspicions were right, she hadn't eaten a single thing since arriving.

"Do me a favor and clean that up," I said to the Beta in wolf form. "I don't want anyone catching her scent yet." Because that would only shorten my timeline even more.

Lars bobbed his head in acceptance, then picked up the meat with his teeth. I wasn't sure if he planned to eat the steak or toss it into the water. I didn't stick around to find out, my inner animal roaring in anger that the Omega had disobeyed a clear command *to eat.*

I'd given her a safe space to heal and hide. An abundance of resources, too. And she'd thanked me by destroying the furniture and tossing a perfectly good piece of meat off the balcony.

Right.

Time for a lesson.

If she couldn't take care of herself, then I'd do the job for her.

I keyed in the necessary codes, and within minutes I stood outside her door.

Silence met my entry, and a quick scan of the kitchen proved Kari hadn't touched a single morsel of food. The bowl of water I had left for her was turned over on the carpet, where the liquid had soaked into the fibers of the floor. Yet another fun mess to clean up later.

But I had a disobedient Omega to punish first.

I didn't bother calling for her. Instead, I followed my nose and found her curled into a tight ball of fur on the balcony.

"Shift," I demanded.

She didn't move. Didn't even lift her little head. But she was definitely awake. I could tell by the shiver of her shoulders that not only was she very aware of my presence, but a smart part of her was also worried about what would come next.

"*Shift,*" I repeated, giving her one more chance to do this willingly.

When she refused, I growled, low and commanding, and compelled her to return to human form through sheer force of will alone.

She whimpered as her body reacted to my dominance, doing exactly what I told her to do. Her lack of food was evident in how fast she complied, her weak state unable to put up even a semblance of a fight against my wolf.

Bones cracked as her legs extended, her animal crying out in pain at being forced to retreat.

Then she began to tremble, her terror a pungent scent that made my nose twitch.

She curled tighter into a ball, her arms encircling her legs as she tried to hide.

"Kari." Her name rolled off my tongue on a growl, causing her to flinch. Then she began to roll to her back, her legs stretching out along the floor and parting in what most would consider to be an invitation to fuck.

My wolf perked up, curious.

But the man in me recognized the beaten expression of submission.

She'd been trained to react this way, to anticipate an Alpha's need to rut, and to just lie there and take it. My heart panged painfully in my chest, all my frustration and ire at her not taking care of herself leaping off the balcony to join that imprint of steak on the ground.

This poor girl had been through hell and anticipated the worst from my anger.

All I wanted was to take care of her, and I suspected no amount of words would convince her of that. So I would need to approach this through actions only.

I crouched down beside her and gently slid my arms beneath her shoulders and knees to lift her from the ground. Her slight weight told me just how fragile she was, her stomach empty from who knew how many days of starvation.

Cradling her against my chest, I began to purr and took her inside.

Unlike last time, she didn't cuddle into me. She remained limp, her eyes falling closed as though she were already dead.

I pressed my lips to the top of her head and carried her to the bedroom. She didn't react; she barely even breathed, already resigned to her fate.

But I didn't set her on the bed.

Instead, I took her into the bathroom and set her on the marble counter. I leaned her back against the mirror, then held a hand out, half afraid she might fall to the side. But she remained seated with her eyes closed and her lips shut.

This was an Omega who had fallen into a dark space inside her mind, allowing the Alpha to do whatever he wanted. And I didn't like her in this state at all. I preferred the disobedient growls from yesterday, or even the quiet comfort she'd achieved the other night when I'd first brought her up here.

Something had happened. Some sort of switch in her mind that just gave up, and I suspected she'd been on the verge of that since she'd arrived. Giving her space had been the wrong move. I wouldn't do it again.

She needed nurturing and replenishment to gain some trust.

As well as a bath, I thought, eyeing the tub.

Given her lethargic state, that didn't seem like the best choice, so I flicked on the shower instead. I'd worry about feeding her once she was clean and bundled up in a warm towel.

I kicked off my shoes and socks and stripped down to my boxers, then ran my fingers through my hair in an attempt to tame the unruly strands.

The locks promptly fell back into place around the sides of my face.

It was at that length where I couldn't really tie it back, nor could I seem to hold it behind my ears.

Giving up on trying, I tested the water's temperature and found it already heated despite the cool winter climate outside. Leaving the glass door open, I stepped over to pick Kari up again, my purr vibrating loudly to keep her as calm as possible. But she didn't seem to notice. She was too far gone in her mind to even seem to realize what was happening.

Forcing her back into her human form must have been the breaking point. It hurt to be ordered to shift, and something told me she'd purposely driven me to that point so I would remove all her choices. She wanted me to be the bad guy in this world, to show her my worst side. I wasn't sure how she benefited from that. Maybe it was a way for her to define her new normal.

I drew my fingers through her hair as I moved us beneath the warm spray from above, allowing the water to soak into her blonde strands and pale skin. Her lack of movement confirmed she'd fallen into a state of unawareness. She could stay there for now while I took care of her, but I'd need her to snap out of it eventually to be able to eat.

Balancing her weight with one arm, I held her against my chest and used my opposite hand to shampoo and rinse her hair. Angling proved to be a bit of a challenge, but her slight frame was easy enough to manage. I repeated the action with the conditioner, then soaped her off thoroughly by moving her around against me.

Not once did she move on her own.

Nor did she bother to open those pretty blue eyes.

Her heart rate remained steady, her breathing shallow, but she wasn't asleep. Just… vacant.

I allowed the water to run over both of us for a bit, ensuring all the suds went down the drain before turning off the shower. My chest continued to rumble in that tranquil, rhythmic sound, hoping it would lull her out of this state.

But nothing seemed to work.

I wrapped her in a big fluffy towel, combed her hair, and dried myself off, without any success in rousing her.

Sighing, I whispered, "All right, little one. You win." She couldn't eat like this, and I didn't want to risk driving her further into this state by forcing her to snap out of it.

Instead, I set her on the floor of the bedroom while I remade the bed with fresh linens from the closet—because she'd destroyed the other sheets and comforter with her claws—and retrieved some bottles of water from the kitchen.

She remained limp the whole time, her body mine to move and do whatever I wanted with.

Scooping her up from the floor, I carried her to the bed and settled us into the blankets. If she wanted to rest, I'd lie with her.

Spooning her from behind, I allowed her to feel my strength as an Alpha while my wolf vowed through the rumbling in my chest that he would protect her in this weakened state for as long as she needed.

Mine, he hummed. *This Omega is intended to be mine.*

CHAPTER SEVEN

KARI

My wolf yawned and stretched inside me, her contentment radiating through my foggy thoughts. I felt rested, yet weak.

An odd sensation. Not the weak part, but the rested part.

And safe, I realized, my body tingling with foreign warmth.

A hum of sound reverberated through me, heating my veins and causing my wolf to rumble back in kind. She liked that repetitive sound, the soothing tranquility of it appealing to her baser senses.

What is it? I wondered, searching my clouded mind for a source. *Where am I?*

I often woke in this state of confusion, unaware of my surroundings and the horrors that had just been unleashed upon me. But I couldn't recall ever feeling this satisfied, like I'd slept peacefully for hours.

After a few seconds of contemplation, I pulled up my last tangible memory—the one of Alpha Sven forcing me to shift.

I shivered, the horror of the moment prickling goose bumps over my arms.

Except that vibration heightened, causing my skin to

smooth out in the next breath. *I really do like that noise*, I thought with a mental sigh. *Such a hypnotic, beautiful rumble.*

My lips almost curled.

But that memory lingered in my mind, the one of Alpha Sven demanding I return to human form. I'd pushed him too far, which had been the point. I wanted him to hurt me. To provoke his Alpha out to play so we could just get this dance over with.

Examine me.

Present me to the other Alphas.

Or just kill me.

Wait… I frowned. *Is that why I feel so good? Am I finally dead?*

My eyes were too heavy to lift, my body too relaxed to move.

Oh, and that gentle purr had me wanting to bury myself deeper into the warmth around me rather than roll away from it.

I definitely didn't feel *examined* or *used*. In fact, I wasn't sore at all. Just hungry. Something my stomach confirmed by growling with need.

Do stomachs do that when you're dead? I wondered, my brow furrowing.

Something soft drifted over my skin, smoothing out the wrinkles of my forehead before skating down along the edge of my face to my chin. "You need to eat," a deep voice murmured, his words underlined with that addictive rumble.

Alpha Sven.

"We've been in this bed for almost a day, little wolf," he continued. "That's three days without food, and who knows how long before that. And your stomach tells me that not only do you know that, but you're also aware of it.

So open those pretty eyes, and we'll solve the problem together."

The gentle touch stroked the space beneath my eyes as a band of steel tightened around my torso. His finger drifted back into my hair, combing through the strands in a knowing manner that sent tingles down my spine.

How…? I trailed off, unsure of what I even wanted to ask. I couldn't remember anything that had happened after he'd made me shift. I'd shut down, anticipating the worst. But the clean scent and warmth on my skin weren't signs of a rut.

I felt… *clean.*

And safe, I thought again. *Very safe.*

But that didn't make any sense. He'd been so angry and demanding, his growl one I'd heard so many times before. *Shift so I can fuck you. Shift so I can knot you. Shift so I can own you.*

However, my thighs weren't bruised. My insides weren't aching, apart from my stomach cramping from a lack of sustenance. And my skin felt refreshed and unblemished.

No part of me hurt except for the pangs of hunger.

"I don't…" My voice came out raspy, my throat unbelievably dry.

Alpha Sven moved, jostling me from my haven of comfort and eliciting a soft protest from my wolf. I tried to hide it, to banish my inner animal's sounds, but the Alpha must have heard me because he softly hushed in my ear as he moved around me.

My eyelids refused to rise, leaving me blind to whatever he was doing.

Then a plastic bottle met my lips. "Drink," he ordered, sending a shiver down my spine.

I complied because I needed the water. It burned down

my throat, causing me to wince. He purred in response, clearly pleased with my acquiescence.

What the hell happened?

Alphas didn't do this. They didn't care for me after fucking me. They left me drenched in their seed for the next male to find.

But the blankets beneath me were so *soft*.

And this male was *hot*. He reminded me of the sun, his heat soaking into my skin and swathing me in a sea of protection that threatened to overwhelm my wolf. She wanted to lose herself in him, accept his strength, and beg him to never leave.

This has to be a trick, I thought. *Some sort of game.*

The plastic left my mouth, his thumb catching a droplet from my lip along the way. Then he moved again, and this time my eyes opened to allow me to watch him reach across me to set the bottle on the nightstand beside us.

He was shirtless, and his blond hair was messy and sticking out at odd ends. His purr rolled over me as he went back to his position in front of me, his head sharing the same pillow as mine. He had one arm beneath me, his forearm a band of fire along my lower back.

I was naked—a fact that didn't surprise me, considering what we'd probably done in this bed.

Except I didn't smell my slick or his seed. The sheets were clean with a subtle underlay of soap and water. Alpha Sven's masculine aroma surrounded me as well, his mark upon my skin one of sweat and *man*.

But not in the way I usually experienced.

He'd branded me in a foreign manner, his touch oddly tender.

His thumb stroked my chin, drawing my gaze up to his. "Are you ready to eat something?"

My wolf nodded inside me, begging me to accept his offer. However, I knew what would come after food, and just because I couldn't remember our first rutting session didn't mean I wouldn't remember the second one. Especially if he made me eat. It was hard to escape into my mind when my body demanded I expel the contents from my stomach.

His blue eyes flared, his expression darkening. "Hmm, I see." He pulled away, his purr leaving me as he rolled off the bed to the balls of his feet.

The animal inside me mewled at the loss of contact while my mind fought to find another escape before we started whatever this was again.

"I guess we're doing this the hard way," Alpha Sven said, walking toward the door.

Shit, I need to hiii—

Hold on. Why isn't he naked?

His muscular back tapered into a lean waist, his skin smooth and pale all the way down to his black boxer shorts.

I gaped at his firm backside, confused.

Then he disappeared through the doorway without another word.

I grappled for the sheets, my hand moving slower than I wanted, thanks to a lack of energy, and eventually lifted the fabric to reveal what I already knew. *I'm naked*.

But he wasn't.

He'd been holding me while wearing underwear.

What Alpha does that?

I dropped the blankets and rotated onto my back to stare up at the ceiling. *Did he not…? What did he…?* The unfinished questions revolved in my head, my mind unable to ascertain an appropriate response.

For once in my life, I tried to remember what an

Alpha had done to me. But my brain refused to cooperate. I'd shut down as soon as I'd completed my shift. Then I'd woken up warm, comfortable, and *safe*, in his arms. I couldn't remember the last time I'd felt that way.

Maybe before my first estrus. When my mom had been allowed to spend time with me and my sister. I'd felt complete then. Innocent. Happy.

My sister had just found her mate, and my mother had been so hopeful.

Until my father had killed Savi's Alpha.

And taken me from my mother to introduce me to my new purpose and life as an Omega.

My stomach twisted as I recalled the pain of being stolen from my safe place and tossed into the dungeon to be broken and used and spiritually gutted.

Maybe that was the purpose of this game—to show me a glimpse of safety, just to rip it away. But to what end? What did Alpha Sven win by placating me one moment, only to break me in the next?

I was already shattered.

Beaten.

Owned.

He could do anything to me, and I'd allow it. He could kill me, and I wouldn't even fight back. Why bother with the purring or the baths or the—my nose twitched at the blossoming scents in the air—*food*?

Unless he knew that it would keep me awake afterward. To experience whatever darkness he possessed.

I considered shifting into my animal form, to hide from whatever he intended, but his footsteps reverberated through the suite, alerting me of his approach.

My heart skipped a beat. *If I call my wolf, then*—

"Don't," he said, entering the room. "I don't want to

hurt you, Kari. But I will force you right back into this state and make you eat."

I blinked at him, alarmed. *How did he know my plan?*

"I could feel your energy humming along my skin," he explained, again reading my expression or thought or *energy* and addressing my unspoken question.

I wasn't sure how I felt about him being so in tune with me that he could pull words out of my head.

He set a tray down on the bed, the plates on top of it holding enough food to feed an army of pups. My stomach growled in excitement, my wolf pacing eagerly inside me, dying for something to eat.

But we both knew what would come next.

Which meant I could only have a little bit, or I'd seriously regret it later.

It was always this way, leaving me in a perpetually weakened state. However, I preferred to starve over regurgitating all my meals during or after sex.

"It's dark more hours than light this time of year, so breakfast always feels appropriate." He started pointing to items on the tray, describing each dish.

There were eggs, smoked salmon, various cheeses, and a plate of sliced vegetables. None of it sounded appetizing when I considered the intended outcome of this experience.

Alpha Sven noted my reluctance with a raised brow. "I will start feeding you if you don't pick up a fork and do it yourself."

My jaw clenched, some part of me wanting to deny him on principle alone.

It was an inane reaction, one that would absolutely earn me a death sentence, and a painful one at that. But I couldn't help it. I knew what would come next, and I didn't really want to spoil my previously content mood.

Part of me wanted to ask him to purr again and to fall back asleep in his arms, just for a few more minutes of peace.

Assuming that was all we'd done. But given how I felt, it seemed the only likely scenario. A male the size of Alpha Sven would leave bruises and marks all over my much smaller form. If he'd fucked me, I'd be able to feel it. Particularly as he'd said I'd only been asleep for a day or so.

Three days here, I thought, recalling what he'd said. *Yeah, I would—*

"Kari." My name came out on a warning growl.

Slowly, I pushed myself upright to a seated position against the headboard. Then I reached for a celery stick and chewed on it.

His jaw ticked, but he didn't say anything. Just watched.

After swallowing, I picked up another one, and his eyes narrowed.

The motions continued for three more rounds before he caught my wrist. "I don't know what game you're playing, Omega, but you need more than rabbit food."

"You brought the plate of vegetables," I pointed out under my breath.

His brows rose at my comment. "They're a side garnishment. Eat the salmon."

"Then just give me the salmon instead of a tray of options," I replied, uncertain of where my backbone had suddenly come from. It was the kind of tone I used to give my sister when we were younger and more comfortable. It definitely wasn't the sort of response I'd ever given an Alpha before.

I shifted backward on instinct, only then remembering the plank of wood at my back. *Shit.* My eyes lowered as I mumbled an apology, but it was too little, too late. Alphas didn't appreciate disobedience. They killed Omegas for less.

Alpha Sven caught my chin, and I closed my eyes, accepting my fate.

"Look at me," he said sternly.

So it'll be like that, then, I thought, resigned. Forced to watch my punishment. And now that I had a little food in my stomach, I'd probably stay coherent through all of it.

Of course, it was what I deserved. I knew better than to speak my mind.

"*Kari*," he snapped, impatience underlining my name and jolting my eyelids upright.

Twin storms of blue blazed down at me as he knelt beside me on the bed, his expression fierce. "I'm not going to hurt you." The words were a punch to my senses, his irritation stirring goosebumps along my skin. "But I also won't let you hurt yourself. So you will eat until I am satisfied."

He released me, only to take over the space beside me and settle the tray across his massive thighs. I felt so small in his presence, his size dwarfing mine at least two to one.

That wasn't anything new for me, but his handsome features had a gentleness to them that other Alphas lacked. It didn't make him any less masculine so much as easier to look at. He didn't have the barbaric sternness many of the Bariloche Sector Alphas possessed. He appeared almost regal. Godly. Otherworldly.

"Staring at me like that isn't going to get you out of this, sweetheart," he murmured, his full lips quirking up on one side. "Although, I don't mind having your eyes on me."

I blinked, confused. Then I realized I'd been admiring him for an unknown amount of time, just studying the planes of his face and appreciating the elegant square cut of his jaw. Rather than stop, I continued my perusal, noting the strong tendons of his neck and the bulk of his shoulders.

Most Alphas were solid muscle. Sven was no exception. But his veins didn't protrude like the others', his arms sleeker and more athletic rather than harsh and intimidating.

He interrupted my perusal by bringing a fork to my mouth. I opened for him because there was no other choice. A smoky flavor touched my tongue, my wolf growling in approval at the obvious high quality of the meat.

It'd been a long time since I'd indulged in more than table scraps. This sort of cuisine would probably upset my inner balance, making me sicker than usual when he took me later. But I couldn't help the groan of approval as I swallowed, because it really did taste decadent.

He purred in response, that sound a hypnotic caress that lulled me into a passive state. I stopped worrying about being sick later, choosing to enjoy the moment for however long it lasted instead. *I'll just need to make sure this is worth it*, I thought, savoring the flavors. Eventually, my stomach began to protest, my appetite small and unrefined due to years of barely eating.

Alpha Sven didn't push me, instead finishing off the food himself while maintaining that soothing rumble in his chest. Then he set the tray on the floor and studied me.

My heart sank, my body already aware of what would come next.

I wanted to ask for more time, to at least have a few minutes to digest the food before we began, but I knew better than to make a request.

So I lay down instead and spread my legs the way I'd been taught to do, and waited.

Alpha Sven took in the view before stretching out

alongside me and propping himself up on his elbow. "I'm not fucking you in this state, Omega," he said. "You can't handle me yet. So you can relax."

My brow crinkled. *What?*

He stroked his fingers along my jaw, his purr intensifying as he gently brushed the slope of my neck down to my sternum to trace a line between my breasts.

"I won't lie to you, Kari," he murmured, his fingertips drifting down to my stomach to circle my belly button. "My wolf has already staked his claim on you. Therefore, I intend to make you mine. But I won't do it until you're strong enough to take me."

I shivered, unsure of how to reply to that. There wasn't a choice here. He wanted me, so he would have me. Just like all Alphas. And when he tired of me, he'd give me to someone else.

I used to dream of escape. Of running. Finding my own life somewhere else. Or just dying in the woods on my own.

Maybe I could revisit those desires here. He'd given me a rather large cage to stay in, plus food that might actually allow me to build some strength to run.

What would happen if I broke the windows on the balcony and jumped into the ocean? Would it kill me on impact? Or would my wolf be able to heal me? In my current state, I'd die. But if I kept eating and regained some of my natural shifter tendencies, I might be able to survive.

And do what? I wondered, thinking of the cold air outside. *Become an ice cube?*

Alpha Sven's touch drew lower to my shaved mound and over to my hip. Such a feather-soft stroke, his hands exploring a body he'd already decided belonged to him for however long he desired it.

The realization twisted my gut, reigniting my hatred of all wolf-kind and the cruel hand fate had dealt me.

But I couldn't deny that his fingertips evoked a certain warmth beneath my skin, one that paired nicely with the deep reverberations coming from his chest.

He was lulling me into a submissive state, one meant to bend to his will. I wasn't strong enough to fight him, so I absorbed the strength he offered instead and allowed my mind to dream of alternatives. To consider another way out.

Alphas had used me all my life.

What would be the harm of using this one now?

It seemed only fair, considering everything I'd endured. If he wanted to strengthen me to take him, then I'd allow it. When the opportunity presented itself, I'd use that renewed power to my advantage.

And run.

CHAPTER EIGHT

KARI

I STIRRED to awareness beside a blanket of heat, my mind fighting to remember when I'd fallen asleep. Alpha Sven had petted me for what had felt like hours, his hands exploring my body but never touching me anywhere truly intimate despite my splayed thighs.

He'd merely warmed my skin, teasing me with a sense of security and warmth that my wolf had craved all my life. While my mind knew better than to fall for his tricks, I couldn't deny the comfort of his presence.

I opened my eyes to find my head pillowed against his chest. His strong arms were wrapped around me as he continued emitting that amazing soft rumble of noise. He'd been purring nonstop for days, or so it seemed. It was addicting and hypnotic and a sound I would very much miss whenever this ended.

His fingers combed through my hair as he said, "It's time to eat again."

I nearly groaned. This male was obsessed with food. I felt like I'd just eaten ten minutes ago, but the slight growl in my stomach told me it'd been much longer than that. Perhaps even a full day. Time was elusive here in this nest of warmth and lulling purrs. At some point, I'd shifted the blankets around to create a wall of sorts, like I was trying to trap us in this bed so we could never leave.

His lips pressed into the top of my head as he tried to disentangle himself from our cocoon. I growled in annoyance, his movements disrupting my carefully crafted barriers.

He paused and I hummed in approval, nestling deeper into the vibrations of his chest.

"You're not going to distract me from feeding you, Kari," he warned.

I ignored him, not sure what he meant, and continued to press myself against his hard body to find the contentment I'd experienced before he'd moved.

He sighed and pulled me into him again, then drew his fingertips down my spine. It was heaven. Or maybe hell. Because I knew it wouldn't last, and with every breath, I anticipated the worst.

But the longer he held me, the more I relaxed. Then I reached out to fix the blanket he'd touched when trying to leave and closed my eyes once more.

Minutes passed.

Maybe hours.

And the big Alpha tried to dislodge me again.

I growled.

This time he growled back.

My wolf whimpered.

He kissed my forehead and moved away despite my protests, leaving me in the fort I'd created. It was strange, yet natural. I recognized the signs of nesting, something I'd witnessed in other Omegas but had never experienced myself.

I'd never owned my own space, nor had I ever been able to access so much luxurious bedding. My cell had been more like a cage back at Bariloche Sector. The only times they'd let me out had been when an Alpha had wanted me in a bed, and that bed had never been my own.

This one isn't mine either, I thought, frowning.

But that didn't stop me from fluffing one of the pillows and situating the blankets where I wanted them once more. I left a space for Alpha Sven. Which was strange because he definitely didn't belong in my nest. Yet I liked the way his scent marked the sheets. And his warmth, too.

I was just putting the finishing touches on my wall when it parted to reveal Alpha Sven and another tray of food. He set it inside, making me snarl in annoyance. I picked up the tray and threw it on the ground with a low growl of warning.

Food does not go in the nest! I shouted at him in my mind.

"*Kari.*" Fury poured off of him in a palpable wave that upset my inner wolf. But I didn't back down. He'd tried to soil my space with *fish* and—I sniffed—*beef*.

I glowered at him, not at all caring that the food was now decorating the floor. Better the carpet than my sheets.

"You will *eat*," he demanded.

I snorted. This had nothing to do with me eating and everything to do with him disrespecting our nest.

"I mean it," he said, his tone ice cold and his purr long gone. "I'm done with this self-harm bullshit."

He wanted to talk about harm? He tried to put *food* in my *nest*. "You're a terrible Alpha." He should know better than to destroy such a cherished space. *My space*. Something I'd never had before. Maybe that was part of his game—this desire to make me feel at home only to remind me that I wasn't home, or safe, and entirely under his control.

My heart skipped a beat.

Yes.

That had been the point of this lesson. He'd allowed me to feel a few days of comfort just to rip it away by—

"A *terrible* Alpha?" His ire spiked across my senses, quieting my inner turmoil for a second.

Did I call him that? I couldn't remember. I was too focused on my nest and the situation and... *Why am I acting like this?* I'd never been territorial before. And I knew better than to consider this bed mine, let alone to make a nest.

"I've bathed you, fed you, purred for you, offered you warmth and protection, and you think I'm a *terrible Alpha?*" His voice rose to a roar of sound that had me shrinking inside the nest and calling to my wolf on instinct alone. Fur sprouted across my skin, shifting me into my animal state faster than I'd anticipated.

Because of the nourishment, I realized.

Already I was feeling stronger, and Alpha Sven had barely given me much more than comfort and food.

A furious growl followed my transformation, the Alpha angrier than I'd ever seen him. "You will shift back right now," he commanded. "Or so help me, Kari, you will *not* like the consequences."

Crap. I'd really made him mad. Like, way madder than the other times. And he was going to truly destroy me now.

I leapt out of my nest, afraid that he might grab me and pin me down.

Which was the wrong thing to do because he lunged toward me on a snarl, his wolf shining in his eyes. I'd not only insulted him, but I'd also provoked his predatory instincts.

This was bad.

Very, very bad.

I ran into the living area, trying to get away from him, and knocked down several items along the way. He roared in my wake, then froze beside the couch, his attention going to the door.

My hackles rose as a sweet scent touched my nostrils.

Omega.

Competition.

Dislike.

The reaction came from my inner wolf, her snarl one that Alpha Sven shot right back at me as he marched toward the bedroom and pulled on a pair of jeans and a shirt before heading for the main door.

I growled, irritated that he was leaving me for another Omega, only to freeze as he snapped, "*Stop.*"

The door slammed shut behind him.

My inner animal rioted, furious that he'd cut me off to be with another female. Meanwhile, my head spun in confusion, trying to figure out what the hell had just happened and why.

I'd created a nest.

He'd tried to soil my nest.

I'd thrown the food on the floor.

Then I'd called him a terrible Alpha.

And now he'd left me to be with another woman.

I sat on my rump, blinking into space, trying to sort through the emotional chaos erupting in my psyche. He'd left me. Wasn't that a good thing? My wolf didn't think so. Part of me wanted to stomp off into the bedroom and destroy the safety he'd helped me create there. Meanwhile, another part of me wanted to skulk into the bedroom and cry in my safe haven.

I'd… screwed this up.

Sort of.

Maybe.

I couldn't figure it out. Alpha Sven didn't act like the wolves I knew. He… he offered me food. Sanctuary. *Purrs.*

And now he was punishing me by playing with another Omega. Another slave? Did he own several?

My nose twitched, the scent still strong. It was then that I realized he hadn't fully left yet. He was standing in the hallway outside the door, just like he'd done the other day with Alpha Ludvig.

The hum of voices met my ears, causing them to twitch in irritation at the sickly sweet sound of… *Hold on…* I recognized that tone.

Snow Frost.

But she was a Beta, not an Omega.

Did she have an Omega with her?

I scented the air, searching, and only found the fragrant perfume of competition mingling with my Alpha.

My eyebrows rose. *My Alpha? Whoa, no, no, no. Not* my *anything.*

A grumble in my chest stirred in disagreement as my wolf retorted, *My Alpha.*

I shook out my coat, trying to regain my mental faculties because I'd clearly lost my mind. Then I settled my rump again on a pile of shredded cushions. *These might look good in my nest. Maybe—*

The door opened, and the scent of competition floated into the air, drawing a growl from my wolf. *Competition!*

"We're not done with this conversation," Alpha Sven said, his blue eyes landing on me. "Consider this a gift of time, Omega. You now have at least two hours to fix your attitude."

My attitude? I thought back at him, snorting. *You're the one flirting with another Omega in the hallway!*

"You will eat while I'm gone," he continued.

Food? This has nothing to do with food, I grumbled. Not that he could hear me since I was in wolf form, but he might be able to read the thoughts from my eyes like he had before. *And where are you going for two hours? To play with your new Omega?* Just the thought of it had my hackles rising in response. An entirely irrational reaction, but nothing about this situation was rational.

"Starving yourself isn't an option," he snapped, clearly unable to read my mind this time. Or maybe his new Omega was clouding his judgment.

I hate you.

"I will force-feed you just like I did yesterday," he added, giving me pause. "Your choice, Omega."

He considered that experience to be force-feeding me? At what point did he make me do anything? He'd just brought the fork to my lips, and I'd done the rest.

Wait a second. Now you're distracting me with your food obsession. I glared at him. *This isn't about food, you dumb Alpha.*

He placed his hands on his hips. "Two hours," he said. "Eat, bathe, and be human when I return."

Why? So you can use me as a secondary sleeve after you play with your new Omega? I demanded, uncertain of where all this fury inside me had come from, but indulging it nonetheless. I'd never felt possessive over an Alpha, and I had no idea why I suddenly experienced it with this one. Maybe because he'd been nice to me for a few minutes after a decade of torment.

There's something different about him, though, I thought, contemplating it as he squatted down in front of me to meet my gaze.

"I've been lenient because of your situation. That will end when I return, and this behavior will be sternly corrected." He uttered the words slowly, like he thought I might not understand them otherwise.

It made me want to growl at him, but instead, I held his gaze to show I wasn't afraid. He could correct me now if it meant not going off with the other Omega.

64

What the hell is wrong with me? I wondered, delirious with this bizarre change between us. A sudden urge to lunge at him and bite his shoulder left me dizzy and incapable of responding.

Mine, my wolf raged.

Why? I demanded in response.

Alpha Sven stood abruptly, his annoyance a whip in his wake that only provoked my urge that much more. *Do not leave*, my wolf wanted me to say. *You belong here. In my nest.*

Stop, I begged. *Stop this insanity.*

"Talk some sense into her, will you?" he said, confusing me even more.

Could he sense my wolf's need to mark him? Was he telling me to get it under control?

Of course he would want that. As a sterile Omega, I couldn't actually claim him, or vice versa. This whole situation was—

"I need to go make sure Kazek doesn't kill half the fucking sector," he added from the hallway, making me frown inside.

What?

The sound of the elevator shutting agitated my wolf. He'd just left with that Omega, ensuring I'd know exactly what he intended to do for the next two hours.

I growled, knocking over the coffee table beside me, and bounded toward the door, ready to claw up the corridor walls.

Only to freeze in the hallway at the sight of Snow Frost standing before me.

She was the source of the Omega scent.

CHAPTER NINE

KARI

MY INNER ANIMAL snarled in recognition and annoyance at knowing our competitor. A royal princess. A former Beta. *How did you become an Omega?* I wanted to demand. *And what do you want from my Sven?*

He is not mine! I shouted back at myself.

Fuck, I'm delusional. I've completely lost my head over this man.

Snow snarled back at me, the sound equally fierce and underlined with a hint of concern. "I'm not in the mood, Kari," she said. "But I'm glad to see you're all right."

I paused, stunned by her words. *You're glad I'm okay? Why?* We barely knew each other. I'd been a gift for her betrothed. An Omega to knot because Snow couldn't... *But she's an Omega now.* I could smell it all over her. Just like I scented another Alpha embedded in her skin like a claim.

She stalked through the door, clearly done with our conversation, and started to explore.

I followed her, curious, and a little bit annoyed that she felt like she could just invade my space. *Not my space*, I corrected for the thousandth time as she investigated the kitchen. There was another tray of food there, one I suspected had been meant for Alpha Sven to enjoy after he finished feeding me.

Oops.

"Wow," she breathed, admiring the fridge.

I followed her gaze, not sure what she found to be so impressive.

Then she eyed the claw marks I'd left in the dining table—something I'd done the other day in my effort to redecorate the suite—and then she went into my room.

Hmm.

I called upon my human form, wanting to tell her to stay away from my nest. "Okay…" she said, turning right into me as I finished my shift.

"What are you doing?" I demanded, my tone a bit more aggressive than I'd intended. But she was standing too close to my nest.

"Trying to find the outside area Alana mentioned," she replied.

I wasn't sure who *Alana* was, so all I could do was say, "Oh." Then I nodded and showed her to the door at the back of the room that led to the outdoor patio. "It's a greenhouse," I said, noting the trees. "I suppose it's all right for a glorified prison cell." Which left me wondering why she was here. I'd sensed her on the plane the other day but had thought it might be my imagination. And I'd forgotten all about her since arriving.

The memory of it had me asking her why she'd snuck onto the plane. To which she countered, "Why didn't you tell them I was there?"

I blinked and admitted I wasn't sure if she'd been real or not. Then I glanced around and added, "I'm still not convinced *this* is real."

It was all so strange and foreign to me, and my inclination to claim Alpha Sven only further drove that point home.

At least he didn't leave with an Omega, I consoled myself.

Then I nearly growled because that shouldn't appease

me. I should hate him. "They're not good men, you know," I said, more to myself than to Snow. "*He* continues to lie. To trick me. But I know better. All Alphas do is seek and destroy, and I won't let him destroy me."

There. I'd said it. That made it true.

Then why is my chin wobbling?

Gah!

I swallowed down the urge to scream and took a step away from her, only to stiffen as the sounds of Alphas howling in the distance graced my ears. *Oh no. Oh, no, no, no!* I knew that sound. *Battle. Destruction. Aggression. Fuck.*

The Alphas of Bariloche Sector often engaged in violent acts with one another to expel some aggression, only to need an outlet to soothe that aggression later.

It's happening.

They're coming.

Sven left me here… because he intends to introduce me properly now.

My knees buckled as I scooted as close to a corner as I could, my arms covering my head as I began to rock. *It'll be okay. I haven't eaten today. I'll survive the pain.*

Fuck, I shouldn't have pushed him away. I should have… I should have just… I wasn't sure. I wasn't sure at all!

Snow's voice echoed around me, but I couldn't hear her over the howls on the wind. They were so angry. So violent. So savage.

The Omega beside me started talking.

I didn't understand, her words gibberish when mingled with the snarls below.

But after a few minutes, her statements began to register. She said something about Alpha Enrique, how he'd planned to kill her, causing my lips to curl down.

Alpha Enrique would never do that, I thought. *Unless it was to protect you.*

Maybe he knew she was an Omega and planned to put her out of her misery before the others could use her like me and Savi?

She continued into how she went into estrus after arriving, something about suppressants hiding her true nature. Which explained her Beta scent.

Then she told me about Alpha Kazek, how he'd claimed her. And now he was being punished for taking an Omega without permission—an act that confused me even more. Weren't all Alphas allowed to take without permission? Or maybe because he'd claimed her without approval from the Sector Alpha?

"I think that's why they're howling," she concluded. "He said I'd be able to hear it but not see him."

I wasn't sure who *he* was, or what exactly she meant. But her explanation soothed me a little because it implied this wasn't about me at all.

It's about her.

Ice drizzled through my veins because that was almost worse. She didn't seem to understand what was going to happen to her next. She was innocent and unaware of the fate Alpha Enrique had tried to save her from.

Poor Snow.

I no longer considered her a rival, but a companion.

An Alpha began speaking below, his voice loud and carrying and showering goose bumps down my arms. He sounded big. Powerful. *Terrifying.*

Then I recognized his voice from the plane. *This must be her Alpha Kazek.* He spoke his name half a beat later, followed by his position, confirming it was him.

He continued into an explanation of whom he'd taken as a mate—*Snow Frost of Winter Sector.* Snarls followed that

69

announcement, the wolves disapproving. But he remained undeterred, saying he was ready for their challenges. Then he warned them that he would duel to the death before submitting and concluded with, "I welcome your blood on my hands."

I trembled. "*That's* your mate?"

"Uh, yeah. That's Alpha Kazek."

I blanched. "He sounds terrifying."

She didn't reply, but I caught the agreement in her features. I suddenly felt fortunate that it'd been Alpha Sven who had tried to nurture me, not Alpha Kazek.

"What happens to you if he loses?" I wondered out loud, my voice soft.

"I'm claimed by a new Alpha," she whispered back.

That didn't make sense. "But if he dies, the shattered link will destroy you." I glanced up at her, aware of what that would do to her. Because I'd watched it happen to my sister. "The bonds are supposed to be unbreakable."

"Unbreakable?" she repeated, her tone confirming that she had no idea what was coming for her.

When Alpha Kazek lost... she'd become a slave. A broken Omega passed around and taunted and fucked until she longed for death. And only a kind Alpha would give it to her.

Of which, I'd only ever really met one. *Alpha Enrique.* He'd already tried to save her and failed. Just like he'd failed to save me.

Because I'd been taken before he'd been given a chance.

"Yes," I whispered, confirming the unbreakable bond. "I used to believe my father ruining me was a blessing because Alphas won't claim a broken Omega. Not bonding means my soul will never be connected to another, you see. But I found out the hard way that

Alphas can destroy me in an entirely different manner."

"Your father ruin—" Her words cut off on a sharp gasp, her midnight eyes flaring wide with panic as she crumpled to the ground and curled into a tight ball.

My eyes prickled with tears, the memories of my sister falling into that exact same position all those years ago flashing in my mind.

Her mate… she senses her mate…

"Snow," I breathed, unsure of how to help her but feeling obligated to try. The howls outside grew, the angry aggression whipping across my senses and making me want to fall and hide alongside her. But I had to be strong, to help my new companion. It was all we had. All I could do.

I stayed with her, occasionally whispering her name and trying to offer comfort. She screamed, her agony piercing my heart. It went on and on, the scene eerily familiar. My heart broke for her, for my sister, for my mom. For all the Omegas who had suffered.

My cheeks were damp, my lungs aching from lack of breath.

Snow eventually stilled, her shoulders softening and no longer shaking. *Too soon*, I thought. *Too soon to develop that dead look.* It'd taken my sister months to reach that state. She'd screamed and cried and tried to kill herself so many times. But Snow… she calmed too quickly. And the howls outside subsided, too.

What's happening? I wondered, glancing around and trying to discern the change in atmosphere.

"Snow?" I whispered. "A-are you…?" I couldn't finish it, uncertain of what to really ask. *All right* seemed too weak a phrase. Of course she wasn't—

"I'm okay," she rasped, her voice deteriorated from all the screams.

I gaped at her, shocked by the miraculous recovery. Did that mean her Alpha had survived? Would he be used against her? To force her submission and compliance?

I didn't dare ask, her posture and demeanor telling me she was hurt enough. I remained by her, offering her what little strength I had, attempting to bond.

Then froze as a strong presence taunted the edge of my psyche.

Incoming Alpha.
Dominant.
Powerful.
Fierce.

My wolf immediately took over, shifting me into animal form and ignoring the restructuring of my bones. I couldn't let anyone touch Snow in this state. She was too fragile. They could deal with me instead. I'd take it. I'd be the punching bag for their aggression.

Snow curled into a tight ball, terrified.

And I stood before her, ready to face whoever entered.

It was a blond male, tall, broad-shouldered, and the spitting image of Alpha Sven. *His father*, I realized with a snarl. *You won't touch her!* my wolf told him, taking up a defensive position.

He growled in reprimand, clearly unamused by my posturing.

And that was all it took to send my animal running off to the corner, my need to submit overpowering reason. *I hate you*, I thought at him, curling into a ball. *I hate all of you!*

"Don't make your punishment worse than it already is, Omega," he replied, a note of warning underlining his tone.

My wolf whimpered and tried to disappear into the wall. I wanted to call her a coward. But I couldn't. This was the Alpha of Norse Sector. The age radiating off of him intimidated me, as did his air of superiority.

I could see where Alpha Sven had gained his own power.

These two were forces of nature that I stood no chance against. And I told him that by curling into as tight a ball as I could.

He watched me for a moment, then switched his focus to Snow.

And started to purr.

The sound wasn't the same as Alpha Sven's, and it irritated my wolf because he wasn't the one I wanted to hear. I wanted *my* Alpha, the one my wolf had grown comfortable with over the last few days.

I'm in so much trouble.

CHAPTER TEN

SVEN

I STOOD IN THE HALLWAY, waiting for my father to finish his discussion with *Winter*. The Omega princess had changed her name from Snow Frost to Winter after Kazek had claimed her. A fitting action, one I knew he'd prompted. It was just like him to suggest a new identity to erase the old.

Fortunately, he seemed to be mostly under control outside. When Winter had told me about the punishment my father had organized, I'd worried for my fellow packmates. Setting Kazek loose like that was a dangerous move, but seeing him pace the field with those agitated strides had told me why my dad had orchestrated it.

Kazek only had one flaw—he doubted his own ability to lead. He failed to see himself the way others did, always assuming the pack considered him a mutt more than a worthy Alpha.

This test would prove what my father already knew: the pack would respect Kazek's claim.

A few of the hungrier Alphas had tried to fight him, mostly because they weren't mature enough to ignore a chance to expend some aggression. But they went down quickly and instantly submitted.

It would be a long three days for Kaz now while he waited to be reunited with his mate.

And my father intended to keep her here with Kari.

I sighed, leaning against the wall. I'd warned him on the way up that Kari was still denying food and partaking in activities that promoted self-harm. He hadn't been happy and had told me to fix it.

Then he'd told me to wait here while he spoke to Winter.

He didn't want our combined energy to overwhelm the Omegas inside. I also suspected he wanted to evaluate Kari for himself since he hadn't officially met her yet.

You're a terrible Alpha.

Her words reverberated around my skull, the punch behind them battering my heart on repeat. She'd sounded so fierce and angry when she'd uttered that statement, like my very presence in her life affronted her.

Most of my fury had melted into confusion because I'd done everything an Alpha should for her other than knot her. Was that why she'd lashed out at me? Because I hadn't fucked her yet?

My jaw clenched.

She wasn't ready for me, her frail body too weakened from a lack of food and maltreatment. I wouldn't take her in this state. She'd just have to deal with it. It was my job as an Alpha to monitor her development and ensure her comfort. If that meant she would consider me *terrible* and hate me for taking care of her, then so be it.

Although, it would severely impact my ability to claim her if she didn't choose me back. Which was a problem since we now had less than three days to work out these differences between us.

"Once the trials are over, we'll host a celebration for our newest additions to Norse Sector and finalize Kazek's claim," my father had announced to the sector less than an hour ago.

Whispers of Kari's presence had trickled through the

ranks, her scent impossible to hide. Especially when I seemed to be wearing it like a perfume on my skin. Several Alphas had tried to ask me about her outside, but my father had chased them off when he'd told me to escort him to the guest suites.

Word of her location would now spread through the sector, as everyone would know this area could only be used for one purpose—to safeguard someone precious.

Now there were two Omegas up here, mandating a need for a guard. I intended to take that role, but I suspected Alpha Alana would be helping. Or she might stay outside with Kaz to ensure he didn't seriously hurt anyone. He'd displayed an impressive amount of control when Joel had pissed him off earlier, but that didn't mean he wouldn't snap after a few days of being without his new mate.

Fuck. Kaz has a mate, I marveled, blowing out a breath. Now his urgency for me to leave the plane with Kari made sense. I'd anticipated needing to fight him for her, but he'd let me go. I should have known it was for his own reasons.

I pushed away from the wall as I sensed my father approaching the door, waiting for whatever order he'd give me.

He entered the corridor and shut the door softly behind him before cocking a brow. "You failed to mention the new decor."

I cleared my throat. "Well, I told you she's been difficult and refusing to eat."

"She's also trying to push your buttons, perhaps to provoke your anger in hopes that you'll hurt her or kill her."

I gaped at him. "What?"

"She's clearly suicidal, Sven. I don't know what that female has been through, but her wolf is a shaking mess out on the patio right now. Although, she admirably tried to protect Winter. It only lasted for a second, but it's the effort that counts."

I frowned. "Protect Winter from what?"

"Me," he replied simply. "She fears Alphas."

Well, that I had already determined. "And you want to unleash her on the sector."

"No, I want to introduce her to the sector so she can see what life here is like before she makes any long-lasting decisions," he retorted. "I'm not going to allow anyone to court her in that state. *Including you*."

"She's already mine," I replied without missing a beat. "And you won't be able to stop my wolf from staking that claim."

He looked me over, his gaze calculating. "You might be my son, but I'm still your Alpha."

"While I respect that, I'm telling you that she's mine. I will take care of her. I will heal her. And when she's ready, *I* will court her." There wasn't anything he could say or do that would talk me out of this path. My wolf had made up his mind days ago, and I wasn't going to deny my instincts.

"Sterile Omegas can't be claimed," he reminded me softly.

"My wolf says otherwise." She might not be able to conceive. She might not be able to even go into estrus. But there was something about her that called to me, and I refused to ignore it.

"Then I hope your wolf is right," he replied. "See what you can find out about her sterility over the next few days. We'll talk before the celebration and determine what's best for her introduction."

"You have no doubt that Kaz is going to win."

He snorted. "Of course I don't. He's the one who

doubts himself. Everyone else knows he's more than capable."

"And you're using this as a way to teach him that."

He merely smiled. "I've never been fond of the Queen of Mirrors. Perhaps Kazek will do something about it."

"With the appropriate push, I think he just might."

My father studied me for a moment. "Hmm, yes. He just might." Something told me he was talking about me more than Kaz now. But he didn't elaborate, just wandered over to the wall panel to key in a series of numbers while saying, "I'll send Alana up to watch over Winter, as I suspect you'll have your hands full with Kari."

He stepped into the elevator as it arrived, and faced me once more.

"There's a fine line between gentle and firm. Master it and you'll master her." He pressed a button, causing the doors to close as he softly added, "Good luck."

CHAPTER ELEVEN

KARI

ALPHA LUDVIG's parting words rolled around through my mind.

"Alpha Kazek will be hungry when he's finished the challenge, and I don't mean for food. So prepare yourself, Omega. He'll be demanding and ruthless, and he'll require complete obedience."

Snow didn't seem to understand what he'd meant, her shoulders hunched over as she remained in a submissive stance long after he'd left. I shifted back into my human form, intent on warning her. But as she glanced up at me, I could see the determination in her eyes. She wasn't broken or scared. She was strong and ready to face the future ahead.

I saw my sister in her expression—the sister who had died when our father had killed her mate.

For Snow's sake, I hoped her Alpha survived.

Although, I wasn't sure that would be much better for her in the end. Perhaps he'd be possessive and refuse to share, then all she would have to do is take his knot for eternity. Maybe he'd develop feelings for her and purr for her.

My mom used to say it was possible for an Alpha to love and cherish his Omega.

However, I'd never witnessed it myself. Not in Bariloche Sector, anyway.

Snow turned her gaze away from me, her dismissal evident. She wanted to be alone. I understood that need, so I quietly left her on the patio and debated my next move.

Alpha Sven wanted me to shower and eat and be human when he returned. It would be wise on my part to obey, mostly so I could be in reasonable shape to help Snow if she needed me.

We were companions now.

As her companion, I owed it to her to be there for her if the worst should happen.

Mate-bonds tied the souls together, ensuring the pair felt each other's pain. It was why my sister never truly recovered. Every time I saw her, she had this glassy look in her eyes like her soul had died long ago and all that had been left behind was her body.

The Alphas didn't care. They enjoyed having a broken doll in their beds. It was why I often played the same role, choosing to hide inside my mind while they rutted between my thighs.

I shivered, my stomach souring at the thought of Snow suffering a similar fate. I didn't know her. I didn't owe her anything. But as a fellow Omega, I felt for her. I would do my best to help her in any way I could because I knew what it was like to be all alone in this world.

There was no one there to help me. Not then. Not now. Not ever. I'd accepted that fate long ago, but Snow wouldn't have to.

I'd never hoped for an Alpha's survival before, but I hoped for Kazek to win. If anything, to ensure Snow maintained her mental faculties.

With a shudder, I knelt to pick up the tray on the floor by the bed and did my best to pull the items off the carpet and put them back on their designated plates. Then I ate a few cold bites, ignoring the unsanitary appeal of the food and forcing myself to finish as much of the sustenance as I could to satisfy Alpha Sven.

My eyes fell closed while I chewed, my imagination conjuring up the meal of eggs and salmon that we'd shared yesterday. I pretended it was his fork, not my fingers, touching my lips as I fed myself the steak.

I didn't stop until my stomach protested.

Then I stood and walked dutifully to the shower to bathe.

It wasn't until I opened the glass door that I realized Alpha Sven was there, watching me. He had a pained expression on his face, one I didn't quite understand. Was he upset that I hadn't showered yet?

I jumped inside the enclosure, my hands roaming over the marbled wall to locate the handle. A burst of icy spikes hit my skin, making my jaw clench, but I didn't dare move away. I didn't want to upset him further. He'd told me to eat and shower before he returned, and he was already here before I'd been able to finish.

If he punished me now, I wouldn't be able to help Snow, and that—

His big hand closed around the back of my neck, yanking me from the cold spray and into his hard, hot chest. He'd stripped out of his clothes again, leaving him in just a pair of boxers as he reached around me with his free hand to do something to the handle. "Left," he whispered against my ear. "Left is hot water. Right is cold."

My teeth were chattering too violently for me to respond, so I just nodded.

He didn't release me but instead slowly walked me back beneath the warming water. Then his arm came around my lower back in a semblance of a hug.

We stood like that for several minutes, saying nothing. The goose bumps along my limbs gradually melted away, the hot liquid soothing an ache I hadn't realized was there.

Alpha Sven kissed my temple before pressing his mouth to my ear again. "You didn't need to eat off the floor, but thank you for feeding yourself."

I trembled, tears prickling my eyes.

I didn't understand this Alpha or what he wanted from me or why he was so kind to me. It was messing with my mind and confusing my sensibilities.

I wanted to fall into him in relief, beg him to purr again, and ask him to just hold me. But I also wanted him to fuck me and get it over with. Because that was all Alphas ever really wanted. All this other heartfelt kindness would just haunt my dreams through an eternity of pain.

Which only made me cry harder because I wanted to enjoy this, yet I was terrified to indulge in too much.

Alpha Sven caught me as my knees buckled, his strength holding me upright as he purred against my ear, soothing me in the way a dominant wolf should.

I hated him for it.

But a tiny piece of me also adored him and wanted to stay like this forever. To indulge in his protection and power and never fall into the hands of cruel predators ever again.

I suddenly understood how my sister felt about Joseph. He'd been this beast for her, an Alpha possessive and adoring of his Omega. He'd promised to slay the world for her. Only to be tricked and subdued and later killed.

"He never stood a chance," I whispered to myself. "No one ever does against *him*."

"Who?" Sven asked in a rumble of sound.

"My father." My voice was barely audible. I almost wondered if I was even speaking at all or if it was just a fantasy in my head. Why would I bother telling this Alpha anything? What could he possibly do? "It's already done. He killed him."

"Your father?"

I nodded, giving in to the foreign urge to speak. To voice the atrocities of my life. To… to *cry* and scream and rant and rave. Only, my voice wasn't loud at all, but soft and unequivocally broken as I said, "He killed Savi's mate. Alpha Joseph promised her the world, and my father killed him for it." My heart thundered in my chest, the world fracturing into water droplets through my damp eyes.

"Why?"

"Competition," I hummed, tilting my head back to look up at him, to will him to understand. "Alpha Carlos doesn't like competition. He slaughters them all. But never fairly." At least from what I'd observed. "He cheats."

Just like he had with Alpha Joseph.

A knife in the lower back.

A wolf dying on the ground.

Alpha Sven froze against me, drawing me from the violent visual and forcing me to focus on the handsome lines of his face. "Alpha Carlos is your father?"

I nodded, my lips twisting to the side. "He created me. All of me. Down to every last detail." I pressed my palm to my abdomen as though to show him the scars deep inside. "He ensured I'll never take a mate so there couldn't be another threat like Alpha Joseph."

I must have fallen asleep, I mused. *Why else would I talk about such things?*

Because of Snow.

Restored energy touched my limbs, reminding me of my renewed purpose—to protect my companion. "She's an Omega now? Snow?" I still didn't quite understand that.

83

Except, she'd mentioned something about suppressants. I'd never taken them. But sometimes the Alphas in Bariloche Sector used them... to tighten... to... to make Omegas...

Focus, I thought, breaking out of the memory spiral. *Focus on Snow. She needs me to be strong right now.*

"Snow's an Omega now," I repeated, not as a question but as a statement.

Alpha Sven studied me for a moment, like he was trying to understand my mind. Maybe he'd already confirmed my question. If he had, I hadn't heard him.

"Yes," he replied slowly. "And she's chosen a new name, too. Winter."

"Oh." I considered that, momentarily appeased by the distraction. "It's a good name for her." Her skin was as pale as snow, but her hair was as dark as night. *Winter* made sense. It was a strong name for my companion.

But that won't be enough to save her, I thought numbly.

"I... I hope her Alpha survives." It was a harsh truth, one I'd never intended to voice out loud. I hated all Alphas. They were vile, ruthless creatures who took... took... *took*.

My jaw clenched, my eyes squeezing closed.

Omegas need Alphas to survive. It was an ageless requirement, an intrinsic *need*. And I loathed it. But for Snow... *Winter*... I could accept it. Her Alpha had to live for her to stand any sort of chance in this life now.

"Kaz will be fine," Alpha Sven murmured. "It's the rest of the sector that should fear for their lives now."

"Wh-why?" I stammered, distracted by his comment.

"Because he's a determined son of a bitch and one of the fiercest Alphas I've ever met."

My stomach churned. *Poor Winter.* "Maybe she'd..."

No. I couldn't say it. "She needs him now to survive." Without him, she'd go insane… just like Savi.

My throat worked over a quiet sob, my heart breaking for them both. One was regulated to a life of purgatory without a mate, and the other would suffer eternity with one.

Omegas were never given a choice. We were always only owned.

"What do you mean, Kari? Why does she need him to survive?"

I glanced up at him, startled by the questions. Did he not understand what this meant? Alpha Kazek had destroyed Omega Winter for eternity by claiming her.

"The bond," I mouthed, my vision blurring with the sadness those two words inspired. "It… it breaks an Omega when the Alpha dies. My sister…" I swallowed, my gaze falling to his collarbone. "I don't even know if she's alive. He promised to tell me if I went to Norse Sector. But then you… you took me."

My brow furrowed, my mind racing with indecision. I wasn't sure what had prompted me to start talking, but now I couldn't seem to stop.

"Alpha Enrique was supposed to help me. But you ruined it." And I should hate him for that because now I would never know what happened to my sister. I would never be free. I would always be used and knotted and discarded and *hurt*.

"Help you?" he repeated, his voice distant in my ears. Like I was running through a tunnel.

Only, I could never escape. This was all real. No dream. Just fate.

Still, I nodded, my mouth replying as though hypnotized by the Alpha before me. "He's Joseph's twin," I admitted, thinking about Enrique. "He promised to save me." It came out on a whisper, my heart breaking as I realized that would never happen now.

I was at the mercy of this new Alpha, this Alpha I didn't understand with his tender touches and rumbling purr.

Even now, he held me like I was special.

Like I meant something to him.

Like he didn't want me to break.

"But it's all a lie," I told myself. "Everything is a lie."

"What's a lie?"

"*You*," I accused him, my hands balling into fists with a foreign urge to hit him. "This. *Everything*. And I don't understand why you're doing it!"

I nearly collapsed beneath the wave of anguish that followed, my hands loosening as I realized there was no strength left for me to survive in this world. I could barely stand... I couldn't even fight Alpha Ludvig... I couldn't... I couldn't protect Winter or myself.

Because these Alphas had turned me into *nothing*. Yet the one holding me kept threatening my resolve. He taunted me with the notion of *hope*, and I didn't know why he even bothered.

"I'm already broken, Alpha. I'm already a doll. I'm already willing. Why give me this just to... just to..." I couldn't find the right words, my heart shattering in my chest as a fresh wave of tears flooded my vision.

"Just to what?"

"To knot me," I breathed, my legs giving out completely.

He lifted me into his arms, cradling me against his big chest while I cried beneath the warmth of the shower spray. I cried for myself. For Savi. For my mother. For Winter's future. For my own life. I wept... and wept... until I was reduced to a puddle of sobs in his arms.

And it felt... *good*. A release I didn't know I craved. One I needed to be able to breathe again.

But I didn't understand the point. I didn't understand why he kept holding me and allowing me to *cry*.

He said nothing for the longest time, just purred and held me and protected me from the world.

A peaceful moment underlined in agony. The perfect end to my torturous life.

Except he didn't try to kill me or hurt me. He just... *purred*.

Who are you? I almost asked.

But he spoke first, his statement one only an Alpha would voice.

"Omegas need the knot," he said softly. "Why would you not want mine?"

Just rut me, I almost begged, wanting this anguish between us to end. Hope was futile. Kindness was dangerous. And yet, I found myself uttering the truth, my will so broken that I could no longer find the strength to hide.

"It hurts," I admitted. "It's painful inside me. It's..." I trailed off, exhausted and depleted of thought. Why bother explaining it? He wouldn't care. I was wasting my breath and time, prolonging the inevitable, and somehow weakening myself even more along the way.

Maybe I was wrong. Maybe I hadn't been fully broken. Not until now. Not until an Alpha introduced me to a sliver of kindness. A gift I would never receive again. A memory I would forever cherish while loathing my very existence.

"He promised to help me," I whimpered, thinking of Alpha Enrique. "And now I don't know where I am or what to expect. And I can't figure out how to properly please you."

"You talking pleases me," he whispered against my ear. "I want to know more about why it hurts to take the knot."

"Why?" I asked against his chest. "Alphas don't care. They rut." Another thought occurred to me shortly after that, one that had me stilling. "Do you want it to hurt?" Had I just given him the information he desired to finally knot me? Would he fuck me harder, knowing it would put me in a perpetual state of agony?

He growled against my ear, the sound sending a shiver of panic down my spine. "I've vowed not to harm you, Omega. And I haven't, have I? What have I done that makes you think I'd ever *want* to hurt you?" ⋅

My throat felt like grating rocks as I tried to force myself to swallow. But there wasn't enough saliva in my mouth to comply. "Alphas... *hurt*."

"Not all Alphas."

I shook my head. He didn't understand. "They do."

"Not me." He threaded his fingers through my hair, tugging my head back and forcing me to meet his blazing blue eyes. "Give me three days."

I frowned. "Three days?" The change in topic pulled me out of my mental fog, only to drown me beneath a sea of confusion. "Three days for what?"

"Give me three days to prove it to you. Let me show you what life with me is like. Then we'll go from there."

I blinked. "Wh-why?"

"Because I want you."

Okay... "Then take me." It was simple and straightforward. I wouldn't stop him.

He shook his head. "Not like this. I want you to be mine."

"Until when?"

"Until forever."

My lips moved without sound, his statement not

making any sense. "But… but I'm sterile. He made me sterile. I can't take a mate."

"Who made you sterile?"

"Alpha Carlos… m-my father…" I hated calling him that, but it was his role in my life. "He… after Joseph… he made sure…"

"That you couldn't take a mate," Alpha Sven finished for me. "By sterilizing you."

I nodded, my lip wobbling as I remembered the pain of the procedure. But the worst part was the residual agony every time an Alpha knotted me. "It feels like needles… the knot… it pulsates… and…" I shuddered, my shoulders hunching. I needed to stop talking, but I heard myself adding, "The knot goes too deep inside. It touches whatever he did to me."

"And the Alphas don't feel it?"

I shook my head. "They like it too much to notice."

"Fuck," he breathed. "For how long?"

"For always," I admitted. I went through several estruses alone while my father prepared the procedure. He'd tested it on other Omegas first, wanting to guarantee the survival rate before putting me through the treatment. "I was sixteen." Not that it mattered, but I felt the need to say that out loud.

"How old are you now?"

I considered the question. "Twenty… four?" It was a guess. I'd stopped celebrating birthdays long ago. "Time is meaningless."

"Time is everything," he countered. "Will you give me three days? To show you that not all Alphas are cruel?"

"What happens after three days?"

"You meet the others in Norse Sector."

My heart plummeted. He'd spoken about keeping me for forever, which apparently was only three days. "Oh."

"It's not like that, Kari. Alpha Ludvig, who is a much better Alpha than your father, wants to introduce you to all the wolves in our pack. He wants to make you part of Norse Sector."

"To be available for all his Alphas," I whispered, recalling what he'd said that first night. "I understand."

"I don't think you do," Alpha Sven replied, palming my cheek. "You'll only be *available* for them if you want to be, and given what you just told me about taking the knot, I don't think you'll be available at all."

I frowned. "I don't understand."

"Yeah, I've gathered that," he murmured before pressing his lips to my forehead. "But I'll use our time together to try to better explain, and I'll show you how Alphas can be different. We'll start by finishing this shower."

CHAPTER TWELVE

SVEN

IT HAD TAKEN several hours of purring, petting, and eating to calm Kari down enough for her to sleep. She snuggled into her nest, her hair sprawled across the pillows in a fan of blonde strands. I combed my fingers through them for a moment before shifting a little to focus on my wrist.

A twisting motion brought the watch to life, the technology programmed specifically to my genetics. It shifted with me and only responded to my touch and command. I pulled up a blank message screen and a keyboard below it. Then I silently typed out a note to my father while keeping an eye on Kari in my peripheral vision. She was out cold, her nose pressed against my chest as she lost herself to my purr.

I gave him all the details from our conversation and asked if we could arrange to have a physician evaluate her statements about the procedure her father had inflicted upon her.

Just typing it had my jaw clenching all over again, my ire a hot prick inside my psyche that demanded I react. However, I swallowed down the urge, aware that what Kari needed right now was a tender Alpha, not an angry one.

Alpha Carlos Is Her Father, I typed as the subject of the

email. That would grab my dad's immediate attention. Because it had certainly captured mine.

I'd never met the Alpha of Bariloche Sector, but I was aware of his brutal reputation.

He'd subjected his own daughter to a life of servitude by *sterilizing* her. I gritted my teeth, my wolf bristling beneath my skin. She'd said it hurt to be knotted as a result, which suggested whatever he'd done wasn't permanent.

If he'd removed her uterus, she would have healed over time. Perhaps even grown it back, given our immortal tendencies. Although, we stopped aging and growing around our twenty-fifth year. So if he'd mutilated her as a teenager, then she might not have been able to regrow the organ because her immortality wouldn't have kicked in yet.

Whatever the case, she needed to be medically evaluated. But not today. We would need to work up to that. I'd establish some trust first, then go from there.

I reviewed my message, adding a note at the end requesting that Alana bring up some essential supplies— like more food—and hit Send.

Kari didn't stir, her full lips parted as she slept peacefully against me. I adjusted slightly, curling toward her a little more, and firmly wrapped my arms around her back.

She released a long sigh, one heavy with the torments of her past. Then she nuzzled my chest again as though asking me to increase the volume of my purr. I kissed the top of her head and obliged, giving her the vibrations her wolf craved, and closed my eyes to rest with her.

The Omega began to stir several hours later, causing my wolf to go from a sleeping state to alert in an instant. I wasn't sure what would happen when she woke up, and I wanted to be ready for her.

A subtle buzz on my wrist told me I had a missed communication—likely a reply from my father—but I didn't risk pulling it up. I wanted to give Kari my undivided attention in case she started crying again.

However, when her eyes opened, they were clear crystal-blue orbs filled with apprehension, not torment. She studied my face for a moment, glanced down at my chest, and then rolled a little to her back in an obvious need for space.

I didn't follow her, just continued to emit a low purr, and released my hold on her. She didn't try to move away from my arm beneath her shoulders, and her side still aligned with my torso as I remained on my side. Her eyes flicked around the nest, a frown marring her brow at finding one of her sheets slightly bent from her movements.

She reached out to smooth the edge, then began to rearrange other blankets while I watched, going to her knees to pull all the sheets into place exactly as she wanted them. My eyebrow arched as she slipped from the bed, and I rose to my elbow to watch her disappear into the bathroom.

Kari returned after a minute with our towels from the shower and my clothes from yesterday, and quietly added them to her safe haven in little nooks that she'd clearly created for them.

It was all silently done, her expression one of severe concentration.

I slowly lowered myself back to my side, waiting to see what she would do next.

She ran her fingers over the edges, checking each piece, then slowly settled back into my side and pressed her nose to my chest. I'd never experienced this side of an Omega before, but it had my wolf fully engaged within me, guarding her while she worked and purring in gratitude at including him in her space.

"This is my first nest," she whispered. "May I keep it for a while?"

"You can keep it for however long you want," I promised her.

Her head bobbed a little in a satisfied nod. I waited for her to say more, but she seemed content to just lounge in silence. At least until her stomach informed us both of her need to eat.

"Do you have a food preference?" I wondered out loud.

She stiffened in response, causing my instincts to fire.

"Kari, you have to eat," I said, my voice a little sterner than I'd intended. But I wouldn't repeat what had happened yesterday. "Please don't make me force-feed you."

She remained silent for a long moment, agitating my wolf. "C-can we eat in the other room?" Her question was so soft, reminding me of a feather floating in the air and just barely brushing my ear.

I frowned and went to my elbow to look down at her as she rolled onto her back. "The other room?"

"O-or just outside th-the nest?" she stammered, looking a little bewildered and scared at the same time, like she expected me to yell at her for even asking.

I studied her for a moment, understanding working its way through my mind. "Is that why you threw the tray on the floor yesterday? Because I set it in the nest?"

She swallowed, her chin bobbing subtly in a small nod. "Y-yes. I... I'm sorry. I didn't mean, or I don't... I'm sorry." Her eyes drifted to the side in a show of clear submission, her voice having dropped to a whisper by the end.

I palmed her cheek and drew her focus back to me. "Don't apologize for my mistake," I told her in as gentle a tone as I could muster. "*I* am sorry for not respecting your nest. I won't do it again."

Her statement about me being a terrible Alpha suddenly made sense. She hadn't meant it in the way I'd interpreted it; she'd just meant it in the heat of the moment, that I'd tried to spoil something special to her by not asking before placing something in her safe haven.

She gaped at me, suggesting she'd never heard an Alpha apologize before.

I was willing to bet there were a great many things she'd never experienced with an Alpha, considering everything she'd told me.

My gaze fell to her mouth as I wondered if she'd even been properly kissed. A deep rumble inside me urged me to find out—not by asking, but by taking.

I ignored the instinct, aware that she wasn't ready yet.

But then her little pink tongue snuck out to dampen her lower lip.

I slowly lifted my eyes to hers and found her wolf gazing at me through widened pupils. Her breath shuddered out of her as the subtle hint of her heartbeat escalated between us.

Interest, my inner animal recognized. *Mutual interest*.

One kiss wouldn't hurt. It might even help. Because I would show her how a real Alpha treated his intended Omega. I wasn't one of those cowards from her home sector that had to torment and hurt a slave to get off. No, I was an Alpha worthy of her wolf.

I ran my thumb along her lip, warning her of my intent.

Her irises thinned as her wolf continued to watch me with an intensity I felt to my very soul. I gradually lowered my head, holding those twin orbs of intrigue the whole time, and pressed my mouth to hers.

She stole a quick breath, her lips parting on impulse, but I didn't dive in and immediately take control. I let her inhale. I let her taste our embrace. I let her exist. I let her experience the sensation without tongue. A gentle meeting of mouths meant to entice and express adoration.

She didn't immediately return my kiss, her body utterly still beneath mine, like she expected me to force something from her.

But after a beat, she relaxed, and her lips more firmly met mine.

I drew my teeth along her bottom lip, skimming the plump texture and testing her reactions. Her mouth parted, not on an exhale this time, but to allow her tongue to caress the place my teeth had just stroked.

All the while, she held my gaze, her pupils full-blown and enticingly aroused.

She lifted a hand to my neck, her touch tentative as she grazed my skin on her way up to my hair. I purred as she drew her fingertips through my strands, combing them in a way similar to what I'd done to her countless times throughout our night together.

Kari kissed me again, this time with a little more force as her wolf took over and drove her actions. I sensed the animal rioting beneath her skin, needing to revel in my presence and take what I had on offer.

It was an Omega's natural instinct to submit to an Alpha.

But that wasn't what I wanted here.

I wanted her willing and eager participation, and the flick of her tongue against my lip told me I had it. Even if it was her wolf, more than the woman, reacting to me, it demonstrated our compatibility.

I touched her tongue with my own, then slowly entered her mouth to begin a sensual dance meant to erase any and all males who had come before me.

This female was mine.

And I wanted her to know what that meant.

She closed her eyes, giving in to our kiss and allowing her body to lead her mind. I purred louder, ensuring she felt my approval, and indulged her in a heated kiss meant to brand and claim without leaving marks. Without harm. Without hurting her. But assuring she felt my vow for more, my promise to keep her, my need to declare her as mine.

A soft whimper left her throat, not one born of fright or pain, but an intrinsic need that rippled through me and ignited a fervor in my wolf.

I wanted her more than I desired anything or anyone else in my existence. This female had staked a claim so deep inside me that no one would ever be able to touch me again because I knew she was it for me.

Such a bizarre and insane inclination. However, my wolf had always been stubborn and unerringly focused. Impulsive, even, but always with a logical purpose.

And that purpose right now was Kari.

Everything I did from this second forward would be for her, for us, for our wolves.

My abdomen tightened as her slick permeated the air, her arousal an aphrodisiac on my tongue that I swallowed with a kiss. I wouldn't take her. Not today. Not even tomorrow. Not until she was ready. But I would give her whatever she wanted.

Her fingers slid to the back of my neck, her nails digging into my skin as she tried to pull me closer. She parted her thighs in welcome, and I settled between them on instinct, my cock hard and ready against her heat.

My boxers acted as a barrier, protecting me from doing something I shouldn't. However, that didn't stop her from arching up into me, her little whimper turning into a moan as her sensitive flesh pressed into my shaft.

"Kari," I warned, drawing my teeth along her lip once more.

She released an adorable growl in response, then froze beneath me like she couldn't believe she'd just allowed that sound to pass through her lips.

I smiled against her mouth, then dipped my tongue inside to stroke hers once more. She didn't return the embrace with the same enthusiasm, her movements turning more rigid, like she was trying to harness her wolf.

Rather than push her further, I ran my nose along her cheek and pressed my lips to her ear. "No food in the nest," I murmured. "Rule acknowledged and understood. Let me know if you have more rules." I nibbled her earlobe and went to my knees between her beautifully splayed thighs.

She stared up at me, her cheeks flushed and her chest heaving with exertion. Then her gaze dropped to my groin, and her nostrils flared.

I remained like that for a moment, allowing her to study every inch of my torso and lower body. Renewed interest pooled between her legs as her body prepared for my entry.

But rather than take advantage of her excited state, I merely bent down to place a kiss at the center of her mound. She jolted beneath my touch, her fingers gripping the sheets on either side of her hips.

"If you need pleasure, tell me," I whispered against her heated flesh. "I'll oblige you with my tongue." I demonstrated with a single lick, tasting her slick and groaning as I swallowed the delectable essence.

My wolf paced inside me, needing more.

But when she didn't reply—at least not with words—I sat up again. A hint of fear lurked in the blue rings of her irises, but her pretty blush remained, as did her widened pupils.

Definitely interested, I mused.

I could work with that.

Later.

She needed food first.

"Pizza," I decided, needing a distraction before I devoured her instead. "Everyone likes pizza."

Some of her fear melted into confusion.

Rather than explain, I carefully maneuvered myself out of her nest without disturbing her crafted walls and headed toward the door. "Meet me in the kitchen," I told her. "We'll eat there."

And if you want, I'll enjoy you for dessert.

CHAPTER THIRTEEN

KARI

My heart wouldn't stop pounding against my rib cage.

What was that? I thought, bewildered as I squeezed my thighs together and rolled onto my side. *Why did I react like that?*

I'd experienced arousal before. But never like *that*. Never with a few soft touches.

And that kiss…

I touched my lips, stroking the place his teeth had skimmed my skin. It tingled, the reminder of his invisible brand steering my flesh and my mind.

It felt… It felt… *good*.

As did the lick between my thighs.

Oh God… A spasm twitched in my lower belly, my need spiking as I recalled the way his scruffy chin felt against my sensitive folds. And his tongue.

I wanted more.

I wanted less.

I wanted to scream.

I wanted to cry.

I couldn't decide up from down or right from left. My mind was a riot of foreign sensations and desires that I never knew were possible. Alphas didn't seduce me. They used toys or buzzing wands to stimulate my flesh, and then they rutted. Sometimes I came, but never by choice.

However, Sven made me want to orgasm for enjoyment alone.

What is happening to me? I wondered, looking around my nest and realizing I'd fortified it with *his* clothes. I saw this space as *ours,* not just mine.

This is dangerous, I decided. *So very dangerous*.

Because it provoked a glimmer of hope and questions that started with, *What if…?*

I swallowed. *No*. I couldn't afford to dream.

But he wanted three days, of which I'd just spent the majority of our first one lounging in our nest. What would the rest of our time together include? More licks? Kisses? Soft strokes? Purring?

I shivered. Even if it was all a ruse, or some twisted game, I'd have the memories to cherish in my darker hours later.

Or maybe they would torment me, show me what life could have been for another Omega.

An Omega like Winter.

I froze, my senses on high alert. Then a single sniff of the air told me she was still here. *Is she all right?* I wondered, concern tightening my gut.

Alpha Ludvig warned her that she had seventy-one hours to prepare for what came next. *Alpha Kazek will be hungry when he's finished the challenge,* he'd warned. *And I don't mean for food.*

My lips twisted to the side. I needed to check on her.

Slipping out of my nest, I went in search of my companion and found her out on the patio, sleeping in a tight ball of white fur.

An Alpha howled in the distance, causing the hairs along my arms to dance in response, but Winter seemed to sigh in contentment and curl even deeper into the bed of shredded clothes she'd created.

A warm presence behind me had me spinning around, ready to defend Winter. Sven raised his hands in a show of peace and took two steps back into the suite before cocking his head for me to follow.

He still wore his boxers, but he had a shirt in one of his hands.

I followed him, my eyes on the material, curious what he intended to use it for.

Shutting the door softly behind me, I approached him and froze as he tugged the shirt over my head. "Alpha Alana brought me some clothes," he said, his voice low to keep from disturbing the sleeping wolf outside. "I thought you might want to borrow some."

The cotton tickled my thighs, the shirt more like a dress on my smaller frame.

He pulled my hair out from the neck, then ran his fingers through the strands before tucking them behind my ears. "Pizza's in the oven."

This Alpha was very strange. And he had an obsession with food.

He gently tugged on the strand of hair hanging near my breast and started backward toward the living area. I followed him on instinct, hungry for whatever he intended.

But when we reached the room, a new scent touched my nose, and my wolf perked up with an irritated growl.

Alpha female.

"Alana," he said before I could embarrass myself by asking. "She's my father's third-in-command. And apparently she has a penchant for cleaning up messes." He gestured to the spotless living room, the couch and chair appearing brand new.

But that wasn't what sent my eyebrows into my hairline.

"Your father has a female general?"

"He has four, actually. But the other three are Betas. Alana is the only Alpha. She's also technically an Enforcer, not a general. However, I suspect she'll become my father's Second when Kazek takes over Winter Sector." He frowned then, his brow creasing. "Assuming he takes the job."

I blinked at him, stunned by the information. No Alpha had ever spoken to me in this manner, like he wanted me to know something other than how to properly take the knot.

I'd also never heard of females being permitted into the general ranks. Alpha Vanessa was the only notable exception, but she'd acquired that role because of her familial relation to Alpha Carlos. She was technically my aunt. Not that I'd ever call her that.

"Is Alana your sister?" I wondered out loud.

Sven snorted. "Not by blood, but she certainly acts like she's my older sibling sometimes. Same with Kaz. They both enjoy testing my limits."

"Testing your limits?" I repeated, not understanding.

"Alpha limits," he rephrased. "They have a penchant for dropping me in zombie nests and timing my escapes."

My jaw dropped. That sounded *awful*. "Why?" I asked, unable to help the gasp in my tone.

He met my gaze, his eyes sparkling. "It's their way of testing my mettle. And it's helped prepare me for challenges within Norse Sector. Alphas are all about hierarchy, and sometimes age can be a discriminating factor."

I studied him. "Age?" I hadn't thought to ask him that

before. He was big and strong and Alpha. Why would his age matter to anyone?

"I'm twenty-five," he said, his tone daring me to insult him. "Some wolves think dominance is about experience. My inner beast and I disagree."

"Oh." I supposed that made sense. Alpha Joseph had been younger. But that wasn't why my father had bested him in a fight.

A beeping sounded in the kitchen, causing Sven to turn away from me. I followed, the aroma coming from the oven making my mouth water.

He pulled out a giant pizza, the cheese and meat sizzling on top.

My eyes rounded at the sight of it. "I haven't had pizza since…" I trailed off, my heart panging miserably in my chest.

"Since when?"

"Since… my mom," I whispered, unable to continue. She'd made pizza for me and Savi a few times, her favorite being a potato and corn one with sausage chunks.

This one appeared to have a different sort of meat on it, the circles a deep red and reminding me a little of bacon.

He didn't ask me about my mom, instead saying, "I wasn't sure what kind you'd like, so I went for pepperoni and ham."

"I don't know that I've ever had that before," I admitted. Ham, yes. Pepperoni, no. And definitely not on pizza.

He pulled open a drawer and drew out a sharp-looking metal wheel. "What kind have you had?"

"Sausage, potato, and corn," I murmured.

He paused, glancing at me. Then he looked at the

pizza and cocked his head. "Huh. That would be interesting to try. Maybe I'll make it tomorrow."

My chest ached at the thought. "I can help," I offered before I could take it back.

He glanced at me, a smile in his blue eyes. "I think I'd like that."

I nodded, relieved that I'd pleased him. It stirred a warm sensation in my veins that helped soothe the pain radiating from my heart and calmed my nerves considerably.

He cut through the cheese and sauce, creating pie slices. Then he put one on a plate for me before grabbing a second slice for himself.

He opened the fridge and pulled out a bowl of diced meat cubes. I examined them, curious as to what he intended to do with them. They weren't cooked yet.

"For Winter," he explained before leaving the room.

I almost followed him, my instinct to protect my companion at odds with my wolf's innate trust in Alpha Sven. She wasn't concerned at all about him approaching the other Omega, entirely content with the notion of him taking care of Winter. She was more concerned about him returning right away—which he did—because she didn't like the idea of sharing him with anyone.

His thumb drew a line over my forehead, smoothing out my skin. "You're frowning," he murmured. "Why?"

"My wolf is confusing me," I admitted.

"How so?"

"She's being… possessive."

"Of me?" he guessed, a smile in his voice. "That's good because my wolf feels possessive of you, too."

"Why?"

"Because you're mine," he replied simply, taking our

plates over to the dining room table. "Do you want water or something sugary?"

I was too busy gaping at him to answer that.

So he chose water for us both, then used a hand on the small of my back to guide me toward the table. "Your claw marks are an interesting decoration," he mused as he settled me into a chair.

I was still gaping at him when he took the seat across from me. "You can't claim me; I'm sterile." The words came out before I could hold them back. "I don't understand what all this is. I'm… I'm not an available Omega. I'm a slave."

"You're a former slave," he corrected. "And you're very much *my* Omega."

"Why? Why me?"

He considered me for a moment and shrugged. "My wolf says you're ours. So you are."

"And what if my wolf disagrees?" I countered.

"She doesn't."

I blinked. *This… How…? But…*

"Eat," he instructed. "We can discuss this more later."

"Discuss what more later?" I asked, slightly miffed. "You've already decided for us both."

"Yes, I have, but I'll enjoy convincing you to agree."

"And how do you intend to do that?" I demanded. Because clearly this Alpha was insane. Why were we even discussing this? There could be no future here. It was dangerous to even consider it. Infertile Omegas couldn't go into estrus, which meant we couldn't procreate and therefore couldn't take mates. Obviously, he knew this. So why—

"I think I'll start by worshipping you with my tongue," he said, interrupting—and entirely *annihilating*—my thoughts.

"Um, what?"

"My tongue," he repeated, his eyes smoldering as he met and held my gaze. "I think that's how I'll start our courtship."

Courtship? I repeated to myself. *Tongue?*

My skin heated at the thought.

"You can't take my knot, but that doesn't mean we can't play in other ways," he continued. "And trust me, Omega, I have an excellent imagination."

"I…" I swallowed. "I can't take your knot?" I was an Omega. Of course I could take his knot. That was the reason for my existence.

"Not yet," he replied. "Not until you've been fully evaluated by a physician. I promised not to hurt you, Kari. And you said knotting you hurts. So my hands are tied."

I gaped at him. "You're… you're not going to knot me?"

"Oh, I'm going to knot you, Omega. But only when it's safe to do so." He gestured to the untouched food on my plate. "Eat. You need strength. We'll discuss this more tomorrow."

CHAPTER FOURTEEN

SVEN

K ARI HAD WATCHED ME CAUTIOUSLY, like she'd expected me to strike out at her at any moment. Her inherent distrust had grated on my nerves.

Which was why I hadn't ended up licking her for dessert after eating pizza together.

And also why I'd refrained from touching her too intimately for the two days that had followed.

We'd shared her nest each night. But even that had taken a certain amount of effort. She had always stripped off her shirt and lain in the center with her legs spread, expecting me to take her. Each time, I'd gently moved her to the side to make room for myself, then pulled her against me with a purr and held her until she eventually succumbed to sleep.

We hadn't discussed my claims on her. Nor had I teased her with my tongue or my kiss. It'd been an excruciating experience that had required an insurmountable amount of resistance on my part, but I'd had no choice. We couldn't move forward until I earned her trust.

Unfortunately, we were on our final hours, and I was nowhere near that point with her.

I'd spent most of our time together talking to her like

any other wolf. That had seemed to work well before our pizza meal the other day, so I'd worked to replicate that easy camaraderie. She'd mostly seemed amenable to it, even choosing to open up a little bit about her mother and sister while we'd made the potato, corn, and sausage pizza together.

But then my father had shown up to check on Winter —and, not so discreetly, on Kari—and she'd completely shut down in response. She'd barely touched her pizza after that, and I'd spent most of our night together purring while she'd slept fitfully in my arms.

I'd messaged him the next morning telling him not to show up unannounced again. He'd replied with a quick agreement, saying we would talk today after the claiming ceremony.

Kari was nowhere near ready to meet the pack. I'd tried to tell her more about Norse Sector over the last few days, including giving her a detailed structure on how the hierarchy worked. It seemed like a good starting place since the female generals had intrigued her the other day. She'd listened and asked a few questions, but I'd sensed her hesitation and concern throughout each conversation.

She was afraid to believe me.

Afraid to trust me.

Afraid to allow any ounce of hope to touch her spirit.

I couldn't blame her in the slightest. What little she'd told me about her history confirmed her life had been one horror after another. She'd spoken about her mother in past tense, suggesting she was no longer alive. And she'd already confirmed she didn't know her sister's fate.

My father was trying to find out what he could, but the Alpha of Bariloche Sector was not one of our allies.

I picked up the skillet to dump the scrambled eggs into a bowl, then set it on the table beside the fruit salad Kari had made. She'd very carefully washed all the berries before assembling the salad, her movements meticulous and perfect, like she'd been afraid to make a single mistake.

The final item was the salmon I'd smoked in the oven, which I added to a new plate and set beside the eggs.

Kari took a seat, but before I could, an alert popped up above my wrist. Her eyes widened as a visual of my father's face appeared. "Alana is on her way up to release Winter," he said without a greeting. "Stay with Omega Kari for now. I'll reach out about tonight."

I frowned, confused by the change of plans. He'd told me just yesterday that he wanted me at the claiming ceremony. "Everything all right?"

"Pheromones," he replied.

"Ah." Kaz must be agitated. He didn't want to risk me absorbing the scent and taking it back to Kari. "Understood."

He gave a nod and disconnected the call.

"How did that happen?" Kari asked, gaping at the air above my wrist. "Can he…? Does he…?" Her eyes rounded, and she looked down at her own arm. "Am I…?"

"It's my watch," I explained, showing her the device wrapped around my wrist. "It's genetically programmed to me and my wolf. So I can shift with it or, in this case, keep it hidden if I want. But it's like a miniature computer tied to my DNA."

She blinked at me like I'd grown five heads.

Amused, I took the seat across from her and pulled up the main screen to start showing her how the watch worked and what it did. We were in the middle of going through the primary applications when Alana arrived for Winter.

"Is there a reason I couldn't just walk her to the elevator?" I asked by way of greeting.

"Yeah, Alpha Ludvig wants me to torture her first," Alana drawled.

Kari's eyes widened, making me growl. "*Alana.*"

"What? It's true. And Kaz deserves it. He gave her my clothes to wear, Sven. Talk about an idiot move." She rolled her big blue eyes and flipped her blonde ponytail over her shoulder. "You'll note that all the clothes I gave you are your own. You're welcome."

She gave a little finger wave to Kari before passing the table and heading out to the balcony area. Kari started to stand, her hackles rising.

"She's not going to hurt Winter."

"She just said—"

"I know what she said, but she meant it figuratively. Winter doesn't like Alana because she's slept with Kazek before. So Alpha Ludvig sent Alana here on purpose, knowing her presence would punish Winter. He's not all that pleased with her for sneaking onto the plane." And my father would be looking for every method he could exploit in punishing the Omega in a thorough manner while not risking any harm to her physically. "I promise she's not hurting Winter."

Just as I said it, a snarl came from the balcony, followed by a low warning Alpha growl.

Kari bolted upward, ready to intercede, when Winter stomped inside in wolf form. She bared her teeth at Alana, which just made the Alpha grin widely. "Oh, I do like you," she said.

Winter snapped her jaws in response, clearly stating the feeling was not mutual.

"Keep your claws to yourself, honey. I don't want your Alpha. He's all yours."

Winter grunted as though to suggest she didn't believe Alana at all.

Which, of course, just amused Alana that much more. "See you at the welcome ceremony later?" she asked as she passed me, her gaze flickering briefly to Kari with an obvious question in her eyes.

"Yeah," I replied. She'd see me. But not Kari if I had my way.

Alana nodded. "Good. Welcome to Norse Sector, Omega Kari. Everyone is looking forward to meeting you."

Kari froze, causing me to groan inside. "Bye, Alana," I said through my teeth.

She just smiled and opened the front door for Winter. "Out you go, little Omega."

The *little Omega* snapped her jaws again, earning another low growl from Alana. "I'm allowing this because I understand your need to mark your territory. But don't push it."

Winter visibly clenched her jaw and darted out the door with Alana hot on her tail. The door slammed behind her, leaving Kari frowning at the table. She was still standing, her hands clenched into fists at her side. "Where is she taking her?"

"To Alpha Kazek."

"Before or after she tortures her?"

"She's already torturing her," I drawled. "Her presence here irks Winter's wolf."

Kari looked at me. "I don't understand."

"How would you feel if I said I'd fucked Alana?" I asked her, genuinely curious as to how she'd react.

She didn't disappoint, her cheeks flushing a deep red as her eyes narrowed. "Why would you fuck her? You have me."

It took genuine effort not to smile at that response. "That's not what I asked."

"Well, I don't like your question."

"And that's exactly how Alana is torturing Winter right now," I drawled.

Kari just continued to glower at me. "I don't want you to fuck Alana."

Okay, so we were stuck on that. I couldn't help the low chuckle escaping me in response, which was clearly the wrong thing to do because Kari growled, placing her palms on the table and leaning forward. "She can't take a knot. *I can.*"

"Sweetheart, that's not the point." I reached forward to cup her jaw, but she caught my palm between her teeth and bit down. Hard. My eyebrows rose. "Did you just mark me?"

Her eyes widened, the twin splotches of red turning white in an instant as she looked down at my hand and then back up at me. "Oh… I…" Her knees gave out as she fell to the ground into a pose of supplication on the ground. "I-I'm sorry, Alpha. I… I don't know what came over me. I… I just *reacted.*"

An understatement.

She'd just claimed me in her own way.

And my wolf was now preening inside me as a result. But he did not like her position on the floor.

I pushed away from the table and walked around to where she remained bowed with her forehead touching the floor.

"Kari," I murmured, crouching before her. "You don't need to apologize or bow. I'm not mad." I gently drew my fingers through her hair, then grabbed a fistful of the strands to tug her head back when she didn't make any move to climb off the floor.

Tears filled her eyes, her mortification evident.

"I was trying to explain to you how Alana is torturing

Winter," I said softly. "Omegas are very territorial of their Alphas, just like Alphas are possessive of their Omegas. It's particularly bad at the beginning of a bond, which means that Winter cannot stand to be in Alana's presence because she's one of Kazek's former lovers."

Technically, she'd just been a *fuck buddy*, but I didn't want to use that term with Kari.

"Come on, little wolf," I said, wrapping my palm around the back of her neck to pull her up from the floor. "We both need to eat, and I'll finish explaining how my watch works."

Her gaze went to my hand and the small teeth marks on my palm. I'd purposely used my other hand to guide her up off the ground.

"Do you want to kiss and make it better?" I offered, trying to lighten the mood.

"K-kiss?" she repeated.

"Yes, Kari. My palm," I said, holding it out to her.

She didn't make a move to kiss the mark, she just gaped at it. But I caught a flicker of satisfaction in her eyes, her wolf pleased with having sunk her teeth into my skin.

With a shake of my head, I dropped my hold on her and lowered my hand back to my side. "Sit down and eat, Kari."

She quickly obeyed, taking her seat and picking up her fork.

Sighing, I returned to my chair and scooped the now-cold food onto our plates.

We ate in silence for a while, then I broke the quiet by finishing my explanation of the technology on my wrist. It was an advanced device that facilitated communication both within our sector and with sector allies. As I was showing her images and surveillance, I noticed her straighten and went back to the album that had caught her eye.

With a small smile, I brought up the photo of my older brother with a little wolf on his shoulders. "That's Ander," I said. "And that's his son, Joaquim. Although, they call him Quim for short. It's a namesake for the language in the Andorra region—Catalan."

I wasn't sure if Kari heard me at all. She was too busy studying the photo.

So I switched to a second one that showed Ander with his Omega mate and their son. "That's Katriana," I told her. "My brother's mate."

Kari leaned forward as though to touch the image. Then her big blue eyes met mine. "She's… she's smiling."

"Yeah, and I think she's pregnant again." I wasn't quite sure because Ander hadn't confirmed it, but he'd been a little more growly than usual on our last call. "I've actually not had a chance to meet her yet, but I hope to soon."

"But… but she's smiling." Kari looked back at the picture. "She looks happy."

"I imagine that's because she is happy," I replied, studying her. "You said Savi had a mate. Was she not happy?"

Kari considered that for a moment, her gaze falling to the table. "Yes. She was happy." Her lips twisted as she bit her cheek. "He made her feel safe."

"As an Alpha should."

Her gaze turned faraway for a second, her expression hardening. Then she looked at the image again, stirring conflict in her features. After a long moment, she cleared her throat and focused on my hand. "I'm sorry."

I smiled. "Well, I'm not."

Her brow furrowed. "You're really not mad." Not a question, but a statement.

I closed the applications on my translucent screen and met her wary gaze. "No, Kari. I'm thrilled." It wasn't a lie. "My wolf is preening inside me right now, pleased that you claimed him."

"I didn't claim him."

"Sure," I murmured. "Are you done eating?"

It almost seemed like she wanted to argue but thought better of it, and then she nodded.

I let her consider everything she'd learned while I went to clean up the kitchen. When I finished, she hadn't moved from the table, and she had a crinkle in her brow that indicated deep thought. "This is our third day," she said quietly.

"Yes."

"What happens next?"

"You meet the sector," I told her. Assuming I couldn't change my father's mind, anyway.

"And then?"

"And then you'll be welcomed into Norse Sector as an Omega under our protection." I wrapped my palm around the back of her neck again. "Let's go shower. My father will be calling soon for a meeting, and I need to be ready."

"You're leaving me here?" she whispered.

"For a little while, yes." I drew my thumb along the edge of her jaw while my palm remained around her nape. "But I'll be back to take you to the ceremony later."

"Where will I go after that?" It was a nearly silent question, her eyes filling with tears again.

"I don't know yet, Kari," I admitted. I wasn't sure if my father intended for her to stay here or if he had other accommodations in mind. Once she was part of Norse Sector, she would be considered a cherished member. No one would dare touch her without his consent or blessing.

And I'd also kill anyone who tried.

Kari nodded, her lower lip wobbling slightly. "Okay."

I pressed my lips to her forehead. "It's going to be all right, little wolf," I promised her. "You'll see."

She didn't reply, her lack of faith in me evident yet again.

With a sigh, I led her to the bedroom.

Maybe the ceremony would be a good experience for her. She'd finally understand how our world worked here, and she'd start to truly heal. Because it was becoming clear that I couldn't handle that part on my own. Not until she trusted me.

Which, at this rate, might take years to accomplish.

My wolf bristled inside me, drawing my attention back to the bite mark on my hand.

Or perhaps it'll be sooner than I think, I thought with an inward smile as I stroked the indentations with my thumb. It would heal soon. But for now, I'd enjoy her little claim.

My sweet wolf, I mused. *One day, I'll bite you, too. I vow it.*

CHAPTER FIFTEEN

KARI

ALPHA SVEN DRESSED IN SILENCE, pulling on a pair of jeans first and then a sweater. When he started to lace up a pair of boots, my heart skipped a beat.

This is it, I realized. *He's leaving me for good.*

After tonight, I'd be given to the other Alphas. And our time here would be finished.

It was just as I'd feared—I had become addicted to his purr, his presence, his *scent.* The memories would haunt me for a lifetime as I returned to my hellish existence.

At least Winter's mate had survived. She still had a chance to live.

But not me.

The healing mark on Alpha Sven's hand proved it. I couldn't claim him just as he couldn't claim me. Not that I had a right to even try.

And he hadn't even been mad.

He'd... he'd been perfect. He'd held me. Kept me warm. Made me feel safe. Shown me what an Alpha could be. While I still didn't understand his goal, it was on the tip of my tongue to beg him to stay.

His watch flickered to life like it had earlier, this time with a message that he swiped away before I could read it. I hadn't noticed the device before, the band having blended into his skin in a manner I didn't know was possible. But I supposed the magical tech would have to exist if he could shift with it into wolf form.

He finished lacing up his boots and stood, leaving the bed.

Leaving me.

Our nest.

This beautiful moment of peace.

"Alpha," I whispered, not ready for it to end.

I was sitting in the middle of the mattress, protected by the wall of sheets that still smelled like him.

He turned, his eyebrow inching upward. "You're allowed to call me Sven."

My nose crinkled, the informality feeling wrong, yet oddly right, too. *Sven.* "Alpha Sven."

His lips twitched. "I don't need the title. I'm very aware of my status, little wolf." He bent to carefully place his palms on the mattress inside our nest and pressed his lips to my cheek. "I don't know how long this is going to take."

My stomach churned at the words and the implication behind them. I wasn't even sure where he was going or if he planned to come back. Our three days were over. Now I would meet the other Alphas. And I knew what would follow.

He'd promised to show me how Alphas could be different, and he'd succeeded. And now he intended to take it away.

I didn't understand.

Had I done something wrong? Displeased him?

I'd given him access to my body each night, but he hadn't taken me. Just purred for me and held me. Was I supposed to do more? Take charge? Offer to pleasure him?

Some Omegas openly begged. I'd heard it through the

119

LEXI C. FOSS

thin walls back home, especially during estrus cycles. But I'd never been one to fall to my knees for an Alpha.

However, I would do whatever Sven asked if it meant even just a few more hours of peace.

He'd asked for three days. He'd talked about forever. He'd claimed that I was his.

So why is he leaving now?

Did he realize I wasn't good enough? Did he finally understand that he couldn't claim a sterile Omega?

Or had I missed a cue somewhere? He'd asked for a kiss earlier. Maybe that was what he wanted—for me to show interest. Parting my legs at night wasn't enough for him. He needed more than a doll.

Could I be that for him? Would that encourage him to keep me? To stay here instead of preparing for the event later? Would I be able to convince him not to give me to the other Alphas?

I have to try, I realized. *I have to do something to make him keep me.*

He started to lift away from me, from our nest, from the safety of this moment, and I reacted. I grabbed him, my fingers sinking into his hair as I pulled him back to me, my lips claiming his in a begging kiss.

Don't leave me.

Don't ruin this.

I'll do anything, everything, be whatever you need! Just stay. Please. Please stay.

The words were chaos in my mind, the tone one of desperation and *need*.

The last few days had been a gift and a curse. A new form of torture. A way to introduce me to a life I'd never known existed, just to rip it away and throw me back to the literal wolves.

I never wanted to leave. I never wanted this to end. I

just wanted him. And I showed him with my mouth that I would give him my own life if it meant just a few more minutes of peace.

"Kari." His voice was a rumble that vibrated my chest.

I silenced him with my tongue, doing exactly what he'd done to me the other day, only with more force and desperation.

I had no idea what I was doing, so I let my wolf lead, giving her the reins over my body and allowing her to show him what I desired. *Him. In my nest. Forever.*

It was a dangerous desire, a foreign hope, a dream I never knew I possessed.

This Alpha had been kind. Gentle. Protective. I wanted to give him all of me in return for just a sliver more of that attention and warmth. Tears streamed from my eyes, my mind a maze of desire and warning.

He'd broken me in a way I'd never anticipated, touching my heart and shredding it to pieces.

Don't leave me, I repeated with my kiss. *Don't make me meet the pack. Don't give me away. Keep me. Please.*

His palms cradled my face, his growl one I felt to my very soul.

But he used his strength to push me back, his gaze twin pools of heat. "I have to go," he murmured. "I'm sorry, Kari. I would stay with you if I could."

My chest cracked open, my breath leaving me in a whoosh of sound. *I'm too late.* I'd already missed my deadline, and now there was nothing I could do to encourage him to stay. "Please," I managed to croak out, my voice an exhale of sound and lacking in resolve.

His lips brushed mine in a gentle caress, a soft goodbye, a whisper of what could have been. "I won't be long," he promised. "I'll be back soon, and we'll discuss tonight's ceremony, okay?"

My hope flickered and burned inside me, the thin threads unraveling and disappearing into ash. "Okay," I mouthed, not meaning it.

Because I didn't want to talk about the ceremony.

I didn't want to join his pack. I didn't want to become *available* for the Alphas. I wanted to stay here in my safe haven.

However, as he kissed the top of my head and left without another word, I realized how foolish I'd been. Sven had said to give him three days to demonstrate how Alphas could be. He'd never promised to remain this way. And I knew better than to expect him to.

I was an infertile Omega.

I couldn't have a mate. All that talk about me being his was just his wolf dreaming of a future with some other female.

Not me.

I had to attend the ceremony tonight. Meet other Alphas. Be available for their knot.

Yet I sat here in this nest, wishing for a different fate. Wishing for a fantasy that would never come to fruition.

What am I doing? I thought, looking around at the sheets and realizing how wrong it all was, how I didn't belong here, how I'd allowed my instincts to override my mind.

I knew better than this.

Alphas couldn't be trusted. They used Omegas. They destroyed them. They knotted them. This was all some twisted game, a cruel punishment I would never understand.

Because it no longer mattered.

Our time was up. I'd used him for memories I would forever cherish, and now... now I had to face the next stage.

I swallowed, my vision blurring beneath a wall of unshed tears. *Who have I become? How did I even get here?*

Just a week ago, I'd experienced a kindling of hope about going to Alpha Enrique.

Yet I sat in a soft bed, surrounded by another male's scent.

I grabbed his shirt, yanking it over my head and tossing it to the floor. *Enough.* I wouldn't fall for his trickery anymore. I wouldn't be this wolf. I wouldn't allow myself to believe that Alphas could be kind. I'd remind myself of their true nature. I'd be the Omega my father had created.

Sterile.

Worthless.

A sleeve.

With a scream, I ripped the blankets up off the bed and threw them to the floor. But it wasn't enough. The scent was everywhere, the pull to re-create the safety of my walls strong and nearly overwhelming.

My wolf whimpered, begging me to go back, to fix my mess, to hide in my nest and wait for Alpha Sven to return.

What's the point? I demanded, a sob breaking from my chest. *He's just going to introduce us to the Alphas and leave us for them to fuck!*

She growled in my mind, negating the words.

But I was too far gone to hear her. I was done with this game. This trickery. This horrible, wicked display of kindness.

No more.

I leapt off the bed, glaring at the twisted stack of sheets. It beckoned me to return, to rebuild, to be what an Omega should be.

But I wasn't that Omega.

I'm nothing.

I'm just a tool for the knot.

An Omega without a mate.

How many times had my father told me my purpose? How could I forget it so easily?

I almost laughed, my chest inflamed with hatred and despair. *There's no hope for you here, Kari*, I thought, the inner voice deep and reminiscent of my father. *You're weak. An Omega. A thing to be fucked.*

Tears fell from my wobbling chin, the room spinning as I sprinted toward the door.

I had to destroy it… this hope… this hesitation in my heart that told me to take a breath and think. I didn't want to think. I wanted to disappear. To not feel anything. To not know what was about to happen. To become the doll my father had created.

Lifeless.

Broken.

Dead.

A scream lodged in my throat as I entered the kitchen, my eyes on the knives. I grabbed two and ran back to the bedroom, aiming for the nest, needing to destroy it and everything it represented.

I wasn't allowed to feel. I wasn't allowed to possess this dream, this fantasy, this unrealistic life.

Safety didn't exist.

Alpha Sven wasn't mine.

I belonged to all Alphas, not just one. No mating. No love. No bond. Just a thing to be rutted and marked and *used*.

I'd meant to use him.

But I'd failed. I'd fallen into this unacceptable state instead.

No more. I was done. We were done.

With a cry, I stabbed the mattress over and over and over again, both of my hands working to destroy the scent and our nest. But it wasn't enough. It still lingered, the memories embedded into my heart and soul and drawing me to my knees in the mess.

"Die!" I screamed, needing the nest to disappear, for this feeling to leave me alone, to take me back into a catatonic state and drown me in quiet.

I lost track of time.

Space.

Just kept stabbing. Stabbing. *Stabbing.*

I lost the knives, the mess of feathers and shredded sheets engulfing them in a fluffy cloud that smelled like Sven.

More tears fell, my vision blanketed behind a waterfall of color and pain. I collapsed into the mess on a sob, needing it to end, needing not to feel, only to feel a sharp sensation deep inside that grounded me in the present.

It reminded me of the surgery, the pain unlike any I'd experienced in a long, long time. Worse than the rutting. Worse than the occasional bite.

I clutched my abdomen, crying out in pain, and blinked at the sticky sensation on my skin. Lifting my hand, I noted the deep red color.

Did I rupture something? I wondered dizzily, my vision blinking in and out of focus.

I suddenly felt incredibly woozy. And sick. *Very, very sick.*

I pressed a palm to my mouth, and the other to my stomach, as I curled into a ball to try to calm my racing heart. The pang worsened, my body jolting in response and stirring a low whine in my throat.

Oh God... I couldn't breathe. The slicing pain had slid upward to a lung, forcing me to straighten my legs and roll onto my back.

I couldn't see.

The darkness had engulfed me. But it wasn't the good

kind that numbed my thoughts. No, I felt every ounce of torment shooting through my veins.

I… I think I'm dying, I realized on a wave of understanding. *Will I finally experience true peace?*

I blinked. Or I thought I did.

My heart skipped a beat as my lips curled down.

No, I whispered to myself. *I've already experienced peace. With Alpha Sven.*

A dying wish.

A dying memory.

A beautiful… moment… of hope.

One I would take to my grave. Assuming they even deemed me worthy of a burial. I pictured it, my body beneath a big fir tree, surrounded by snow and ice.

Alpha Sven stood beside me, his big palm cupping my face, his expression sad.

Yes, I whispered to myself. *This is the real fantasy. Having an Alpha care enough… to be there for me… even in death.*

I fell asleep with that dream in my mind.

A part of me hoping to never wake again.

And another part… mourning the loss of an Alpha I really wanted to be mine.

Maybe in the next lifetime.

Or perhaps just in my dreams.

I think… I think I could have loved you, Sven. Thank you for giving me peace. Thank you… for our three days.

CHAPTER SIXTEEN

SVEN

I stood beside my father as Kaz led a sex-high Winter away from the field. Her dark eyes were glazed with passion while he purred in contentment at having officially claimed his female. I'd missed most of the show, having been delayed by Kari's unexpected kiss.

She'd tasted so damn good, but the desperation pouring off her had kept me in check. I wouldn't take her in that state. Nor did I understand what had caused it.

We'd spent the last few days getting to know each other, and not once had she clung to me like that. I was eager to return to her and find out what had provoked her behavior. Although, I suspected I wouldn't like the reason, which explained this odd pinching sensation throbbing in my chest.

I rubbed at it with my fist, willing the discomfort to fuck off. But it only worsened. Like something was wrong and I just couldn't figure out what had caused it.

An inane notion.

But that didn't stop it from irritating my wolf. He prowled inside me, eager to return to the female he considered his mate.

I flexed my hand and glanced at the spot where she'd

bitten me a few hours ago, my lips twitching at the sides. At least until another pang shot through my heart.

"What is it?" my father asked quietly, his focus on the dispersing pack members. That didn't hinder his constant awareness of those around him. It was a trait I admired about him and hoped to perfect on my own someday.

"I feel like something's wrong," I admitted. As he was my father and my Sector Alpha, I never hid anything from him. It was why I'd been upfront and clear on my intentions to claim Kari. "She was very"—I paused, thinking about the right term—"*emotional*, not sad so much as clingy, when I left. And it's not sitting right with me."

"Clingy how?"

"She begged me to stay."

He glanced at me with an arched brow. "That's an improvement."

"Yeah, but it doesn't feel right." And that was precisely the problem. She'd wanted me to stay with her, which should have made my wolf rejoice and preen. Instead, he was pacing restlessly and urging me to run back to her.

He faced me, his expression pensive. "Doesn't feel right in what way?"

I considered how to word what I was feeling. "I should be pleased that she showed progress by wanting me to stay. But all I feel is a deep-seated ache of dread. Like something is really wrong." I rubbed my chest again, wincing as my wolf growled inside me, his patience thinning. "My animal side is demanding I go to her. He's worried about something."

My father's blue irises flickered with his wolf, his pupils flaring. "Have you bitten her?"

I frowned. "No. But she bit me earlier."

His eyebrows lifted. "She bit you?"

"I asked her a hypothetical question, and she

responded by biting my hand. It was a result of her innate possessiveness." Something that had pleased me to no end but felt disturbing now.

Something is very wrong, I decided, glancing at the building only a block away. I took a step toward it without thinking and shook my head to stop myself.

However, my father started moving. "Let's go."

"But the ceremony—"

"Is done," he interjected. "They'll all finish dispersing and head home to prepare for the dessert feast."

I nodded and followed him, my wolf begging me to run.

"You said her father did this to her," he said as we picked up the pace. "He likely didn't make her infertility permanent, which explains your wolf's insistence that she belongs to you."

"I've had that thought," I admitted. Because I'd felt from the beginning that she was mine to claim, even while knowing she was sterile.

"So her biting you might have initiated a subtle link," he continued as though I hadn't spoken.

My heart skipped a beat at his words, my wolf even more agitated than before. "Then that means…" My pace quickened into a jog, instinct taking over.

"You're feeling something through the link. That's how you know something's wrong."

I was running by the time my father finished, his feet moving just as quickly beside me. He was over five hundred years old and could usually beat me in a race, but not today.

I reached the building first, bolting inside and calling the elevator with my watch. My wolf demanded I take the stairs, but it would end up slower in the end.

The doors opened as I approached, my father right behind me as I keyed in the code to her floor.

With each passing second, I felt the increasing dread inside me.

"Did you leave anything sharp in the suite?" my father asked, a screen hovering over his wrist with the contact number for the pack's physician pulsing just over his thumb.

"You think she hurt herself?"

"I warned you that she was suicidal," he growled. "Did you leave sharp objects in the suite?"

"Yes," I whispered, my stance suddenly unsteady. "I… I didn't think…"

"Clearly," he snapped, keying in the code for her floor.

My fists clenched. "She has fucking claws," I hissed. "I can't take those from her."

He glanced at me. "Perhaps that's why they collared her before, to keep her wolf in check."

The notion infuriated me. "They collared her to make her a slave."

The doors opened before he could reply. Not that I was in the mood to listen to him anymore. I sprinted forward, the familiar metallic aroma making my wolf crazy inside me.

It was heavy.

Potent.

And thick in the air.

Oh, Kari, what the hell did you do?

I ran through the door and the living area, following the scent…

To a scene that made my heart drop into my stomach.

Blood.

Feathers.

Shredded sheets.

And a naked Omega passed out in the center of a mutilated mattress.

She'd destroyed our nest. She'd... she'd stabbed herself *in our nest.*

A pained groan left my lips as I fell to my knees beside her. The knife was deeply embedded in her abdomen, the angle likely nicking one of her lungs.

"Fuck," I breathed, my hands roaming over her. "*Fuck!*"

"Don't pull it out," my father said urgently.

"No shit," I snapped back at him. "That's the only thing keeping her alive!"

If she'd pulled out the blade, she would have flooded her lungs. And while wolves could survive a lot, only the strongest could survive drowning in one's own blood.

Considering she'd done this to herself, I doubted she'd try to fight such a thing. She'd welcome death.

In our nest.

My wolf growled in fury, then whined at the sight of her pale skin. She looked so fragile and broken. Barely alive.

Towels dropped down beside me, my father in healing mode. I used them to cover the area around the wound and tried to help stop some of the bleeding.

"Doctor Pal—"

"He's already on his way," my father interjected. "Purr for her. Give her your strength. Make sure she knows you're here."

"Will that even help her?" I asked, gaping at the small female. "*She tried to kill herself in our nest.*" That couldn't mean great things about our future together. My purr might be the last thing she wanted right now.

"Is she yours or not?" my father demanded.

My wolf growled at the implication of his words, his

stance still resolute that this female belonged to him. Even if she was broken and preferred death over being his mate.

"You told me three days ago that it's your job to take care of her and to heal her. So either own it or move out of my way."

There were moments when I loved my father and moments where I hated him. This moment was a mixture of both.

I gritted my teeth and focused on Kari. Not on the carnage surrounding her or the feelings this scene evoked, but on the Omega I considered mine.

Her heart beat unsteadily in my ears, her breaths shuddering out of her petite form. I slid into the mess with her, careful not to jostle her wound, and allowed her to feel my heat. My protection. My strength. My *purr*.

I told her without words that I was here, that I would see her through this. And I fought the urge to consider what would happen next.

All that mattered was her survival.

She needed to know I wouldn't give up on her this easily. My wolf was a stubborn Alpha who refused to walk away from a challenge.

She was mine whether she liked it or not.

Seconds turned into minutes, then a new presence arrived. My father spoke to the doctor in low tones, warning him not to distract me from my process. I was ensuring her spirit survived while the physician saw to her body.

It was a delicate dance. Exhausting. Infuriating. Heartbreaking.

But I did it for her, holding her hand as a team of medics arrived to carefully move her. Brushing the hair from her face as we entered the elevator. Guarding her as we left the building. Blocking the view of her face and mangled form as we made our way to the medical quarters of Norse Sector. Purring louder as the medical team took her to the surgery room. Ensuring my breathing rivaled hers as they operated. And running a cool towel over her forehead after they brought her to a patient room.

It hadn't taken them very long, the wound not as deep as I'd originally thought.

They'd said the blade had entered her with force, but not enough to do serious damage. With her wolf genetics and their advanced medical techniques, she'd be awake in the next few hours, and mostly healed within a day.

However, that was only in reference to her physical wounds, not her emotional ones.

I was angry. Distraught. Confused. And a myriad of other emotions.

Yet I never stopped purring for her.

I put her above my own turmoil, needing her to know I was still here, that I wouldn't leave her to suffer alone.

Except my father had other plans for me. He arrived dressed up for tonight's festivities and hung a suit bag on the door of her patient room. "You're attending," he said. "I'll watch her while you change."

"I'm not leaving her."

"You are," he countered. "But just for an hour."

I glared at him. "My presence isn't needed."

"On the contrary, it's very much needed. Kazek has taken an Omega mate. And not just any Omega mate, but Snow Frost. Alpha Vanessa has sent out a communication for everyone to hear, and I need you there to stand in solidarity with Kazek."

My jaw ticked. "You're punishing me."

"I don't need to punish you, Sven. You've already gone through enough today. I assume you'll know better than to leave sharp objects around your *intended* now."

It took effort not to punch him in the face. Mostly because he was implying that what had happened to Kari was my fault. And while, yes, a part of the blame definitely lay at my feet, *she* had made the choice to hurt herself.

"I will not collar her wolf," I said, unzipping the garment bag. "I don't care how suicidal she is, separating her from her animal isn't the solution." If anything, it seemed that was part of the blame for all this. She didn't rely on her wolf instincts at all.

Well, not unless I provoked them. Like the claiming bite on my hand. But otherwise, she seemed to live perpetually in her head, constantly fearing others despite the obvious sitting right in front of her.

Kari's wolf seemed to like me, at least enough to drive her reactions. It'd been her wolf that had built her nest. Her wolf that had bitten me. Her wolf that had kissed me only hours ago.

Not Kari the person.

"She'll be under observation here until you return," my father said, interrupting my thoughts. "I've already spoken to Doctor Palmer, and he doesn't think she'll wake up for at least another hour at a minimum. So she won't even notice you're gone."

"You're the one who told me to purr for her," I muttered, pulling off my shirt and beginning the tedious process of putting on formal wear.

"And you did. Now she's recovering. Maybe it's wise to let her do the last bit on her own, so she can think about what she's done."

I considered that while I switched my jeans for a pair of dress pants. My mother probably picked the all-black ensemble, knowing it would match my mood. Assuming she knew what had happened today. My parents rarely kept secrets from each other, so it was likely.

"You want me gone when she wakes up," I finally replied, thinking through his ploy. "She'll sense my presence in the scents but know that I've left. And you want to give her that moment to think about losing me and my protection."

His blue eyes gave nothing away. Yet he said, "Now you're thinking like an Alpha."

"I'm always thinking like an Alpha," I retorted. "I'm your fucking son."

"A *Sector* Alpha," he corrected. "The best lessons are the ones taught without much involvement."

"Which I'm guessing is why you intend to showcase Vanessa's message to the sector, to prompt Kaz to act."

Now he smiled. "You really are my *fucking* son, aren't you?"

I rolled my eyes and finished dressing. Then I purposefully set my clothes next to Kari, knowing she would need them when she woke up. "One hour," I told him. "That's all I'm giving you."

"That's all I need," he replied, gesturing to the door. "Let's go make some history."

CHAPTER SEVENTEEN

KARI

EVERYTHING HURT. My head. My body. My heart. I swallowed, but my throat resembled grating rocks.

I groaned, trying to recall what had happened, while also being terrified to know.

An Alpha must have… I trailed off, my nose twitching at the scent of *Alpha* all around me. An image of a beautiful male with blond hair and blue eyes trickled into my thoughts, rousing my inner wolf. *Sven.*

Did he do this to me? I wondered, frowning. *No. No, Sven makes me feel safe. Comfortable. Warm.*

I snuggled deeper into his scent, the soft cotton providing just enough of him to placate my inner turmoil. Just for a moment. A short breath. A glimpse of time.

Until the memory of what pained me struck through my mind.

The nest. I'd destroyed it. Then I fell and something stabbed me.

I groaned again, straining to remember any details, but my brain refused to operate beneath my command. It was foggy. Exhausted. Unable to compute the accident.

Voices filtered through my psyche, a female discussing Snow Frost. I couldn't quite grasp the words or where they were coming from.

My eyes refused to open, but I was awake.

What's happening?

Something about seven days and trying to locate Snow Frost.

Her name is Winter, I thought back at the voice. *And she's not missing.* I'd just seen her... when? My brow furrowed, my concept of time failing me like it always did.

I tried again to lift my eyelids. They slitted, revealing a white wall with people embedded in it. *That can't be right.* I squinted, trying to discern the scene, when a male voice started talking about an Omega on suppressants and how the *Queen of Mirrors* had tried to kill her by having her knotted to death. "She is now Winter of Norse Sector. My Winter. My mate."

Yes, I agreed. *Her name is Winter.*

I tried to clear the rocks from my throat, to focus more clearly on the wall of people, but my body wasn't ready to fully operate yet. I was lost between some state of unconsciousness and consciousness, aware of my surroundings yet unable to respond to them.

My eyes slid closed again, blocking out the blurry scene while I tried to figure out up from down.

But the voices infiltrated again, something about making the Queen of Mirrors pay for threatening the life of an Omega.

Alpha Vanessa? I guessed, frowning. *What am I listening to? Where am I?*

"The decision on how to handle Winter Sector will be left up to Alpha Kazek, as is his right as Winter's mate." The deep masculine tones carried through my room, forcing me to open my eyes again.

Alpha Ludvig, I recognized, his voice unmistakable.

The back of his blond head was on my wall, as were a

variety of others, all dressed in formal wear. *It's a video,* I realized. *Some sort of live feed.*

But I had no idea why I was seeing this, and I couldn't raise my head to look around my room for the source. Nor could I seem to speak.

"Excellent," Alpha Ludvig continued. "I'm pleased we are all in agreement on Alpha Kazek's right to decide, as well as how to proceed in regard to Winter remaining in Norse Sector. Particularly because I've just been notified by Vanessa that Alpha Enrique will be paying us a visit tomorrow to discuss Snow Frost's whereabouts."

Alpha Enrique? I repeated to myself, a spike of hope settling inside me.

"What?" the Alpha who spoke about Winter demanded, his dark eyes narrowing at Alpha Ludvig in a way that made my skin crawl.

Yeah, Winter's Alpha is terrifying, I thought, shivering. I'd already told her that once before, but now I had proof of it staring at me from the wall.

"Yes, it seems he also wants to debate the ownership rights for Omega Kari," Alpha Ludvig said, making my lips part.

"Over my dead body," Alpha Sven snapped, his reaction stirring a sharp inhale from my chest. Several others reacted similarly, their gasps tangible and heartfelt on the screen. He'd just spoken to his Sector Alpha in a dangerous tone.

Goose bumps trailed down my arms as I waited for the older Alpha to react to his son's outburst.

Please don't hurt him, I whispered in my mind. *Please don't hurt Alpha Sven.*

"As Omega Kari clearly has no wish to join Norse Sector, Alpha Enrique is within his rights to negotiate for her release," Ludvig said, his voice cold and underlined in dominance. "I am not accustomed to forcing Omegas to remain in my territory when they wish to leave."

I blinked. *What?*

My mind fractured between two thoughts. *Alpha Enrique wants to negotiate for my release? Alpha Ludvig will allow me to leave?*

That… that wasn't typical Sector Alpha behavior. Omegas were coveted fuck toys. Why would he let me do anything?

Sven bristled, releasing a quiet curse. His angry expression was tinged with hurt. Because his Alpha had just told him he couldn't keep me? Or was there another reason for that look?

I glanced down, frowning. *I don't understand.*

It was a common phrase I'd voiced in his presence, one I heard on repeat in my thoughts now. Not just because I didn't comprehend the situation, but because the notion of having a choice left me uneasy and befuddled.

I can leave if I want to. But do I want to leave?

Alpha Ludvig seemed to think I didn't want to join Norse Sector. However, I'd never said that. Because no one had ever asked what I wanted.

I wasn't a person but a thing. I didn't have choices.

Yet, he made it sound like it was up to me whether I stayed or left.

And Alpha Enrique is coming to negotiate my release.

My heart pounded in my chest, my mind at odds with my desires. The thought should leave me feeling relieved and ecstatic, but Alpha Sven's expression on the screen remained rooted in my thoughts. All I could see was the sadness in his eyes, the soft downward tilt of his lips, and the concerned lines of his forehead. He was mad, but also desperate. Sad. Disappointed.

That wasn't the look of an Alpha about to lose his toy.

It was the look of a man about to lose someone precious. I recognized it because Alpha Joseph had worn a similar expression when Savi had been taken away from him. He'd been furious, yet utterly broken. And she'd felt the same way.

The conversation continued as Alpha Ludvig asked Alpha Kazek how he wanted to proceed. There was talk of time, but I ignored it. Fifteen hours meant nothing to me.

It wasn't until I heard Alpha Sven's voice that I started listening again.

"You're risking your son in this dangerous game," he said quietly, causing me to open my eyes. He stood off to the side of the room with his father while the other packmates indulged in social conversation throughout the ballroom behind them.

This must be the ceremony Alpha Sven kept talking about. It was nothing like I'd imagined, the wolves behind him all in human form and smiling or laughing with one another. They also appeared to be eating a variety of desserts. No hungry or angry Alphas. Just… a pack socializing. Like they were actually friends.

"If Enrique takes Kari back with him, then I'll be forced to go after her," Alpha Sven continued. "My wolf won't allow any other alternative."

"Then I suggest you find a way to tame him," Alpha Ludvig replied. "Or I'll be forced to tame him for you."

Alpha Sven growled, low and deeply, the sound sending a tremble down my spine. "She's mine."

"And yet, her actions suggest she doesn't want to be yours," he returned, his voice soft yet firm. "Is that really what you want in an Omega, Sven? A female who refuses to be a partner? Who prefers to stab herself in her safe haven over being with you?"

My eyebrows lifted. *I did not stab myself.*

But Alpha Sven didn't say that. Instead, his expression fell even further, the despair in his features making my chest ache.

"I don't know what happened. I don't know why…" He trailed off, his throat bobbing over a swallow. "She's been through so much. I don't think she knows what she wants. To say she's refusing to join Norse Sector isn't fair. She doesn't understand what it means yet. She needs more time."

His father considered him for a long moment. "You have fifteen hours."

Alpha Sven's jaw hardened. "That's not enough and you know it."

"Then I suggest you stop wasting time here and go back to Omega Kari. She should be waking up soon, if she hasn't already." He glanced over his shoulder and directly at me. "Perhaps she'll tell you what she needs rather than relying on self-harm to convey a message."

My heart dropped. That message was very clearly for me. Because the screen disappeared half a beat later, leaving me alone and whimpering in the bed. It was foreign. Cold. Sterile. Just like my body.

A throat cleared nearby, making me flinch. And then a male with soft brown eyes stepped around the bed at my feet to walk upward toward my face. "Hi, Kari," he said in a gentle tone. "I'm Doctor Palmer. Alpha Ludvig thought you might want to watch tonight's ceremony. That's why it was playing on the wall."

I blinked up at him, not knowing what to say or how to react. My stomach released a pang of discomfort, eliciting a wince and another whimper from my throat.

"You should heal quickly now that your knife wound is all cleaned up and bandaged. But I wouldn't suggest moving too much for the next few hours. You need to rest, and it's my job to stand here and make sure you don't do anything to further harm yourself. At least until Alpha Sven returns. So don't get any funny ideas."

I frowned at him. *Further harm myself? Like I would do that on purpose?*

"I…" I wasn't sure what to say, his words reverberating through my mind in a confusing swirl of thought.

"All the sharp objects have been removed from your room. If you try to shift, I'm under orders to force you back into human form," he added.

My brow furrowed. *So now I can't shift?*

"While I understand you've been through a lot, stabbing yourself isn't the solution," he continued, a note of censure in his tone.

"I didn't stab myself," I replied, irritated that this wolf who didn't know me was condemning me for something I hadn't done. While the words had come out raspy, he'd clearly heard them, because his eyebrows rose.

"You had a steak knife in your stomach."

"Because I fell on it," I told him, annoyance thick in my veins. *Why would I stab myself? I'm in enough pain as it is. And even if I were to stab myself, it surely wouldn't be in my stomach!*

"You fell on it," he repeated, incredulous.

"I… I dropped the knives…" And I couldn't remember the rest. But I knew I wouldn't stab myself on purpose. "I hurt enough without it."

His brow furrowed, then he nodded slowly. "Yes, I imagine the wires are quite painful."

"What wires?" a new voice demanded from behind me. *Alpha Sven.*

Doctor Palmer immediately straightened, his eyes flashing to the side in a show of immediate submission. He must not have heard Alpha Sven approach, just as I hadn't sensed him. But with his scent all around me, it sort of felt like he was a permanent fixture at my side even while gone.

"The wires in her stomach, sir," the doctor said, clearing his throat. "I noticed them while cleaning up her wound."

"And you didn't think to mention them?"

"I did, sir," the doctor insisted. "To Alpha Ludvig."

Alpha Sven released a low growl. "Of course you did." His heat blanketed my back as he approached the bed. "Did you discuss how to remove them?"

"No, my orders are to take X-rays and send them to Andorra Sector," Doctor Palmer replied. "But not until she's healed from her suicide attempt."

That had my eyebrows hitting my hairline. "*Suicide*?" It came out on a half laugh, half snarl. "You think I tried to… to kill myself?" I no longer felt the ache in my throat, my raspy voice a hiss on the wind. "With a knife to the stomach? The part of me that *always* hurts?" I was furious that he could even consider that as a concept. "*Why* would I do that?"

It made no logical sense.

"I destroyed the nest because we were done… Three days… finished. I didn't… I *wouldn't*…" I trailed off, thinking. Because yeah, I *would* hurt myself. But… "Not like that. Not in my stomach. Off the balcony, maybe. Something quick. Not… not *that*."

Tears blurred my vision, but they weren't born of sadness so much as frustration.

These wolves didn't understand me. And I couldn't even blame them because I often failed to understand myself. Or this situation. Or anything about my life.

I felt lost.

Hopeless.

Alone.

I wrapped my arms around my abdomen as though to protect it and curled into a ball. It hurt, the pain inside me splintering through my veins to my nerve endings and making me choke on a sob. But I wanted to be small. To disappear. To no longer exist.

They think I did this on purpose, I thought, delirious and angry. A whole myriad of other emotions pelted my mind, each one plowing through my mental barriers and making me want to scream in frustration.

I craved death. But I also craved life. I craved *him.* Alpha Sven. His scent. His purr. His touch. I longed for him to wrap his arms around me and keep me safe.

It was all a fantasy. One I'd forever relive in my dreams.

I closed my eyes, willing it to exist, and sighed as I felt the bed shift behind me. His warmth touched my exposed back while the sheets moved around to cover us both.

Magic.

An enchantment.

Bliss.

His purr vibrated my being, his lips ghosting over my neck, his words a whisper against my damp skin. "I'll handle it from here, Doctor Palmer. Get some rest. We'll discuss the X-rays in the morning."

"Of course, sir."

"And, Palmer?" he added, his tone rising a little as though calling to him. "She's my intended mate. You will report on her health directly to me. And I will share the information with my father as I see fit, in accordance with Norse Sector law. Understood?"

"Y-yes, sir."

Alpha Sven nodded, his chin stroking my cheek. "Good."

I kept my eyes closed, not wanting to disturb the moment. Real or not, I didn't care. I was too weak to deny the comfort it provided, and so I allowed myself to soak up his strength, to just exist and *be*.

His intoxicating rumble swathed me like a blanket, tugging me into sleep. *My Alpha*, I thought dreamily. *My Alpha has me. I'm finally safe.*

CHAPTER EIGHTEEN

SVEN

KARI'S ANGER and subsequent despair both pleased and agonized my wolf.

She hadn't been trying to hurt herself with the knives, something Doctor Palmer hadn't seemed to believe, but I did. There had just been something in her voice that had breathed *truth* when she'd uttered the claim about falling on the knife. And that same instinct had resonated when she'd spoken about destroying the nest.

She'd thought we were done, whispering a few words about three days and being *finished*.

I frowned, not following her logic. Why would that result in her destroying her safe haven? Did she expect to have to move it?

She sighed against me, lost to her sleep, while I continued to roll over everything she'd said.

Her irritation at being accused of trying to commit suicide was a good sign because it meant she didn't want to harm herself in that manner. And that implied I'd read her correctly the last few days, too.

While I'd picked up on her sadness, I hadn't sensed her depression running so deep that I'd had to worry about her life.

Thinking I'd missed the obvious tells had tormented

me all through the mating festivities, making it impossible for me to focus until my father had brought up Alpha Vanessa's broadcast.

Then he'd dropped the bomb about Enrique's visit, and I'd just lost it. I hadn't meant to lash out at him in front of the pack; however, saying he would consider giving Kari to another Alpha had painted my vision in red.

She might not want me. She might have sliced apart our nest. But like hell would I let someone take her away from the safety of Norse Sector.

My blood boiled at the thought.

Then her words trickled through my mind once more, her statement about why she'd shredded our sanctuary twisting my heart.

How could she think we were done? She'd just bitten me, her wolf clearly staking a claim. And I'd told her over and over again that she belonged to me.

Yet her statements, and the way she'd spoken them, implied she thought we were finished. Not because she wanted to be over, but because our time had run out.

I ran through all my actions, all our conversations, every possible scenario, long into the night and through the early morning hours. My wolf refused to rest, his need to protect and purr keeping me wide awake and alert while Kari slept soundly.

She moved every now and then, always snuggling closer, and at one point rotating to press her nose into my chest. I'd stripped down to my boxers earlier in the night, my skin needing to touch hers. Now I reveled in the feel of her curled up against me, her petite form dwarfed by my Alpha frame.

Once, she'd stirred, her mouth whispering a need for water. I'd found her a drink, inserting a straw between her lips and watching as she'd swallowed nearly two glasses before settling against me once more. Her eyes had remained closed the entire time, her body healing at rapid speed, thanks to her shifter genetics.

And already the color was returning to her cheeks, her hair seeming to rejuvenate from the water alone.

My little wonder, I mused, holding her to me and sighing in deep satisfaction.

This was how it should be.

Minus the hospital equipment, sterile atmosphere, and solid white walls.

Doctor Palmer had put her in a room with little substance, wanting to keep her from having a way to hurt herself.

The memory of finding her bleeding and unconscious struck my heart, followed quickly by my mind replaying her words. *Again*.

She's not suicidal, I thought, kissing the top of her head. *But she is broken*.

Because she hadn't understood why I'd left, and she'd made that very clear by her destructive scene in the bedroom.

I ran my fingers through her hair, petting her and stroking her and offering her my strength. *I've got you. I'll protect you. I won't let anyone hurt you, including yourself.*

She nuzzled my pec, her palms flattening against my abdomen. "Sven," she whispered, her legs stretching and intertwining with mine. "My Sven."

"Your Sven, hmm?" I repeated, amused and pleased by her statement.

She nodded, her lips tasting my skin. "My Alpha." She sounded dreamy, as though caught in between awareness and sleep.

Using my fingers in her hair, I tugged back her head to study her features.

She smiled up at me with her eyes, the expression breathtakingly beautiful. It struck me then that I'd never seen her smile or grin or display a single hint of joy. Contentment, yes. But happiness? No. Not until this moment as her eyes crinkled in true warmth.

Air caught in my throat, cutting off my ability to breathe.

I wanted to see her like this every day for the rest of my life.

"You're stunning," I whispered, awed.

She shook her head, but her blue irises twinkled from the compliment. "Will you kiss me again?" she asked, making me wonder if I'd indeed fallen asleep after all. Because this version of Kari was one I hadn't met before.

Happy. Slightly confident. *Smiling.*

"Would you like me to kiss you?" I managed to inquire, my voice oddly gruff. She was just so perfect in this state. The type of Omega I suspected lived deep within her soul. A wolf in need of her mate.

"Yes," she murmured, arching her neck to press her mouth to the underside of my chin. "Very much, yes." Her lips moved along my jaw, seeking what she desired as her fingers trailed up my sternum to wrap around my nape.

My wolf rumbled in approval, liking the feistier side of his female. He wanted to revel in the moment, to accept her gift and reaffirm her place in his life.

Mine, he hummed, shoving the image of her bleeding body from my thoughts and demanding I reciprocate her embrace and give her what she desired. *Anything. Everything. Take. Give. Claim.*

I caught her mouth with my own, my tongue sliding inside to indulge in the sweet flavor that was all her. She responded in kind, a moan fluttering from her throat and reverberating against my lips.

149

Cupping the side of her face, I deepened the embrace, taking charge and allowing her to feel my dominance as I rolled her to her back and slid a knee between her thighs. She immediately arched up into me, her needy little body telling me she desired her Alpha.

But I wouldn't take her.

Not like this.

Not here.

She was still healing, her wound closed but still pink around the edges. I'd checked on it after her last glass of water, wanting to ensure she was recovering appropriately. And she was, her body resilient and perfect and very much *mine*.

But not yet.

Not entirely.

Not until we sorted this mess out between us. Not until she *truly* healed. That required her mind to recover just as much as her body, and I would make certain she was completely ready when I took her.

Her tongue dared me to sway from my resolve, her nails digging into my neck as she kissed me harder. "Please, Alpha," she whispered. "Please."

I shook my head, my thumb lying along her jaw as I held her face in one palm. "I refuse to hurt you, Kari," I told her. "And especially not in this state."

"Dreams don't hurt," she breathed, arching into me. "Dreams are whatever we want them to be."

My heart stuttered in my chest, understanding slapping harshly against my senses and jolting me from the moment. *She thinks this is a dream. Shit.*

"Kari," I whispered, but her mouth sealed over mine again, her kiss hungry and demanding as she pushed herself against my thigh.

Her slick permeated the air, her sweet scent beckoning

my animal forward with a soft growl. He wanted to taste her. To devour her. To stake his claim.

Fuck, if she thought this was a fantasy, I couldn't take advantage of her.

But I could make her dreams come true.

I could show her pleasure. Make her realize what being with me would be like. Completely turn all her previous experiences on their head and introduce her to a new world. One where she was a prized Omega. Worshipped. Adored. *Safe*.

I skimmed her lower lip with my teeth, drawing her focus and gently nibbling on the tender skin. "This isn't a dream," I told her softly, needing her to understand that this was very much real. "But I'll make this the sweetest reverie you've ever experienced, if that's what you want."

She pressed into me in response, her needy cunt soaking my leg as she drew her nails down my back. "Yes," she said, the word a demand. "Make me forget. Give me a memory to hold on to. Something to dream about."

"It'll be more than a dream," I promised her. "Because this is real, Kari. You're very much awake."

She giggled—an amused sound that went straight to my soul—then groaned as my lips met her neck. "More," she begged. "More, Alpha, more."

I wanted to make her giggle again. Make her smile. Make her moan my name. Make her feel alive and realize what life could be like with me as her mate.

"Kari," I rasped against her skin. "I need to taste you."

"Taste me?" she repeated.

"Mmm," I murmured against her throat as I kissed a path down to her breasts. I took one of her nipples into my mouth, watching her face as I did so. She closed her eyes and bowed upward, her hand lifting from my spine to the back of my head.

"Oh," she breathed. "I like that."

I nibbled her stiff peak in response, causing her to gasp as though she'd never experienced such pleasure. If she wanted to dream, then I'd join her in that and pretend I was the first wolf to put my mouth and hands on her.

Hmm, yes, my inner beast approved.

With my tongue, I vowed to ruin her for anyone else, drawing sweet little moans from her lips as I tortured her breasts with my mouth and touch.

Then I started downward to the heaven between her thighs.

She was so fucking wet, her Omega instincts readying herself for her Alpha's cock. But she'd have to handle my fingers and tongue instead, because I pledged not to hurt her, and I intended to keep that promise.

My dick would just have to wait.

But tasting her… that I would do now. I'd indulge myself to my heart's content and send her to the stars in the process.

Settling myself between her legs, I pressed a kiss to her smooth mound and inhaled deeply. "You smell amazing, Kari," I told her, loving the way her body responded to mine.

She'd been bathed earlier, post-surgery, leaving behind a citrusy perfume that gave her an almost tangy appeal. But the heart of her was all Kari. Sweet. Alluring. *Beckoning*.

I groaned, unable to hold myself back for another second, my need for her a burn inside my groin that forced me to take action. *I need to taste what's mine.*

My tongue parted her folds, licking her deep and saturating my face in her fragrance. It wasn't enough. I required more. I wanted to feel her tighten around my fingers, taste her glistening slick, and feast upon her pleasure.

Yes, I whispered darkly. *All of the above.*

Her hand remained on my head, her fingers threading through my hair as I allowed my wolf to drive my instincts. Her animal responded in kind, her thighs trembling around my head as she rode my face in a beautiful dance of oblivion.

I watched her face, admiring the blush painting her cheeks, and nibbled her clit to make her lips part on a gasp.

Fuck, she was divine.

My gorgeous, perfect Omega.

Had I known this was what her dreams entailed, I would have done this days ago.

I would have to make up for lost time with my tongue.

Licking her thoroughly, I smiled as she began to tremble, the first signs of a climax quivering around my finger as I slid one inside to test her tightness.

I didn't go in too far, not wanting to hurt her.

And I watched her closely, ensuring she enjoyed everything I did to her.

She mewled, her head flipping back and forth as I sealed my mouth around her clit once more, sucking her harshly into my mouth.

A scream rent the air as she reacted, her stomach tightening as an orgasm ripped through her. But the sound of ecstasy she released soon twisted into one of agony.

I frowned, eyeing the pink mark on her abdomen, worried I'd done something to irritate her wound.

Then she clutched her stomach and began to shake, sobbing as she breathed words I didn't understand.

"Kari," I whispered, tortured by the sight of her falling

apart on the bed after what should have been a beautiful and pure moment.

Tears tracked down her face, her thighs fighting to close.

I moved away from her lower half, allowing her to curl into a protective ball. Magic shivered through the air as she called on her wolf, her shift painfully slow.

"Oh, Kari." My heart broke for her, shame a heavy stone in my gut. "I didn't realize…"

She whined, her blonde fur covering every limb as she completed her transformation. Then big blue irises met mine, terror residing in their depths.

"I'm not going to make you shift back," I told her, guessing the direction of her thoughts. I reached for her, but she flinched away like I might strike her.

So I did the only thing I knew how to do for her.

I purred.

Her reaction was immediate, her ears perking up as her gaze flicked back to mine.

I increased the intensity in my chest, telling her without words that I wasn't leaving her, that I wasn't going to push her, that I wouldn't hurt her.

She didn't move at first but kept her wary eyes on me.

After several minutes of watching each other, she shuffled forward. Just a few inches. Just enough for her nose to touch my chest. This time when I tried to pet her, she let me.

I praised her wolf, calling her beautiful, complimenting her soft fur, and telling her how proud I was of her for being so strong for Kari.

She eventually rumbled in response, the noise one that had my own wolf peeking out at her through my eyes. "You want to meet him?" I offered softly.

Her eyes locked on mine, her response clear. *Yes*.

Nodding, I removed my boxers and smirked a little when her gaze flicked not so discreetly downward. But I was already shifting before she could react to my size, and within a few seconds, I was fully transformed beside her on the bed.

Appreciation brightened her pretty eyes.

My wolf shared in that reaction, allowing her to see through his own irises how he felt about her. Then I leaned in and licked her muzzle.

She released a surprised sound before doing the same back to me.

I rumbled in approval, my purr louder in wolf form.

She nuzzled into me, her fur an aphrodisiac to my wolf.

An idea occurred to me, one I knew my father would despise, but it seemed like just what Kari needed.

A run.

Nothing too strenuous. Just fresh air. Some snow. And a little frolicking.

I returned to my human state—much to her wolf's dismay—and said, "Follow me."

I didn't second-guess it. I didn't even bother with pants or boxers. Just stood on two legs and took advantage of my use of thumbs in this form and walked straight to the door.

When I didn't hear her bound after me, I turned to find her sitting with her head cocked to the side.

"We're going on a little walk," I explained. "Nothing too far or long. Just some fresh air and maybe a little snow." Well, likely a lot of snow. It was winter in Norse Sector and cold as fuck. But our wolves would love it.

She didn't move.

"Now, Kari," I said, making it an order instead of a request. Something told me that was the push she needed to obey, maybe because she'd never been offered this sort of an experience before.

155

With a little huff, she jumped off the bed and slid across the floor to my legs.

I caught her and arched a brow. "Never walked on marble before?" I guessed.

She grumbled, stood up on all four legs, shook out her coat, and nearly fell on her ass again.

Frowning, I considered her stance. She reminded me of a young pup just learning how to walk for the first time.

Maybe it wasn't the floor at all, but her being unused to being able to roam far in her wolf form. That collar had dictated when she could shift. When she was human again, I'd have to ask her how long she'd been wearing it.

Choosing to proceed slowly, I opened the door and led her into the hallway. She hobbled along, her footing still uneasy on the slick white floor. A Beta nurse stepped out, her eyebrow rising at finding us in the corridor. "We're going for a little walk," I told her. "If my father stops by, let him know we'll be back in an hour or so."

"You sure that's wise?" she asked.

"You mean, do I think he'll be pissed?" I replied as we moved by her. "Sure. But that doesn't mean I care."

She laughed in response, making Kari growl low in her throat.

Amusement warmed my chest. "You already claimed me, little wolf. Remember?" I waved my hand at her, and her wolf curled her lip as though to threaten another bite.

With a smirk, I continued down the hall toward the nearest exit.

As soon as we were outside, I shifted. Then I used my head to say, *This way.*

CHAPTER NINETEEN

KARI

Sven was huge. The kind of Alpha I should fear. All lean muscle and beastly size. Both as a wolf… and as a *man.*

I swallowed, my mind flashing to the image of his masculine parts. *Huge* was an understatement. Just the thought of it melted my insides, stirring an ache only he could soothe.

Except he really couldn't.

All pleasure ended in agony.

The moment I'd felt the excruciating pain rip through my midsection, I'd known I was very much awake. However, if I were honest with myself, I'd known that before I'd reached my orgasm. I'd merely allowed myself to fall into the fantasy, wishing it could be a dream and not reality.

It'd felt right… until it hadn't.

And then my animal had taken over, healing me while Sven had purred.

I eyed his rump, admiring the brown and white fur flicking along his back. He moved at a slow pace, leading me down a sidewalk alongside the building we'd just departed. I wasn't sure what he intended, but my wolf was excited.

I didn't fully share in her anticipation, my mind

working through all the ways this could go horribly wrong. I'd never been allowed to explore Bariloche Sector, not even as a pup. And I'd rarely been given an opportunity to shift—only when the Alphas had demanded it. Then I'd usually been put into a cage.

No running.

No playing.

No exploring.

My wolf's ears perked up, taking in all the sounds around us. My nose twitched with the scents. And my eyes scanned for danger.

However, I felt safe in Alpha Sven's presence. Like I knew he wouldn't let anything happen to me. It was a dangerous reliance, a hope I had no right to own, but it was there nonetheless. And my wolf didn't question the sensation in the slightest. She trusted Sven implicitly.

I'd always been somewhat detached from my animal side, allowing me to take control of my instincts rather easily. But not today. She'd taken the reins and was following him without any concerns.

He glanced back at me, his blue eyes rimmed with dark edges, giving him a predatory gleam. His wide shoulders and massive paws added to the image.

And my wolf reveled in it.

She saw him as a worthy mate, a male of stature and grace, and an honest Alpha.

He purrs for us, she seemed to be saying. *He takes care of us.*

I didn't want to listen to her. I wanted to run in the opposite direction. But I couldn't deny that he'd been everything I'd never known existed.

He slowed his pace until I was beside him, then he nudged me with his snout as though to say, *Get out of your head*.

Or maybe that was just my interpretation because it was what I wanted to say to myself.

For the first time in my life, I was being given an opportunity to exist. And I continued to squander it with my frequent worries. I really needed—

My feet froze midstep as a squealing sound pierced my ears. I had one foot in the air, the other three on the sidewalk, and my ears twisted toward the noise.

A giggle followed.

Then a female ran across the street as a male chased her.

My heart throbbed heavily in my chest, my instincts on high alert. *Run, run, run!* I chanted at her, terrified on her behalf. She was just a Beta. The male pursuing her… he looked big… like another Alpha.

And he quickly caught her.

I winced, knowing what would come next.

Until… until he picked her up and swung her into a hug that had her dipping her head back in laughter.

I blinked. *What is he doing?* I'd expected him to throw her on the ground and mount her, not lift her into the air.

She said something that I missed, and he set her down. Then the two began to strip right in the street, shifted, and ran off into the park, playing another game of tag.

This time when he caught her, he pinned her, and they rolled across the ground while playfully nipping at each other.

Another male emerged then, his expression amused as he shook his head, disrobed, and joined in on the fun.

Alpha Sven bumped me, reminding me that he was beside me. Then he gestured with his snout to keep following him.

I wanted to shift back into human form to ask him what they were doing, but my wolf was more interested in finding out what he wanted to show her. So I trailed after him and left the frolicking animals in the park.

We passed several more shifters along the way, many of them pausing to look at me with curious expressions. Sven eventually walked right beside me as though to shield me from their inquisitive glances, and even growled a few times at those who gawked at me a little too long.

Others went about their day, busy with various tasks like shoveling snow, lighting lanterns, or baking. The latter caught my attention because I could smell the delicious scents coming from various doorways. All sweet items that reminded me of the ones I'd seen briefly on the screen last night.

Thinking of that had me recalling what Alpha Ludvig had said. Something about me not wanting to be here. But as I wandered the streets with Sven, I started to wonder if Alpha Ludvig was wrong.

This place seemed… quiet. Nice. Soothing.

A few shifters greeted us. Although, they called me Omega, maybe because they didn't know my name. But none of the Alphas we passed made a move my way. They just watched, their attention more on Sven than on me. Perhaps they were trying to decide if they could take him in a challenge. However, I didn't sense aggression or hostility from them. Merely respect.

After what felt like miles, we finally reached a woodsy area that was much larger than the park behind us. *What are we doing here?* I wanted to ask.

Except Sven wasn't paying attention to me at all.

The moment we reached the edge, he bounded headfirst into a giant pile of snow.

My eyes widened as almost his entire furry form was engulfed in white fluff. Then his head popped out of the top, and he gave me a big, wolfy grin.

He's playing, I realized with a start.

My animal reacted in kind, giving an excited little yip as she joined him.

But my jump was far less graceful. And when I realized just how deep the snow went, I started to struggle and panic as I tried to swim my way out of it.

Teeth clamped into my scruff as Alpha Sven helped me out. I whined in frustration, and he purred as he set me upright again. Then he gestured to a smaller pile with his snout.

My wolf reacted without my permission, bounding right for it and rolling around in the fluffy goodness. It felt cool and soft against my coat, the icy element an exciting sensation to experience. It wasn't my first time touching snow, but I'd never frolicked in it before.

I found another pile of a similar size and plowed through it.

Sven followed, his bulky size destroying the snow towers with ease.

I released a happy yip and dove into several more drifts, loving the way the cotton-like substance parted to allow me entry.

By the time I finished, I was panting, my wolf having expended all my energy. But it felt good. I'd never exhausted myself in such a manner, and I found myself eager to do it again soon.

Sven nudged me with his snout, then gave me a lick on the nose before signaling to trail after him again. Only, he walked beside me, bumping me as he went and flashing me a lopsided grin each time.

At one point, I licked his nose in response, earning me a growl of approval. And by the time we returned to the building we'd come out of, I couldn't stop my own snout from parting in a wolfy grin.

I'm happy, I mused. *Really happy.*

Maybe this whole thing had been a dream after all. But I really hoped it wasn't. Because I wanted this to be true. I wanted to feel this way. I wanted to *live.*

I want to be with Sven, a small voice whispered. My voice. One that came from a place I knew little about—my heart.

An Alpha opened the door for us as we approached, allowing us to enter in our wolf forms. My grin faltered when we walked by him, my innate fear creeping in, but all he did was hold the glass until we were through and then released it.

Sven trotted forward, only to pause at the opening of the corridor. I froze beside him as Alpha Ludvig's familiar scent hit my senses. My eyes lowered on instinct, my entire body supplicating to the powerful aura before us.

He didn't speak, making me even more nervous. His suit pants shuffled, the sound causing my ears to twitch.

And then he was right in front of me, crouching down and lifting his hand toward me as one might do to a stray animal.

I swallowed, uncertain of what he intended. But my wolf gave him a sniff. She wasn't nearly as frightened of him as I was, her instinct to trust the superior male programmed into her DNA.

"Hmm," he hummed, reaching out to gently scratch me beneath the chin. My animal sighed, loving the tender affection.

Sven parked his butt beside me and released a snort, his agitation palpable.

Ludvig chuckled, releasing me and standing once more. "Now you're thinking and behaving like a mate."

I wasn't sure whom the words were for, but he turned and started walking down the hall. Sven stood to follow and bumped my side, encouraging me to walk with him.

So I did.

And the three of us ended up in the medical room I'd stayed in overnight.

"Mila gave me a dress for Kari to borrow," Alpha Ludvig said, pointing to a blue gown hanging on the back of the door. "She grabbed another suit for you as well."

Sven snorted—whether that be an acknowledgment or an annoyance, I wasn't sure. But it made Alpha Ludvig's lips curl upward.

I studied his mouth, noting the similarity to his son's. Then I eyed his cheekbones and blue eyes—the same shade as Sven's—and his thick blond mane of hair. They looked more like brothers, apart from Alpha Ludvig's ancient air.

When I returned my gaze to his, I realized he was studying me just as intently, and I immediately bowed my head in submission again. So he crouched once more and pressed a finger to my chin to lift my eyes from the ground. "You have a decision to make, little one," he said softly. "About whether you want to stay here or return with Alpha Enrique."

Sven growled at his words, but Alpha Ludvig ignored him.

"We would be lucky to have you, but we don't tolerate self-harm in this sector. Even if it's accidental," he murmured, making me frown inside.

"I see Doctor Palmer is still reporting to you," Sven drawled, having returned to his human state shortly after growling.

"I'm Sector Alpha."

"And I'm her intended mate," Sven countered. "By our laws, that gives me authority in this situation."

Alpha Ludvig didn't stand but lifted his gaze to his son.

163

"Only when that intention is acknowledged by your Sector Alpha."

Sven fell quiet for a moment. "You don't acknowledge my claim."

"Not yet," Alpha Ludvig replied. "But you're doing a reasonable job to convince me of it." He drew his knuckles along my snout and scratched me behind my right ear. "Keep walking down this path, and you'll have what you want."

Just like before, I wasn't sure if those words were for me or Sven.

He stood before I had a chance to shift and ask him, his attention falling completely to Sven. "Let's hear Enrique out before we make any decisions. He might be more helpful than you think."

Sven was quiet, making me glance at him. He hadn't put on any clothes, leaving his naked body on glorious display. *Definitely Alpha*, I thought, admiring his strong form and impressive manhood. My wolf almost sighed at the sight, despite my inherent fear of men like him.

"What time is dinner?"

"Unclear, but I'll let you know as soon as Kazek decides."

"Meaning, you're not sure he'll even let Enrique live until dinner."

Alpha Ludvig shrugged. "That's up to him, not me."

I bristled, the thought of harm befalling my former savior enough to send me back into human form. Both men watched my shift, likely having felt the energy of it rolling over my skin.

As Alphas, they could control the forms of others, meaning they were more in tune with the enchantment than someone like me. But without the collar around my neck, I was able to choose my state—human or wolf—as I desired. A nuance I'd never realized I was missing… until Sven.

I cleared my throat and focused on what prompted my need to speak. "Alpha Enrique has helped me before. He was supposed to help me in Winter Sector, too." I couldn't quite meet Alpha Ludvig's gaze while I spoke, my voice a little hesitant but loud enough to convey my point. "He's… he's… not bad."

I wouldn't call him good. Because no Alphas were inherently good.

Except maybe Sven, I thought with a whisper. But I still didn't know what he wanted from me. So I couldn't fully deduce that yet.

"He was going to set me free," I added softly.

"I doubt that," Alpha Ludvig interjected. "But I don't doubt that he wanted to help you. We'll hear him out and see what he has to say about Winter's attempted murder as well."

"Assuming Kazek allows it."

Alpha Ludvig smiled again. "I suspect he will. And as you know, my suspicions are almost always right. Focus on your path, son. Maybe another one of my expectations will come true."

With that, he stepped from the room, leaving me alone with a naked Sven.

His body naturally reacted to mine, his need for an Omega clear in the stiffening of his shaft, but he made no move to try to pin me or knot me. Instead, he reached for me and pulled me into a hug, kissing the top of my head. "Thank you for wandering with me, little wonder."

Little wonder, I repeated in my mind, smiling at how that sounded. I liked it more than *little one* and *little wolf.* It made me feel special somehow. Unique. Like I could actually mean something to him.

"Now I want you to tell me why you destroyed our nest," he said, ruining my momentary happiness. Not because I disliked his demand so much as I didn't want to think about it.

But a small part of me wanted him to understand, to know that I hadn't been trying to hurt myself, that I'd just meant to destroy something I'd considered to be a threat.

It seemed important to tell him. To share that part of me with him. To ensure he knew that I'd valued our time together, that I just... I just hadn't wanted it to end.

"Hope," I whispered, my throat suddenly dry. "It... it resembled *hope*."

He pulled back just enough to stare down at me. "What resembled hope? The nest?"

I nodded. "It... I wanted to stay... w-with you... but our three days were done. And I was upset that I allowed hope inside me." I couldn't look at him while I said it, the words sounding naïve and foolish to my ears.

He cupped my cheek, his thumb nudging beneath my chin to draw my focus up to his alluring irises. "I wanted three days to show you how Alphas can be different. But that didn't mean our time was over, Kari. You're still mine. And you're allowed to hope."

I shook my head. "Hope is dangerous."

"It's also wonderful," he replied in a hush of sound. "Hope is part of life. It provides motivation to move forward, to heal, to *live*."

No, he was wrong. "Hope hurts."

"Hope heals," he countered. "I'll prove it to you."

"In three days?" I guessed.

He chuckled. "No. We won't put a time limit on it. I'll just prove it to you."

I blinked. "How?"

"That's for me to determine," he murmured. "All you

need to do is give me a chance, Kari. And if you could stop destroying furniture, that would be appreciated. Also, no more knives."

I flinched at the last statement, drawing back to glare up at him. "I did not stab myself on purpose."

"I know," he replied, still grinning. "I'm taking away your access to knives to protect our future nest."

My lips parted. "Future nest?"

"Mmm, yes. But not here. I don't particularly care for windowless rooms. We'll find a better one." He spoke like we had a future together.

"But what about being available for other Alphas?"

His grin disappeared. "You're not *available* for anyone, Kari. Until you've healed, you can't be properly courted. And if our earlier activity is anything to go by, that applies to both your physical and mental state. But I can be patient." He bent to press his lips to my ear. "Because my wolf knows you're worth the wait."

I… I didn't know what to say or how to interpret what he was telling me. "Wh-what's courting?" I whispered, unclear on the term. He'd mentioned *courtship* once, too. But I hadn't asked for clarification then.

"It's the term we use in our sector when we want to win the favor of a mate." His thumb lifted from my chin to draw a line along my bottom lip. "You're intended to be mine, Kari. It's my job to convince you of it, too. And I will. Because I never back down from a challenge."

"But I'm sterile," I whispered.

He released my lower back to gently press his palm to my abdomen, his opposite hand still cupping my cheek. "We're going to fix it."

"How?" I breathed.

"By conferring with some of the best medical teams in

the world," he replied. "Trust me to help you, Kari. And I will. I vow it."

I swallowed, my heart fluttering uneasily in my chest. *Trust an Alpha?* I'd tried that with Enrique, and he'd failed me. Yet I'd survived. But something told me if Sven failed me, I wouldn't recover from it. However, a small, weak part of me longed to believe in him.

Hope, I marveled, feeling the light sensation taunting the edges of my mind.

He wanted to prove the value of hope to me.

He wanted to court me.

He wanted to be mine.

A nagging voice whispered this all to be an impossibility, my life not one grounded in fantasy or fairy tales. Yet that flicker of light at the corner of my psyche begged me to consider his proposal, to put my faith in another, to allow myself a glimmer of *life*.

So I found myself giving a short, small nod in reply, my mouth unable to voice my acceptance. However, it seemed to be enough for him because his lips curled up into a breathtaking smile. It was the kind of expression I would forever dream about, his blue irises glistening with pleasure.

I want him to be mine, I marveled, taking in his handsome facial features and beautiful mouth. *I want this Alpha to be my forever.*

It was a hazardous thought.

But at this point, what did I have to lose?

He was the bright light I needed in an otherwise dark and bleak life.

I would be a fool not to gravitate toward him. Because on the off chance he proved himself, it would be worth all the pain I'd suffered. And if he betrayed me, then at least I'd have a memory to fall back on when I needed it.

His lips ghosted over mine, his kiss soft and belying the hardness pressing into my lower belly. His desire was a palpable heat that called to my Omega senses, demanding I go to my knees and satisfy my better. But he held me upright, his palm leaving my belly to touch my lower back, as his mouth continued to gently taste mine.

I caught the hint of my former arousal on his lips, the memory of the pleasure he'd evoked drowning me in a sea of bliss.

Only to end in a torment of pain.

Because we couldn't be together in my current state. Not really. It all led to pain.

He must have sensed my hesitation because he pulled back to study my features. "We'll start with an X-ray and go from there," he said. "I'm going to fix this, Kari. You'll see."

I wasn't sure I believed him. But I nodded again anyway, that warmth inside my soul flickering brighter with each passing second.

Hope.

I realized then that it had never been the nest that provoked the emotion, but him. Alpha Sven.

He… he gives me hope.

CHAPTER TWENTY

SVEN

Kari's nervous energy prickled at my skin. After an afternoon of conversation and comfort, she'd retreated into her previous cocoon of fear as soon as we'd left her patient room.

Trust definitely did not come naturally. She seemed to anticipate the worst at every turn.

"You look beautiful," I whispered into her ear, hoping to calm her a little as we entered an elevator from the underground tunnel. I'd taken her down here in hopes of keeping her warm as we traveled beneath the sector to a building roughly two blocks away from the hospital center. She wore a stunning blue silk dress with thin straps and a long skirt, leaving her arms exposed. I'd offered her my jacket, but she'd declined the offer with a slow shake of her head. I'd almost protested, but I'd suspected she'd needed the cool air to keep herself aware.

So I'd allowed it, instead wrapping my arm around her lower back and letting her feel my heat as we walked.

Now that we were in the elevator, she'd almost frozen from the terror overriding her form.

I crowded her against the wall, forcing her to look up at me. "I'm going to make you three promises," I said, one of my palms caressing her cheek while my opposite fell to her hip. "First, I will remain next to you all night." I drew a little circle against her hip bone as though to embed the vow into her skin.

She shivered in response, her pupils dilating.

"Second, I won't let anyone touch you," I continued, my voice dropping an octave. "Except me."

Another circle.

Another shiver.

"And third," I whispered, my lips finding her ear. "At the end of the night, I'll hold you in *my* bed and purr for you while you sleep."

"Y-your bed?"

"Yes." I kissed the tender pulse point of her neck. "I'll take you to my home after dinner, and we'll see how you feel about building a nest there."

"In your space," she breathed.

"In *our* space," I corrected her, my lips skimming her throat. "You're mine, Kari. I might not be able to court you properly yet, but that hasn't stopped my wolf from deciding. And one day soon, your wolf will pick me, too." Technically, she'd already staked a claim with her little bite, but I didn't want to push her. She was already fragile enough. This would take careful coaxing and a hell of a lot of healing.

Because I'd seen the X-rays this afternoon. I wasn't a physician or a medical expert, but the wires in her abdomen painted a painful tale. Doctor Palmer had claimed that operating would be impossible. However, I didn't believe in impossible tasks. After dinner, I would ask my father if the results had been sent to Ander yet. If anyone could help, it would be the Andorra Sector research team.

"Okay?" I asked, my thumb doing a third circle against her hip bone as I held her gaze. "Three promises sealed with a purr," I murmured, giving her a slow rumble from my chest. "But you'll have to trust me not to break those vows. Can you do that?"

Her lower lip wobbled, uncertainty etched into her features. But she gave a subtle nod, similar to the ones she'd gifted me with during our conversation earlier about hope. It wasn't an emphatic acceptance, but it was a step in the right direction. So I solidified our agreement with the whisper of a kiss, my lips tasting hers and drawing out her wolf with a little flick of my tongue.

Her inner animal's faith in me was palpable, the Omega's need to have a strong Alpha protect her from the hardships of the world a desire she wore in her eyes alone. Kari probably didn't even sense it, but my wolf did. And we would give her everything she needed.

It would take time, healing, and an abundance of patience.

Fortunately, those were all gifts I could provide.

And so much more.

I licked the seam of her mouth, daring her to return my embrace, and growled in approval when she did. Just a sweet little swipe of her tongue, but it was enough.

Fear still clung to her skin, the stench of it irritating my wolf, but I knew there wasn't much else I could do to calm her down. She needed to see me in action to believe my words.

With a lingering brush of my mouth against hers, I stepped back to program our location into the elevator. It spun to life in an instant, the sound causing Kari to grasp my jacket as her arms trembled.

"Three promises," I reminded her. "I won't be breaking them."

She gave another of those nods, her wolf flickering in her

gaze to peer up at me. It'd become increasingly evident to me over the last twelve hours that Kari and her wolf weren't as bonded as they should be. I'd asked her about her collar during Doctor Palmer's exam, and she couldn't remember when it'd been put on her. She thought perhaps it'd been there most of her life, with the few exceptions being when they'd had to exchange it for a slightly bigger one as she grew.

The information had twisted my stomach.

She'd never been allowed to control her own forms. Which meant she hadn't been able to connect to her inner animal the way a shifter should.

The disconnect explained a lot about her behavior. She wouldn't let her natural instincts take over unless she needed her wolf to protect her—such as when she felt pain.

It was one of the items I planned to discuss with my father later. I wanted to find out if he'd ever witnessed something like this before.

The ding of the elevator announced our arrival. I pulled Kari into my side, my lips falling to her ear. "This is just a small dinner party," I told her. "If you're uncomfortable at any time, tell me and I'll handle it."

She trembled, her terror ramping upward as the metal slats parted to reveal the restaurant foyer area.

"I'm right here," I promised her. "Lean on me and my wolf. We've got you."

She didn't nod this time, but her spine straightened just a little beneath my palm. I tucked her more firmly against me, my arm a solid band around her lower back, as I grasped her hip and helped guide her forward.

My chest ached with the need to purr, but another masculine sound echoed through the room before I could begin. Kari's gaze whipped upward, and her eyes filled with tears at the sight of Enrique standing on the marble floor.

"What the fuck have you done to her?" the Alpha demanded, taking a step forward.

I quickly pushed Kari behind me, intent on keeping my vow to her. *No touching.*

Enrique growled in response.

I almost growled back, but Kaz was already speaking. "I wouldn't suggest it," he said conversationally. "Technically, I won Omega Kari. So I'll be forced to intervene, and, well, I already have several reasons for wanting to kill you. Adding another might just tip me over the edge."

And I'd gladly help, I thought, narrowing my gaze.

Enrique glared at the other Alpha, his fury potent and making Kari quiver against my back. She'd clutched onto my jacket with her little claws, her body vibrating behind me.

"This isn't a game," Enrique snapped.

"It's not?" Kaz almost sounded affronted, but I recognized his penchant for sarcasm. "You mean you didn't conspire to kill Beta Snow so the Queen of Mirrors could take the throne without interference? And you didn't plan to become her king? I mean, I imagine that's what was in it for you, anyway. Feel free to correct my assessment."

"Conspiring, yes. But that doesn't mean I intended to follow through on her plan. Which, obviously, I can't prove. However, as to what I wanted, the answer is in this room." His attention shifted to me. "Tell me she's okay."

"I don't need to tell you shit," I retorted, furious that this Alpha felt he could waltz in here and make demands. He wasn't in my hierarchy. And like hell would I report to him.

But Kari had other ideas.

"I'm okay," she said, her voice quivering at the end. "You shouldn't be here."

"Neither should you," he muttered, running his fingers through his thick, dark hair.

Concern radiated off him. Not the kind that suggested negative energy or potential harm, but a familiar kind that told me what Kari had said about him wanting to help her just might be true.

It made me want to hear him out.

Not because I'd ever consider allowing him to take Kari—that item was nonnegotiable—but because I was curious about their relationship and experiences together. She hadn't implied a romantic entanglement existed between them, and I didn't sense any desire from either of them now. Just a hell of a lot of concern tinged with an unhealthy layer of hopelessness.

"It seems we have a lot to discuss," my father mused, his stance relaxed. "And I sense there's a story here that I would be most interested in hearing. Shall we hear it over dinner?" He gestured toward the main doors, where a familiar scent lurked.

Mom, I thought. My dad had probably told her to stay in there to remain safe, just in case Kaz decided to turn the foyer into a bloodbath zone. My lone wolf of a best friend wasn't very predictable, especially when irked. And given that Alpha Enrique had supposedly intended to kill Kazek's mate, it was safe to assume he'd earned a position on Kaz's kill list.

"I do enjoy a good tale," my best friend drawled. "Sounds like my kind of appetizer." A subtle buzzing sound flicked to life, my wolf ears perking up at the odd vibrations. Then the scent of arousal followed, causing me to arch a brow.

Ah, I thought, my lips threatening to curl. *Kaz is playing a game with his mate.*

"Allow me to escort you to your seat, Winter," he said softly, his palm low on her back and brushing her ass as he led her forward.

It struck me then that he intended to taunt the unmated Alphas of the room—particularly, Enrique—and yet, Winter's enticing scent hadn't swayed me at all. All my focus had been on Kari and her fragrance, to the point that I'd barely even picked up the other Omega's arousal.

My brow furrowed at the realization, only for my father to flash me a knowing grin.

He'd been studying me closely this whole time, and I hadn't even noticed.

"Still on the right path," he said as he walked by me. "Continue forward."

I watched him through narrowed eyes as he followed Winter and Kaz into the main dining area. A Beta trailed right behind them, but Enrique lurked by the door, his intense gaze focused on me.

Ignoring him, I rotated just enough to bring Kari back to my side and pressed my lips to her temple. "Still okay?" I asked her softly.

She nodded. "Y-yes."

"Good," I replied, wrapping my arm around her waist once more. "Remember to lean on me."

Her chin dipped once more, then she allowed me to guide her forward.

Enrique's eyes were narrowed, but not with jealousy. He seemed to be evaluating me intently. Then he roamed his gaze over Kari in an assessing manner, not a hungry one.

"I'm okay," she said to him again as we approached. It irked me a little that she seemed to be able to speak to him without provocation, but with me, I had to ask. However, it also suggested that they had a bond of sorts, one that meant she could trust others.

So what had he done to earn her favor?

And what did I need to prove to accomplish the same?

His gaze returned to her throat, his pupils dilating just enough to tell me he approved of what he found there. "You removed her collar."

"Did you put it there?" I countered.

He grunted, his ebony eyes flicking up to mine. "I'm not in the habit of collaring Omegas, so no."

"What are you in the habit of?" I asked. "Killing them as a way of saving them?"

His jaw ticked.

"You're holding up dinner," my father called, interrupting whatever response Enrique had intended. "And you know how I feel about food."

I almost rolled my eyes, but Kari's spiking pulse had me leading her inside without a word or comment. My mother's azure irises twinkled as we approached, her lips curling into a welcoming smile as she spied Kari beside me. However, her expression faltered a little upon sensing Kari's innate fear.

Making a quick seat decision, I placed Kari in the chair across from my mother and took the one on the other side.

It was a rectangular table.

Four and four.

Kari, me, Enrique, unknown Beta.

My mother, father, Kaz, and Winter.

What a strange arrangement we made, but it worked. Because it allowed me to keep Enrique in line, with help from Kaz across from him.

"Well now, let's start with a round of salads," my father

said to one of the Beta waiters. "Rolls, too. Wine, water, the works."

"Coffee," my mother added in a murmur.

"She wants a mocha," he clarified. "With extra espresso."

I smothered a grin; my mother always started her meals the same way. Something that confused many of our visitors because espresso and coffee were typically reserved for dessert. But that wasn't my mother's style, and my father loved catering to her needs.

"Chocolate cake, too," he called after the waiter.

"Of course, Alpha Ludvig," the waiter replied.

Kari stirred a little beside me, her gaze flicking up to my mom before dropping back to the table. Then her eyes darted to a squirming Winter, who was clearly losing herself to the vibrations Kaz seemed to be controlling.

Any other day, I would have smirked at his antics.

But I was too worried about Kari to care about Kaz's games tonight.

I stretched my arm out along the back of her chair, similar to how my father held my mother, and looked to him for guidance on where to start. He wasn't one to beat around the bush or placate guests with formalities. Not when he wanted to know something.

So I wasn't surprised at all when he said, "Tell us why we should let you live, Alpha Enrique. Because an observer of the situation would say you conspired to kill a precious Omega and also intended to take another as a slave. Convince us otherwise and we'll reconsider your fate."

CHAPTER TWENTY-ONE

KARI

Alpha Enrique didn't hold anything back, his explanation one that continued to make me flinch all throughout dinner.

He spoke about my father's treatment of Omegas in Bariloche Sector, how he enslaved them and kept them from their Alphas. He told them about Savi and Joseph. He told them about how he'd intended to save me, how he'd agreed to marry Snow Frost in exchange for *me*, and how it had gone all horribly wrong when Vanessa had put me in that cage.

Alpha Kazek pointed out rather curtly that my treatment here had been a little different from my father's treatment—something I considered to be an understatement.

Then they all started talking about my body and how they might be able to *reverse engineer* my situation. When I'd questioned it, Sven stretched his arm out around my shoulders and started to purr.

"Let's see what my brother has to say, then go from there," he murmured, his chest vibrating with that soothing energy only he seemed to be able to create. "Ander has the best team of physicians and researchers in the world. If anyone can help you, it's him."

It wasn't a question so much as a statement.

They intended to *reverse engineer* my situation.

No one asked me what I wanted because my opinion didn't matter. It was all about how to fix the sterile Omega so she could be properly mated and *owned*.

Part of me wanted to scream in frustration, to demand a choice.

Another part of me welcomed the change. Because wouldn't it be preferable to be a mate than a sleeve?

Unless something happens to my mate, I realized, shivering as I thought of my broken sister. Was that truly a better fate than being used and abused by Alphas for eternity?

The conversation morphed into a continued discussion on my father's politics, how he didn't like competition, and the things he did to keep himself on top.

"Hallucinogenic drugs," Alpha Ludvig repeated, the words sounding foul on his tongue. "Coward."

"Unfortunately, it works," Alpha Enrique replied. "He gives them a heavy dose, making them high out of their minds, and offers them an Omega to take it out on. By the time they finish the rut, they've damaged any potential bond that could be formed there, yet they're addicted to the female. And then Carlos takes her away, locks her up, and tells the Alpha to behave if he wants access to her again."

My stomach soured at the familiarity of the concept. I'd never been subjected to that because my father had ensured I couldn't take a mate.

But the others…

I shuddered, my arms curling around my abdomen as Sven's purr increased beside me. "Do you need a break, little wonder?" he asked softly against my ear while the others continued talking.

I considered it and shook my head because a break

wouldn't help. This was my reality. My life. I hadn't been able to escape it then, and I couldn't escape it now.

He pulled me a little closer, offering me his heat while the conversation rolled onward.

Winter and Alpha Kazek excused themselves, their pheromones telling me exactly what they intended to go do. I tried to ignore them, but my concern for Winter won out in my thoughts, and I couldn't help listening for her.

She whimpered in the other room.

Then moaned.

A heartfelt plea renting the air.

Followed by… a *rut*.

Except, it was unlike any rut I'd ever heard. She was screaming for more, and not because she was in estrus… but because she actually wanted *more*.

My stomach began to twist for a completely different reason, my wolf roused by the obvious enjoyment occurring nearby.

I chanced a glance at Sven, but his eyes were on me, his expression thoughtful.

He leaned down to graze my lips with his own, the touch sweet and providing a comfort I didn't realize I needed. Then he nuzzled my cheek and scooted my chair over so it was right beside his.

I wondered if he wanted to take me into the other room and do the same thing, but he made no move to steal me away from the table. He just kept purring low and warmly in his chest, soothing me as Alpha Enrique went on about life in Bariloche Sector.

He told them about the suppressants used to keep Omegas from going into estrus. He told them about the torture drugs used to make Omegas impossibly tight—to the point where one could die if rutted too roughly. He told them about my mother's death, which had Sven holding me even tighter.

And then he talked about Joseph, how he'd been tortured and taken off to an unknown place to be buried.

"I sometimes wonder if he's still alive," Alpha Enrique whispered. "There are moments when I swear I feel him, but Savi…"

"Is broken," I mouthed. "I… I don't know if she's… he told me if I went to you willingly, he'd tell me if she's still…" I couldn't finish it, nor could I look around Sven at Alpha Enrique. I wasn't even aware that I was talking until everyone around me fell silent.

"He held her life over your head to force your cooperation," Alpha Enrique surmised.

I dipped my chin, my lower lip wobbling at the memory. Sven nuzzled my temple, his mouth at my ear. "We'll find out for you," he murmured. "I promise."

That made four vows tonight.

Four vows that he could shatter so easily.

And yet… he'd kept his word so far. He'd remained beside me all night, and no one had touched me apart from him.

My heart skipped a beat, that dangerous emotion blossoming just a little more inside me. Enough for me to look up at him. "Please," I said softly. "Please don't break that promise."

His expression warmed. "I'll never break a promise to you, Kari."

I wanted so badly to believe him, but a lifetime of distrust kept me in check.

Still, I gave him another of those little nods.

Because I wanted to try.

I wanted to be what he desired, just as I longed for him to be what I needed.

"I can ask him, but there's no guarantee he'll tell me the truth," Enrique said. "He's also not pleased that I didn't finish the deal with Beta Snow."

His comment drew them back to Omega Winter and everything that had happened with Alpha Vanessa.

I stopped listening again, exhausted from all the heartfelt and cruel discussions. I knew it was needed, that these wolves weren't familiar with the ways of Bariloche Sector or the Alphas bred there, but I'd lived it. I didn't need to hear more about it.

My focus shifted back to Winter and her mate in the other room. They'd quieted after a round of loudly moaning each other's names. My senses piqued, my concern returning that she might be hurt.

Only, the door opened a few minutes later to reveal her pinkened cheeks and an odd sort of fury in her expression.

My spine straightened. *What did the Alpha do?* Except he appeared right behind her with a note of concern in his features as she headed right for the Beta male at the table.

"Did you know?" she demanded, causing everyone to fall quiet. My heart skipped a beat, worry thickening my blood at her bold maneuvering. But all her Alpha did was stand behind her as a protective shadow, observing the situation and all the others at the table. "Did you know?" she repeated when the Beta didn't respond.

"Know what?" he finally asked.

"That Ludvig is my uncle," she replied through gritted teeth.

Sven noticeably stiffened beside me, his purr faltering for half a beat before he flattened his palm against my arm and regained control of his reactions. His gaze went to his father, then back to the Omega, and then back to his father again.

But she and the Beta were already having a

conversation. He confirmed knowing about her familial ties to Norse Sector, then the question shifted to who else knew, and tensions escalated from there.

I pressed myself into Sven's side as Alpha Kazek involved himself in the discussion, his distaste of the Beta evident.

At least until the Beta said a few words about his use to the other man.

Then things began to calm, and I watched on in confusion as everyone mellowed around the table.

After several minutes of conversation, I came to a significant conclusion: this was nothing like Bariloche Sector.

The Alphas here were very much in control, but considerate. And from what I had observed of Alpha Kazek and Alpha Ludvig, they were considerate of their mates, too.

Winter stepped in front of Alpha Kazek at one point, whispering his name to calm him down, and he immediately melted for her. Despite the conversation having been something about the Beta touching her previously. And the conversation before that had been all about how that Beta and others had failed her, which meant the Alpha was already riled up. But one comment from his Omega, and he softened. Then the conversation intensified once more when Alpha Kazek warned the Beta never to touch her again.

And Winter countered with, "Hugs are allowed."

Alpha Kazek responded with a retort that she quickly opposed, placing them in a standoff unlike any I'd ever witnessed between an Omega and an Alpha.

Omegas bowed.

Alphas ruled.

But that wasn't the case at all. He *nodded* in agreement,

conceding to her on her point, causing my lips to part in shock.

He kissed her, much like Sven liked to kiss me, and held her close before turning to face the table.

"You'll do," the Beta, who I'd learned was named *Grum*, said.

"Was there ever any question?" Alpha Kazek asked.

"Yes. About a thousand of them," Grum replied before turning to address the table. "Now, are we going to talk about taking down the Queen of Mirrors or continue to posture? Because I'm fucking tired of bowing to that bitch."

I gaped at him briefly before studying Winter and Kazek again. My wolf was deeply intrigued by their unique dynamic.

Except, as I considered the table, I realized it wasn't all that unique because Alpha Ludvig was the same with the female beside him.

Sven's mother, I guessed, her scent familiar because of my dress. She had pretty white-blonde hair and blue eyes just like Alpha Sven and Alpha Ludvig. Pale, too. And her elven features gave her a kind appeal, while her petite stature was very Omega.

She caught my gaze from across the table and gave me a small smile.

I tried to return it, but my mouth refused me.

So I blinked and tried to speak through my eyes instead.

She seemed to understand, because she tilted her head a little and gave a slight nod before whispering something in Alpha Ludvig's ear. All his focus immediately went to her, like the rest of the room didn't exist, as he listened to what she had to say.

I didn't eavesdrop, instead choosing to glance at Sven. But he was watching his parents intently.

Alpha Kazek and Alpha Enrique began discussing plans for a return to Winter Sector and Alpha Kazek claiming his rightful throne. Since Snow Frost was a princess and the direct heir to their convoluted hierarchy, it made Alpha Kazek the proverbial King of Winter Sector.

I wasn't sure how all the politics worked because it was a different sector from my own, but I understood the implication of the concept—Alpha Kazek intended to challenge Alpha Vanessa for sector leadership.

And he was demanding that Alpha Enrique help.

I wasn't certain where that left me, but I didn't appear to be an item of discussion.

However, Sven became one, his duty becoming clear as the other Alphas spoke. "He's the best damn pilot on this side of the globe," Alpha Kazek insisted. "He'll fly us in."

"Sure," Sven drawled. "Volunteer me for duty."

Alpha Kazek snorted. "Don't make me take you back to Copenhagen, Mick."

Sven grunted, but it was an amused sound, not an annoyed one. "Drop me in another nest, Kaz. I dare you."

"Severely tempted," the Alpha replied. "Because apparently you've forgotten your place."

Sven rolled his eyes. "Just tell me when and where."

"And now you're back on track. Look at that," Alpha Kazek praised, earning another amused sound from Sven.

He leaned into me and kissed my temple, then looked at his parents. "I agree with your idea, Mom."

"Oof, I've taught him not to eavesdrop, haven't I?" she asked, her tone aghast yet matronly at the same time.

"I'm pretty sure you've taught him the opposite, love," Alpha Ludvig murmured. "After all, it was you who introduced him to my office door."

Her eyes widened in shock. "I would never…"

He chuckled and nuzzled her cheek before pressing his lips to her ear. Whatever he said had her cheeks pinkening and Sven groaning beside me. "And that's how you teach our son not to eavesdrop, Mila," he said, loud enough for me to hear.

"We're leaving now," Sven announced, standing abruptly.

Alpha Enrique moved as though to follow, but a low growl from Alpha Kazek kept him seated. "I need to know your intentions with her."

"You don't need to know anything," Sven countered. "But if you prove useful on this trip with Kaz, I might enlighten you."

"I came to negotiate her release," Alpha Enrique said, a low growl in his tone.

"No, you came to ensure she was all right, which we have more than proven to you." Sven slid his chair into the table, then looked directly at Alpha Enrique. "You request her freedom to go where, exactly? Winter Sector? Is she truly going to be safer there than she already is here?"

"She will be with Alpha Kazek on the throne," Alpha Enrique muttered.

"Yes. But he's not on the throne yet. So what do you want?" Sven pressed. "Are you suggesting Kari accompany us on the mission to reclaim Winter Sector? Because I can tell you right now that I refuse to let that happen."

Alpha Enrique's jaw hardened. "You speak as though you own her."

"She's mine," Sven returned without missing a beat. "So I'll tell you what's going to happen. Kari will remain with my mother, where she is *safe*, and if you prove useful to me, I may allow you to see her again later. That's my only offer. Take it or leave it. Because I won't be negotiating."

My lips threatened to curl down, my lack of a choice in any of this nagging at my mind.

Since when do I even care about my right to choose? I've never been allowed to decide anything for myself. Why should this be any different?

Because he is supposed to be different.

And yet... would I even choose to do something differently?

I tried to shake my head to clear it, the rioting thoughts making me dizzy.

Part of being an Omega was allowing Alphas to make decisions on their behalf. And part of being a mate was trusting her Alpha to make the right choices.

Everything Sven had just said was exactly what I would want for myself anyway, so why be bothered by him voicing it without talking to me first?

My jaw clenched a little, my mind befuddled with strange *what-ifs* that I'd never considered before.

I squashed them, focusing instead on the two Alphas beside me.

Alpha Enrique glared up at Sven, but I caught the flicker of defeat in his expression. He knew Sven was right, just like I did.

Except, I wasn't thrilled by the notion of Sven leaving. What they were planning sounded dangerous.

Which left me wondering, *What happens to me if he doesn't come back?*

CHAPTER TWENTY-TWO

SVEN

KARI EXPLORED my two-bedroom condo on bare feet, her toes sinking into the carpet with every step.

She started in the living room, her fingers brushing the suede upholstery of my couch and chair before taking in the view of the forest through my back wall of glass windows. A balcony lined the exterior that could be accessed by a pair of double doors, but she bypassed them to wander into my adjoining dining area and the chef-style kitchen beyond.

Her eyes ran over the knife block before flicking her gaze back at me over one shoulder, daring me to say something.

I didn't.

But if she tried to touch one, I would.

She circled the center island and left the kitchen area to explore the back hallway off the living room.

It led first to my office.

Then to a guest bedroom.

And finally to my bedroom.

She peeked in the first two before entering the last one. Her wolf seemed to be leading her movements, taking her first to the bed for a sniff test before meandering into my bathroom and my walk-in closet.

I leaned against the double doors that separated my bedroom from the bathing area and waited for her.

A rustle of fabric sounded, followed by the opening and closing of the drawers of my wardrobe dressers.

Zip.

My eyebrow cocked, intrigued by whatever she was doing.

Then my mouth parted as she exited wearing one of my white T-shirts.

And nothing else.

She strolled right by me with a stack of my laundry and went to the bed as though in a trance.

I didn't interrupt her, intrigued by the Omega at work. She climbed into the bed and shuffled around, finding a place she liked best, and started moving sheets out of her way and creating a makeshift wall.

I guess this means she approves of building a nest here, I mused to myself.

She worked in silence, her concentration resolute as she moved everything to where she needed it. I remained utterly still, even as she maneuvered around me to walk into the bathroom to retrieve a few towels and a set of sheets.

Her small hands moved with a precision that pleased my inner wolf, her instincts a sight to behold. *So beautiful. Utterly magnificent. Definitely mine.*

I was content to watch her do this all night, but she eventually slowed her pace, shifting just a few items around at a time, and eventually lay down as though to test the space.

I held my breath, waiting to see if she would invite me inside.

However, she instead popped back up with a frown, her blue eyes narrowing in my direction.

It was on the tip of my tongue to ask what she needed, but she slipped out of her nest and walked toward me with a purpose in mind. A purr hummed in my chest as she unbuttoned my suit jacket and took it to the closet. She returned less than a minute later to unfasten my shirt, her nimble fingers pulling the fabric down my arms before clutching it to her own chest and inhaling deeply.

A satisfied sound echoed from her throat as she took it to the nest.

I toed off my shoes, causing her to sharply glance over her shoulder, a look of censure in her features.

So I casually pushed them to the side as she watched, then I leaned against the door once more, waiting for her next move.

She studied me for a long moment, as though to ensure I wasn't going to do anything else. Her lips twisted a little to the side before she returned to her efforts on the bed.

I fought the urge to smile, her wolf not only in charge but also in an authoritative mood. I'd allow it. For now.

Once she finished her ministrations, she returned for my pants. Heat sizzled through my veins as I remained painfully still for her. My body reacted naturally to her nearness, my cock throbbing with need, but I didn't make any attempt to touch her.

I let her lead.

Watched as she set my pants along the wall of her nest.

And inhaled slowly when she turned around to survey me from head to toe. She nibbled her bottom lip as she considered my groin, her nostrils flaring at the sight of me. "I…" She trailed off, swallowing.

I waited, not wanting to push her.

Her wolf peeked at me again, her pupils dilating in response, and she took a step forward.

Then another.

And another.

Until she was right in front of me again.

It took all my self-control not to take advantage of the moment, to grab her and push her back into her nest and spread those pretty thighs. But I sensed the importance of this moment to be about her.

I also refused to cause her pain.

So I waited with bated breath to see what she would do next.

Her fingertips slid over the light dusting of hair along my lower abdomen, following the trail downward to my boxers and hooking her finger in the material. My stomach tightened as she drew her touch gently sideways to my hip.

Biting her lip, she tugged a little, adding her other hand to my opposite side to draw the fabric down my thighs, stripping me entirely. She tossed the undergarment into the heart of her nest before taking a small step backward, her eyes on me, beckoning me to follow.

I moved with her, matching her stride, and paused when we reached the bed. She lifted a piece of fabric, telling me without words to enter her nest.

My chest rumbled in approval as I slid inside, my wolf telling me to lie down for her on my back—right on top of my boxer shorts. Her eyes ran over me with interest before she joined me and fixed the blankets in her wake.

She looked so small in here, almost fragile, but as she straddled my thighs, I realized just how much power she possessed. I wanted her with a ferocity I couldn't indulge in, and it took considerable effort not to act. Particularly as her slick center settled over my arousal.

"Shit," I breathed, fighting the urge to arch into her.

The white T-shirt she'd put on disappeared, the fabric added to the wall around us, and Kari began to move. It was tentative at first, her body learning mine and kissing me intimately. Then she leaned down to kiss my neck, her tongue slipping out to taste my skin.

I fisted her hair in response, needing to touch her, to hold her, to give myself a distraction before I flipped her and fucked her to oblivion.

I curbed the urge by remembering her reaction earlier, picturing her face and the agony of her features. It was enough to keep me in check, but not enough to dissuade my mood. Because I wanted her. My Omega. My intended mate.

"Need more," she whispered, licking my throat as she started downward. "Need your seed."

My grasp tightened in her hair, my opposite hand going to the bedding beneath me to squeeze. Because *fuck*, that killed me. She'd given up complete control to her wolf, going on instinct alone. And now she wanted to season her nest.

With me.

I was so damn hard and ready for her to do just that, but I couldn't knot her. I couldn't make her come. I could barely even touch her.

And that realization threatened to strangle me.

I was so lost to it that I barely noticed her kissing a path downward, and it wasn't until her mouth closed over the head of my cock that I realized what she intended to do to me.

"Kari," I whispered reverently, arching into her mouth as she took me deep without any warning at all. Her hand wrapped around my base, her fingers unerringly finding my knot and massaging it in a way that had my balls tightening with expectation.

This Omega was magical.

This woman, an enigma.

This female… *so fucking mine.*

LEXI C. FOSS

I groaned as she drew her teeth along the underside of my shaft, her wolf ensuring I knew she was very much in charge right now. It made my inner beast growl in response, his desire to dominate riding me hard.

But I had to let her do this.

I had to be still for my Omega.

Let her guide. Let her learn. Let her—

Fuck.

She swirled her tongue around me with a skill I felt to my goddamn soul, my veins igniting with a fury that nearly undid every ounce of my resolve. "*Kari.*" Her name left my mouth on a snarl of sound, underlined in a strong purr of approval that had her doing it again.

I looked down to find her eyes on me, a hint of wonder in her gaze that highlighted my newfound nickname for her.

She really was a *little wonder*. So unique. So beautiful. So fucking *skilled*.

She knew exactly when to squeeze, when to suck, when to lick, when to use teeth, and when to swallow.

I arched, unable to stop myself, my fingers a tight fist in her hair. She didn't complain, just kept moving her head, bobbing up and down and forcing the climax from me.

Each squeeze of her fingers against my knot ensured it would be that much bigger of an orgasm, her Omega instincts guaranteeing I would gift her with as much seed as possible without fully lodging myself inside her.

I couldn't knot her throat.

Only her pussy.

And fuck if I didn't want to do that more than anything right now. Her slick sweetened the air, taunting my instincts and begging me to fuck what was mine.

No, I thought, groaning with *need. No. Knotting. No claiming. No… fuck!*

194

My chest vibrated with sound, both purr and growl, my wolf demanding his due as Kari shoved me off a cliff with her too-skilled mouth.

An explosion ripped through me, unexpected and entirely uncontrolled, as I emptied myself onto her sweet, torturous tongue.

She shoved me deeper into her throat, taking it all and more, her fingers working my knot to prolong my sensuous torture.

I couldn't stop coming.

And she didn't stop swallowing.

It seemed to go on… and on… and on… a week's worth of sexual frustration and need emptying inside her on repeat as my muscles spasmed and my wolf soared to another state of being.

Everything around me was hazy, my mind lost to a strange sort of oblivion no woman had ever been able to take me to.

But a soft, warm tear drew me back to the woman between my thighs.

She continued to milk me, her throat and fingers working, even while the agony of swallowing so much of me strained her features.

My fist reacted on instinct, yanking her off my cock and pulling her up to me as I continued to throb with unrestrained pleasure.

She gaped at me, confusion replacing her strain, and I tucked her beneath me, my cock slipping between her folds in a sensual caress that allowed me to continue my climax but onto my female. Her slick pooled with my cum, creating a sensual fluid that painted both our bodies intimately with the scent of sex and need.

Kari arched, a moan lodging in her throat as the essence provided her with a strange sort of nourishment.

Then I kissed her to give her something else she obviously needed—*adoration*.

She'd made this all about me, taking my pleasure to the point of clear agony, swallowing when she couldn't even breathe, and would have stayed like that had I let her. Probably because some Alpha had taught her to keep taking it until he'd finished.

But I wasn't that Alpha.

I was *her* Alpha. This was about us as a unit, not me as a man.

I tasted myself on her tongue, as well as the salty essence of tears, and showed her with my mouth what we would be together.

Her arms wrapped around my shoulders, her petite frame cushioning mine in the nest as I gave and took and gave some more.

Without her fingers on my knot, my pleasure eventually subsided, leaving us drenched in our passion and officially christening our shared nest.

This would be her space now, as well as mine, and if I had it my way, she'd never leave.

Except *I* had to leave her soon, to help Kaz with the issue up north. I silently vowed with my mouth to hurry back to Kari and our new haven. Whether she understood or not, I wasn't sure. But I had a few days to ensure the point was received.

And after that, we would head to Andorra Sector.

Assuming my older brother knew how to help.

PART II

ANDORRA SECTOR

CHAPTER TWENTY-THREE

SVEN

EUROPEAN AIRSPACE

Kari sat beside me, her attention on the windows around us. When I'd asked if she wanted to join me in the plane's cockpit, she'd hesitated, then nodded. It'd seemed like a good way to distract her from the trip ahead.

After a week of helping Kaz with the Winter Sector situation, and spending countless hours coordinating plans with my brother, Kari and I were finally on our way to Andorra Sector. His physicians had already reviewed her initial X-rays, and they were preparing a team for our arrival. We still had no idea if operating was even plausible, but without an in-person evaluation, it was impossible to tell.

Doctor Palmer felt it was a lost cause.

But he wasn't the best in this field of study.

Doctor Riley was. As an Omega and a physician with over one hundred years of experience, she was the one I wanted to evaluate Kari. No one else.

I hadn't told Kari about her yet, mostly because we hadn't spent a lot of time speaking out loud since I'd introduced her to my home.

Everything between us had become instinctual with her

choices being driven by her wolf. She preferred to remain in or near her nest throughout the day, pulling me into it most nights to pet and lick every inch of my body. I wasn't complaining, as I rather liked the change of events. It felt natural, apart from my inability to properly knot and please her in return.

The only night that had varied our plans had been the one I'd spent in Winter Sector with Kaz and the others. It'd been an efficient and bloody trip, but it had ended quickly with Kaz and Winter on their rightful thrones.

I'd been able to return in the early hours the following morning, and when I'd arrived, I'd found Kari curled up in a fluffy ball on the couch in my parents' suite. My mother had wanted to spend some time with her, and my father had stayed elsewhere for the evening to give Kari and my mom privacy.

Unfortunately, Kari hadn't spoken much, preferring to remain in wolf form in the living room while she'd waited for me to return.

My mother had suspected it'd been Kari's response to a fear of me not returning. Which had explained her overzealous reaction when I'd gone to find her.

As soon as we'd returned to the nest, she'd shifted back to human form and all but ripped the clothes from my body before demanding I lie down. She hadn't even given me a chance to shower, her need to reacquaint herself with my scent too strong.

I'd done exactly what she'd wanted and held her all day afterward.

When I'd told her last night we were heading to Andorra Sector today, she'd just nodded. No questions. No obvious concerns. Just a bleak sort of acceptance.

I couldn't figure out what was going through her head.

Her emotions at the moment were a mixture of contentment and worry. She no longer flinched away from my touch—she actually seemed to seek it out for comfort now—and she'd called me *Sven* during the few times she'd spoken to me.

"Do you have a lot of experience with planes?" I asked her, attempting to engage in some conversation. As much as I enjoyed her animal being in control of her actions, I rather missed her voice. And I really wanted to know what she was thinking about right now that had her both happy and worried at the same time.

She shook her head. "Just the one from Bariloche Sector to Winter Sector, and then Winter Sector to Norse Sector."

I nodded. It wasn't the brightest question, considering her upbringing and slave status, but at least she voiced a sentence. "What do you think of it right now?" I wondered out loud, gesturing to the clouds and blue sky.

We'd chosen a rather beautiful day to travel, giving us a clear path all the way to Andorra. Of course, that'd been purposeful on my part. The weather forecasts for the rest of the week weren't great, so I'd pushed Ander into letting us come today rather than next Monday as originally discussed.

"It's very freeing," she said softly. "But I find your ability to navigate it more interesting."

My lips curled. "I love flying. Almost as much as I love a long run with my wolf."

I glanced at her before refocusing on my task. With her in the cockpit beside me, I was being extra vigilant and careful up here. I didn't want to risk anything happening to her. But there was no one I trusted more for the task of piloting her than myself.

"I've been operating planes since I was nine," I added. It'd been my passion as a kid. My father had put me in touch with the pack's lead aviation expert, and the rest was history. "I'll have to introduce you to Alpha Garland sometime. He's an old general in Norse Sector who loves to fly just as much as I do. Taught me everything I know, too."

"Why would you want me to meet him?" she asked warily.

"Because he's important to me," I explained. "Not because I expect you to be *available* for him." The latter part I added on instinct because I suspected her mind had run off to a dangerous place at the mention of another Alpha. "I'll also introduce you to his mate, Jacy. She likes to fly as well. They actually met in a human military, but I can't remember which one. Something to do with flying, though."

"Human military?"

"Yeah, pre-Infected era." I shrugged. "I don't know much about it other than the movies I've seen from Kaz's stash, and the occasional book."

"Movies?"

"Films," I said, peeking at her sideways. She had a cute little frown marring her brow, and that air of worry seemed to have disappeared. "I'll show you sometime. When we're back in Norse Sector, and assuming Kaz leaves some of his stuff behind."

She studied my profile for a moment, making me wait to speak more. She had something she wanted to ask. I could feel it in my gut.

Go on, little wonder, I wanted to say. *Voice your thoughts for me.*

"Is… is that the plan?" she asked quietly. "To return to Norse Sector? Together?" I almost missed that last word, her tone so soft that the airplane engines nearly drowned her out.

But I caught the hesitancy in her tone, and the slight shiver as she finally voiced an inner thought for me to devour.

She's worried that I plan to leave without her, I realized. Probably because we hadn't thoroughly discussed what was about to happen. And now that she was away from her nest, the reality of our changing situation was settling around her in a discomforting manner.

My wolf urged me to reassure her, to pull her into my arms and purr for her. But I couldn't do that while operating the plane. Which meant I had to give her words and hope she trusted them.

"We're in this together, little wonder," I promised her. "We'll see what Doctor Riley thinks and go from there. My brother has made arrangements for us to stay for as long as we need. And when we are done, we will head back to Norse Sector together."

I reached across the small space between us to squeeze her thigh, needing her to physically feel the vow in my words. She didn't grimace or shiver, just placed her small palm over my hand and gave it a little returning squeeze.

"Okay," she replied, the single word causing my breath to falter.

Does that mean she believes me? That she's agreeing to have a little faith in me? My heart warmed at the thoughts, and I withdrew my touch from her jean-clad thigh to focus on the controls once more.

We were almost there, which meant I needed to begin to prepare to enter the Andorra Sector dome. I explained a little bit of the high-tech atmosphere to her as we went, telling her how my brother's sector was the most advanced in the world—at least in terms of X-Clan wolves—and how he'd shared a lot of his technology with my father.

"But we haven't created a dome," I concluded, gesturing to the glass orb lurking ahead. "It's not needed since we have water as a border on one side. But we have developed some sonar-tech walls around other boundaries to keep the Infected from crossing. And we have our night patrols, too."

With Andorra Sector being situated in the middle of the mountain, the added protection was very much needed. There were numerous nests in the nearby cities, and those fuckers were starving for fresh meat. They'd travel hundreds of miles for a taste, including traversing rough terrain like the snowy ice caps around us.

Kari remained silent for a moment before saying, "Alpha Carlos has a pit of infected creatures in Bariloche Sector. He throws wolves in there who misbehave."

I blanched. "*What?*"

She winced, and I immediately grabbed her thigh again. "Sorry, Kari. That's just… that's just so wrong… I reacted instinctively."

"So there are no punishment pits in Norse Sector." She didn't phrase it as a question, more of a relieved statement.

"I don't think those exist in any X-Clan sector." Except, apparently, they did in Bariloche Sector. "Alpha Carlos needs to be put down." An Alpha like that shouldn't be allowed to breathe, let alone lead.

She didn't reply, just stared at the dome in front of us. "How do we get inside?" she whispered, a slight tremor in her tone.

I allowed the distraction to soothe my temporary anger and told her how the opening worked. Then I radioed ahead to tell one of the tower agents that I was on my final approach.

The dome began to shift, creating a space at the top for me to fly through to reach their airfield. Kari said nothing, but I sensed her marveling at the way it all worked. Then she reached for my thigh, her fingers digging into the black denim fabric as we touched down only seconds later.

"Apparently, old planes used to speed along long tracks," I told her conversationally as I gestured to a runway beside us. "But these new jets function like rockets by shooting straight up and coming down in a similar fashion. It makes takeoffs and landings easy. At least to me."

She glanced sideways at me. "You're a very skilled pilot."

My chest threatened to puff up with pride at her compliment. Although, I suspected she didn't even realize that her words would be taken in that manner because she'd spoken them like a fact, not praise.

"Ready to meet my brother?" I asked as I flipped all the controls into place to hold the plane steady and keep it parked appropriately.

She didn't reply.

"He's intimidating," I admitted, placing my hand over hers on my thigh. "But he won't hurt you. He'll protect you."

"Why?"

"Because you're precious," I told her softly. "Andorra Sector doesn't have many Omegas. They worship them here. You'll see what I mean when you meet his mate." I lifted my touch to her chin, tilting her face toward me. "Remember the red-haired Omega from the photo? The smiling one?"

She gave a little nod.

"That's his mate, Katriana. And you'll also meet Doctor Riley."

She frowned. "Another mate? To your brother?"

I smirked. "Definitely not. Doctor Riley is an Omega, and she's very much claimed by Jonas."

Her eyes widened. "An Omega doctor? Like Quinn?"

Now it was my turn to frown. "Who's Quinn?"

She considered me for a moment, like she was debating whether or not to say more. It almost seemed as though she was afraid to explain herself, or maybe was surprised she even mentioned the name at all.

"Who's Quinn, Kari?" I asked again, this time with a hint of demand. I didn't want her to stop talking to me now, not after all the progress we'd made.

"An Omega back home," she whispered. "She has healing powers, but Alpha Carlos doesn't know. She helps the others."

My eyebrows lifted. "Healing powers, like she knows medicine?"

She shook her head. "No, like magic. Her touch… it *heals*."

"And she's an X-Clan wolf?"

Another little shake. "V-Clan."

Shock jolted through my system. "Alpha Carlos has a V-Clan Omega?" *Holy shit…* "*How?*" They were incredibly rare, the V-Clan existence having been severely impacted by the Infected era. The majority of those left lived in highly guarded colonies up on islands throughout the Arctic Circle. And they were frequently at odds with the vampires in the Greenland area because of their shared need for human blood.

"He has all kinds of Omegas," Kari replied. "Ash wolves, X-Clan, V-Clan, even a few non-wolves, too. He collects them."

My jaw clenched at the casual way she'd said it, like it was perfectly natural to just keep a clan of Omega slaves.

But to her, it was normal. Because she'd lived it. And then she saw it again with Vanessa in Winter Sector with her unwilling harem of Omega males. Alana had stayed with Kaz specifically to help those used and abused wolves. I suspected she might end up mating one herself, but only if he chose her. Or maybe they all would.

Regardless, they were safe.

Meanwhile, the slaves in Bariloche Sector were very much the opposite.

"How many Omegas does Carlos have?" I asked, completely losing sight of what we were supposed to be doing right now. She'd captured my entire focus with this line of discussion.

"A lot," she replied softly. "Some are mated. Some are not."

"Are they all… sterile?"

She shook her head. "No. Only me."

I wanted to be relieved by that, but somehow it only made her condition worse.

"The others can take mates," she added, more to herself than to me.

"You'll be able to take one soon," I said, certain of it. "And that mate will be me."

She didn't reply, just chewed on her cheek and gave a little nod.

I would have given anything in that moment to hear her thoughts, but she'd cut them off again, her demeanor quiet once more.

Since I'd already pushed her to give me information on Bariloche Sector, I didn't try to pry more words from her now. Instead, I reached over to unbuckle her from the copilot chair, then unfastened myself. "If you feel overwhelmed at any point, squeeze my hand," I told her as

I laced our fingers together. "I'll pause whatever we're doing to make sure you're all right. Okay?"

She gave another of those nods, which I translated to be a bit noncommittal. However, I allowed it for now. I'd just have to monitor her breathing and heart rate and go from there.

CHAPTER TWENTY-FOUR

KARI

What happens if they can't fix me? I wondered for the thousandth time. I wanted to ask Sven, but I was afraid of his response. He clearly wanted a mate. So what would happen to me if I couldn't be that wolf for him?

His questions about Bariloche Sector and the Omegas painted an uneasy picture in my mind. He'd asked if they were sterile, probably because he was considering taking one of them as a backup plan.

I didn't like that.

I wanted to be enough for him, but I wasn't naïve. He needed an Omega he could properly knot, and given that he hadn't once tried to do that with me, he clearly didn't find me worthy of it in my current condition.

Because he doesn't want to hurt us, I reminded myself.

Unless that's an excuse, a voice whispered back, the uncertainty in those words leaving me uneasy as he led me off the plane.

Three Alphas stood near the bottom of the stairs, their stances intimidating and causing me to instinctively squeeze Sven's hand. He paused immediately, his gaze meeting mine. "They're not going to hurt you."

I swallowed, unsure of what to say. It was a natural response to the sight of three massive predators.

Sven pulled me closer, his lips going to my ear. "The one on the left with dark hair and the vibrant gold eyes is my brother, Ander. The one in the middle with pale skin and light hair is Jonas, Doctor Riley's mate. And the third one is Elias, my brother's Second. He's also mated to an Omega named Daciana. None of them are a threat to you. I promise."

I wanted to tell him that just because an Alpha was mated didn't mean he couldn't be a threat to me. I'd been with enough of them to know. But my wolf demanded I trust Sven to keep me safe. If he didn't think this was a dangerous situation, then I needed to believe him.

So I dipped my chin and loosened my hold on his hand just a little.

He brushed a kiss against my temple and continued down the stairs at a slower pace. His protective energy wrapped around me in a soothing wave of heat, keeping me warm despite the cool air and making my shoulders relax a little more.

"I told you he still looks like a pup," one of them said conversationally.

"Careful, Elias, or my brother might challenge you for your position as Second," the other replied in a deep tone that sent a shiver down my spine. *Definitely a Sector Alpha*, I thought, recognizing the aura of dominance radiating off him.

The one who spoke first—Elias—snorted. "I welcome him to try."

"I have no desire to live in the mountains," Sven replied. "Your position is safe. But call me a pup again, and I'll spar with you just to make a point."

"Oh, now that could be fun," Elias mused. "Shall we make a date of it?"

"So I can hand you your ass? Sure," Sven agreed. "So long as Ander doesn't mind his Second being out of commission for a few days."

The Sector Alpha grunted. "If he's naïve enough to underestimate you, then he deserves a time-out."

"Ye of little faith," Elias drawled, his big hand covering his heart as though wounded by the conversation. "Maybe I should relinquish my position right now."

"Your ego won't allow it," Alpha Ander replied, his tone holding an edge to it. He didn't seem angry so much as just… *cold*. Like he was always this way, regardless of who stood around him. It made me wonder how his Omega could have possibly smiled in that photo. Maybe he demanded her to do it?

"Jonas," Sven greeted.

"Sven," the blond one returned icily.

Alpha Ander sighed. "He didn't mean to upset your mate."

"Doesn't change the fact that he did," Jonas returned sharply.

"The X-rays?" Sven guessed.

"Yes. *The X-rays*." Alpha Jonas sounded furious. "She's been crying for two fucking days."

Sven winced, but it was his brother who spoke. "I'm the one who gave them to her. Blame me."

"Oh, I do," Jonas replied flatly. "I very much do." The bulky Alpha folded his arms across a thick chest of muscle. "Fortunately, she's engaged in the challenge and intent on helping." His demeanor seemed to soften fractionally as his attention shifted to me. "She's looking forward to meeting you, Kari."

"Yes, she wanted to be here to greet you, but Joaquim bit his own tail earlier," Alpha Ander said, the edge of his voice softening a little. "Kat insisted on Riley reviewing the matter with utmost urgency."

"Was he chasing it?" Sven asked, his tone amused.

"Unfortunately," Alpha Ander muttered. "He's either chasing himself in circles or posturing with me."

"He's the one I'm afraid of challenging me for my role as Second," Elias interjected, earning a snort from Alpha Ander. "Little dude loves to wrestle in his wolf form."

"And bite," Alpha Ander added. "I'm just glad it was his own tail and not Kat again."

"He's bitten Kat?" Sven sounded surprised.

"By accident," Alpha Ander replied. "She didn't even bleed, but he felt bad and spent the night cuddling her in our nest. There was barely enough room for me to join them."

"And yet you've already created another one with her," Alpha Elias said, a playful note to his words.

"So she is pregnant," Sven said, sounding proud.

"Yeah, which is why she's overreacting to his tail injury," Alpha Ander grumbled. "Hormones."

"But those hormones during sex…" Alpha Elias trailed off, clearing his throat. "Daciana isn't pregnant again yet, but soon. Definitely soon."

Sven released my hand to wrap his arm around me, which was when I realized this conversation had made me shiver with the cold.

Because I would never be an Omega Sven could talk about like this.

I was infertile. Broken. Incapable of giving an Alpha the one thing they would always crave—an heir.

Their conversation continued, but I stopped listening,

my mind taking over and shoving my wolf's instincts to the back of my psyche. She clawed at me, demanding to be free, to drive my actions, but I didn't want to listen to her right now. I needed this dose of reality to remind myself why Sven and I could never work.

Unless he finds a way to fix me.

But I'd overheard Doctor Palmer telling him it was impossible the other day. It was why I'd allowed my wolf to take over, my need to hide behind her hope a necessity to keep on breathing.

I'd realized the other day that, at some point, I'd already started relying on Sven. It came from that part of me that considered him to be mine. It was a dangerous notion because he couldn't be mine… not in this state.

And it would be best to remind myself of that.

This passing infatuation would be just that when he realized I was incapable of being what he wanted.

"Kari," he whispered against my ear, drawing me back to him and the other Alphas. "Let's go inside."

I nodded numbly, my spine prickling with awareness of being surrounded by dominant males. I could feel their eyes on me, the pity radiating from them almost worse than the hunger I usually felt from wolves of their standing.

Sven's fingers wove through mine again, giving my hand a squeeze that I didn't return, and led me toward a building made of glass. The architecture and surroundings reminded me a bit of Norse Sector with all the snow, pristine sidewalks framing glassy exteriors, and clean white lines, but the backdrop of the mountains here was a bit different.

I idly wondered what it would feel like to run up those peaks in wolf form.

Would I slide? Fall? Tumble to my death?

My stability in wolf form was weak at best, mostly because I hadn't experienced much freedom throughout my life. The walk with Sven the other day in Norse Sector had been one of the longest of my life. And I'd definitely never played in the snow like that either.

"We can explore later, if you want," Sven offered, following my gaze to the mountains.

I glanced at him in surprise. "We can leave the dome?"

"Of course," he replied. "The glass walls are to keep the Infected and other unwanted guests out, not to trap everyone inside."

"Oh." That made sense to an extent. "Even Omegas?"

Alpha Ander stepped up to my opposite side as he said, "Omegas roam with their Alphas. Not because we don't trust them to wander on their own, but because it's in our nature to protect. And there are dangers in the mountains that could potentially hurt our Omegas, so our wolves demand we run with them."

"Daciana loves exploring," Alpha Elias added. "We run together almost every night. Or we did, until she had our daughter. Now we only run when Jonas and Riley watch little Brenna for us."

"Brenna," I repeated. "That's a pretty name."

"Yes," he agreed. "For a very pretty little wolf."

I blinked then, realizing I'd just spoken to an Alpha who wasn't Sven. And that he'd replied to me… *casually*.

My wolf pushed me into Sven's side on instinct, needing to remind herself whom she belonged to. He released my hand to wrap his arm around my shoulders.

Alpha Elias and Alpha Jonas moved in front of us to open the door to the glass building, leading us inside.

Light pooled all across the interior marble floor, creating an array of sunshine that seemed to heat the air naturally. *Another technology advancement?* I wondered, feeling the warmth through my sweater and jeans.

I'd borrowed the clothes from Sven's mother. We were similar in size, making it easy to repurpose her wardrobe. But she was just a little more filled out than me, her curves healthy. However, I'd noticed while trying on her clothes that I'd gained some weight while being with Sven, the regular meals having caused my body to heal in a way I hadn't realized it could.

The male led us to a bank of elevators similar to those I'd seen in Norse Sector and keyed in a series of codes to call the car down to us.

My heart skipped a beat as the metal doors slid open, and all three of them stepped inside, followed by me and Sven.

Four Alphas.

One broken Omega.

I shivered, and Sven pulled me into his chest to hold me throughout the ride. His scent surrounded me, holding me captive and shielding me from the others.

It was then that I realized I couldn't smell them at all.

Only Sven.

He was a beacon to my wolf, her proverbial safe haven even outside our nest, and all I could do was cling to him.

We eventually arrived at a white corridor lined with windows on one side and a solid wall on the other with pale wood doors spaced out every twenty paces or so. When we reached the end, Alpha Ander pressed his wrist to Sven's invisible watch, causing it to beep. "I thought you might want a larger space this time around."

"An upgrade?"

"Contrary to what Elias wants to believe, you're no longer a pup. And you have an intended mate to care for, too." Alpha Ander clapped Sven on the back, the gesture affectionate in a manner that seemed dominant, too. I wasn't sure I understood the meaning, but it appeared to please Sven, because he smiled.

"Thanks," he murmured.

Alpha Ander nodded. "Get acquainted with the space. We'll regroup in three hours for dinner downstairs so Kari can properly meet the others."

I stiffened. *Others?*

"Kat left some clothes for Kari, too," Alpha Ander added. "In case she wants to borrow them. But dinner will be informal, so no need to change." He pitched his voice lower as he murmured, "If you need something more, just let us know, Kari. We want you to be comfortable here."

I wasn't sure how to reply, so I looked to Sven.

"We'll let you know," he responded before waving his hand over the handle of the door. It clicked and moved like magic, then opened with a swish of air. "Thank you for your hospitality."

"Anytime," Alpha Ander replied, starting down the hallway. Alpha Elias trailed after him, but Alpha Jonas remained for a beat.

I glanced up at him, wanting to read his expression, and found him staring right at me. "My mate is a genius. If anyone can help you, it's her," he said with a seriousness I felt to my very soul.

He held my gaze, forcing me to look down again in submission.

I shivered when he didn't move or speak, uncertain of what he intended.

"You're a good wolf, Sven," he said after a beat. "Riley will do her best."

"I know," Sven replied, his tone soft. "Thank you for letting us meet with her."

"Oh, don't thank me. That was all Riley's choice.

Thank her." With that, he left and joined the other two males at the elevators.

Then Sven led me through the door into a room decorated in white colors and glass. And my wolf immediately reclaimed control.

CHAPTER TWENTY-FIVE

SVEN

Kari prowled the guest suite throughout the afternoon, her wolf ruling all her actions. She sniffed the kitchen, checked the fridge, eyed the dining table set for two, and climbed all over the furniture in the living room. Then she explored both bedrooms, choosing the larger one with a display of rolling on the king bed before jumping up and heading out onto the wraparound balcony.

I followed her, not saying a word. She needed to find comfort here, so I purred while she attempted to turn this place into a temporary haven.

She eventually slowed and returned to the bed to curl up in a ball. I lay with her, soothing her with my heat and the rumble in my chest. But the hours ticked by quickly, leading us to dinner.

Her wolf didn't relinquish her control, keeping Kari quiet all through the meal. She barely ate, her attention on her plate and not those around her.

It was like she didn't even see the other Omegas or the two children at the table. It left me confused and a little wary. Because if anything should snap her out of her fog, it should be an experience showcasing Omegas and Alphas loving each other. But all it did was drive her further into despair, forcing her animal to remain as a shield of sorts.

After dinner, I took her back up to our suite, where she promptly stripped and went straight to bed. I went with her, allowing her to take comfort in my body the way she'd done almost every night since I'd first taken her to my condo. When she finished, her petite frame drenched in slick and seed, she finally relaxed and fell asleep while I purred.

I didn't follow her into dreamland, disturbed by what seemed to be a regression of sorts.

Riley and I had been communicating via notes, so I pulled up the files on my watch and added a log of her behavior today. Then I read a few observational notes Riley had made after dinner.

Subject appears to be disconnected from her wolf, likely as a result of having her animal nature controlled for so long.

I added a note beneath that, saying I'd noticed this as well. Then I summarized what my father had said when I'd asked him about it earlier this week.

She's using her wolf as a crutch because she's afraid, I typed. *Alpha Ludvig says that she's never been able to rely on her animal, which is a natural instinct for many of us, so it's almost like she's making up for lost time. But because she's not properly socialized with her beast, she's unable to balance the control. So her wolf takes over entirely, despite her being in human form.*

And since her wolf seemed to trust me and like me, she did things she probably wouldn't agree to in a normal frame of mind. It was a thought that nagged at me, making me feel guilty for allowing her to take my seed, but I also recognized that she needed it.

My poor little wonder was broken.

But I'm going to heal you, I promised her, kissing the top of her head. *I promise.*

A private chat message popped up while I said it,

Riley's name scrawling across the screen. *Can you talk?* was written beneath it.

Yeah, just need a minute, I sent back to her.

Kari didn't move or make a sound as I extracted myself from her. She just curled into a tighter ball, her fingers finding my discarded shirt and pulling it into her chest.

I kissed the top of her head again and quietly stood to find one of the robes from the en-suite bathroom. Then I stuffed my feet into a pair of slippers and headed out to the balcony to message Riley.

She called a few seconds later, her hair mussed as though she'd just climbed out of her nest. When Jonas appeared shirtless behind her, I knew that was exactly where she'd come from.

He didn't say anything about her being on the comm, his presence a subtle display of his dominance and ownership and enough to appease his wolf. It probably helped that she appeared to be wearing his shirt, too.

"I saw you adding notes, so I knew you were awake," Riley said by way of greeting. "But I have some thoughts on her behavior."

"Things that might help?" I asked, hopeful.

"Maybe." She cleared her throat and twisted her lips to the side. "The disassociation is clear, as we've both already noted. It's easier for her to cope with her situation when her animal is in control because her wolf seems to trust you. But I'm worried that's going to cause longer-term issues because she's blocking the fears of her mind and failing to communicate her concerns as a result."

I nodded. "I've noticed that. But I'm not sure how to fix it."

"You need to control her wolf," she said softly. "You're being the protector she desperately craves, so it's easy for her to fall into a pattern of reliance. However, she needs your dominance, too. You'll have to push her, Sven. It won't be easy, but she needs it almost as much as she needs your safety. Make her talk to you."

"Oh, is that all?" I couldn't help the note of sarcasm in my voice.

Jonas clearly understood my plight, because he snorted in the background.

"I know; I'm making it sound simple. And I'm very aware it won't be. She's terrified of Alphas, and I'm asking you to become the thing she fears. At least, that's how she'll see it at first. But she needs to talk to you for her to start healing."

She was saying things I already knew, which frustrated me a bit because her advice might create a full-blown divide between me and Kari. At least her wolf accepted me right now. If I turned on her and tried to force her to open up, I risked that connection.

"She's afraid of something," Riley added. "I could sense it at dinner, and I don't think it has anything to do with being surrounded by new Alphas. There's something upsetting her that goes much deeper than a fear of being knotted. That's what she already knows. Her reaction tonight struck me as a new terror, something… something she doesn't understand."

I frowned. "Like what?"

"That's what you need to find out as her Alpha," Riley replied. "Make her talk."

My teeth ground together at the order. I knew she was right, but I didn't particularly appreciate it coming from an Omega in that tone of voice. Wolves had an established hierarchy for a reason. Alphas required obedience and respect, and my wolf rankled at her clear disregard for my superior position.

She's the physician on Kari's case, I reminded myself. *Listen to her. Don't bite back.*

"And there's one more thing," she continued, the little spitfire clearly oblivious to my irritation. "You need to prepare yourself for the very real possibility that this can't be undone."

My world stopped as I narrowed my gaze at her. "What did you just say?"

"I might not be able to fix her sterility, Alpha Sven. You need to be prepared for that outcome."

Such blunt words.

Such… *frustration.*

"Then you should be prepared for me not accepting that alternative," I countered. "Have a good night, Doctor." I hung up before she could comment, and before I could say something I would soon regret.

The audacity of that damn wolf not only giving me an order but also telling me to accept an impossible fate.

I wasn't willing to consider an alternative, and neither was my wolf. Everyone else could doubt the situation as much as they desired. I had enough hope and faith on my own to withstand an army.

Kari will heal.

She will become the wolf she was meant to be.

And she will be mine.

I knew all this because even without the bite, I'd already claimed her. And I refused to let her down.

You'll see that I'm right, little wonder, I thought. *One day soon, you'll believe in your fate just as I do. Everyone will. I'm sure of it.*

CHAPTER TWENTY-SIX

SVEN

Six Weeks Later

I PACED the hallway of Andorra Sector, my heart in my throat.

After over a month of preparation, Riley finally opened Kari up for surgery, and the scene inside… *Fuck.*

My fist drove into the wall on instinct, my chest aching with the mess Kari's father had made of her abdomen. *Wires*. He'd used fucking *wires* to twist her reproductive system into knots that left her not only infertile but also in constant pain.

Tears threatened my vision, my wolf raging to be let free, to run, to *shred*.

I wanted to find Alpha Carlos and fucking throttle him. Then eat him. Then shit all over his damn grave. And do it all over again… and again… until I was satisfied with his death.

Alpha Enrique stepped into my path, the asshole having come in for the surgery today. He'd wanted to be here to offer support, but all I really desired at the moment was a punching bag.

Kari hadn't progressed at all over the last month. No.

She'd gotten worse, withdrawing into herself and refusing to talk to me.

Every movement was led by her wolf as she became more and more withdrawn. I'd tried to make her talk to me, but I couldn't bring myself to be forceful with her. Not after everything she'd endured.

However, I was starting to think that Riley might have been right.

This disconnect between Kari and her wolf was only worsening. And without her mind fighting to survive, she'd end up wallowing in pain and living in a shell of an existence.

We slept together every night, our wolves content to cuddle and play.

But the Kari inside refused to embrace me.

I'd asked her countless times to tell me what was bothering her, demanding she let me fix it, and each time, she'd withdrawn with a "You've already done enough for me."

The worst had been when she'd thanked me for helping her, like she'd been bidding me farewell with her gratitude. I didn't understand it. I'd ensured she knew I intended to make her mine. So why would she feel the need to say goodbye?

I ran my fingers through my hair, tugging at the uneven strands. It'd grown to my chin over the last month and a half, leaving me in dire need of a haircut. But I couldn't focus beyond a daily shave to keep my chin smooth. The rest would just need to wait.

"How could the Alphas in Bariloche Sector let this shit happen?" I demanded, rounding on Enrique. "It's your fucking job to protect Omegas. Not damage them beyond repair."

"I didn't do this," he countered, straightening his spine. "And I've been trying to protect her for years."

"You did a shit job of it."

"I'm aware," he tossed back on a growl. "Very. Fucking. Aware."

That just made me want to punch him more. He'd provided invaluable intelligence to my father, to Kazek, and even to me, but I really wanted to kill him right now. "Riley's in there sewing her back up because she can't even operate. What the hell am I supposed to tell Kari when she wakes up?"

"That you still want her," Enrique replied without hesitation. "That she's not unworthy of protection and adoration just because her father ruined her."

His words gave me pause. "Why would she even think that?"

"Because it's what she's been taught her whole life, that she's just a fuck toy to be passed around, not claimed by an Alpha. She's too damaged to be cherished. That's the rhetoric she's heard all her life."

I stopped pacing, my mind whirring with this information. "You're just now telling me this?"

"I assumed you would have deduced it yourself after spending time with her. Surely she's told you that this is her view of herself."

"She barely talks to me," I admitted, grumbling to myself. "She lets her wolf take over."

He fell silent, making me look at him.

"What?" I demanded.

"She's protecting her mind," he replied. "She's suffered years of unspeakable torment. You're probably the first male to ever make her feel something outside that pain. Consider how terrifying that must be for her."

"It should inspire hope."

"Hope isn't a concept she's ever been able to trust," he countered. "If anything, she's only learned to fear it."

He had my attention. "Keep talking," I demanded.

He sighed. "All right, consider this perspective. Making her hope leaves her even more vulnerable than she's ever been because it introduces a world of *what-ifs*, and she's been trained not to ever consider that for herself. She also witnessed firsthand what that potential fate did to her sister —who, by the way, I've heard is alive. But I'm not sure Kari will want to know that."

My teeth ground together, yet I nodded in agreement. Because yeah, now wasn't the time to tell her that her sister was still being tortured daily.

However, that wasn't even the part that captured and held my focus—it was Enrique's comment about Kari's perspective. *Hope makes her vulnerable.* "When she was in Bariloche Sector, she knew what to expect," I said, thinking it all through out loud. "But she feels vulnerable here with the potential unknowns. Because she doesn't trust me yet to follow through on my word."

"Have you told her what's going to happen next?" Enrique asked.

I considered the question. "Not in full detail, just that we're going to fix her and return home."

"And what if you can't fix her?" he countered. "Have you discussed that?"

"No, because that's not an option. We are going to find a way to help her."

"That's not my point," he replied, folding his thick arms over his black sweater. The color matched his eyes as they narrowed to smoldering orbs. "Have you told Kari what will happen to her on the chance that you can't fix her?"

He held up a hand before I could repeat myself.

"I know it's not an option to *you*, but Kari isn't you, Sven. She's a shattered Omega who thinks she's unworthy of a mate because her father ruined her." He paused to let that sink in, his statement causing my words to churn.

Because no, I hadn't thought about it from that perspective. I'd been resolute in our path. We *would* cure her.

"She doesn't have your hope or perspective," Enrique continued. "She very likely doesn't see there being an option at all, Sven. Which means she's only going through all this to appease you—the Alpha she considers to be kind—not because she actually thinks it'll fix anything."

I really didn't like the way that sounded. And yet, I could see exactly what he meant. Because Kari would absolutely see it that way. Which gave all her nodding a new meaning.

"So have you told her what will happen if she can't be cured?" he pressed. "Or does she think you're going to throw her away for another Omega? Because that's exactly the sort of logic that's been programmed into her."

"How do you have all this insight into her mind?" I asked, my wolf stirring restlessly inside me. Kari had mentioned he wanted to help her, that he had ties to her sister's mate, but all his statements made me wonder just how familial this connection between them really was. Because he had an insight worthy of a mate more than a brother.

"It's not her mind I feel a connection to so much as her sister's. Through my twin brother."

I frowned. "Because of their former bond?"

"*Current* bond," he corrected. "I can't prove it, but I can feel it. My brother is alive somewhere."

"Then why did you volunteer to go to Winter Sector? I

mean, I know you wanted to help Kari, but how did you intend to do that and save your brother?"

"I can't help him while she's in the way," he replied. Now he started to pace the way I had moments ago. "Alpha Carlos is successful because he's perceptive. He knows I'm tied to Kari, but he thinks it's a physical infatuation. He has no concept of family."

I snorted. Because yeah, that much was obvious.

"If I tried to go against him, he'd use her against me. So I needed her somewhere safe. I also need more information, which is why I've spent the last decade playing his fucking games and pretending to be a good soldier. It's all in hopes that I'll find a weakness or some sort of clue as to what he's done with my twin."

"And have you found anything?" I wondered out loud.

His expression told me he hadn't found anything of worth. "Not yet."

I recognized the hint of determination in his hardened jaw because it matched my own with Kari.

"But I know my brother is alive, and through him, I sense his pain and Savi's hopelessness. And I've spent enough time with Kari over the last few years to know her mind as well." He looked up sharply as I took an unconscious step forward. "I've never knotted her. So calm the fuck down."

My wolf growled, not appeased by the tone but momentarily placated by the brisk proclamation. "For your sake, I hope that's true," I said in a low voice, meaning it.

"She's like a little sister to me," he gritted out. "If anyone should be kicking anyone's ass here, it's me who should hand you yours. I can *smell* your seed on her skin, Sven."

"I haven't knotted her," I vowed. "But her wolf… likes my scent."

He eyed me for a moment and grunted. "That better be all it is."

"If it wasn't, it wouldn't be your concern since she's *mine*."

"But she's not," he quickly reminded me. "Because you can't claim her, which brings us full-circle—have you told her your intentions should she be unable to mate?"

"No," I snapped. "Because I don't see that as an option. However," I added sharply when he looked ready to interject, "I heard what you said, and I understand that she likely doesn't share in my certainty. I'll address it."

He looked me over, his expression shifting from irritated to a subtle hint of respect. "Good." His arms loosened to hang at his sides, then he drew one hand through his thick black hair and blew out a breath. "I fucking hate this shit. It's all politics and BS. I just want to head back to Bariloche Sector and put a damn bullet through Carlos's head. But no one will challenge him."

"Oh, I wouldn't be so quick on that assumption," my brother said as he entered the hallway with Elias at his side. "I would very happily put several bullets through his skull after everything I've learned about him."

"But it's not just him; it's the other Alphas, too," Enrique said, not at all fazed by my brother's approach. Most Alphas bowed in some way. Not this one. I noticed he was the same with me, confident in his abilities, yet respectful when needed—such as when Kaz or my father demanded it. "Most of Carlos's generals are controlled with drugs, but not all of them."

"Yourself included," I pointed out.

"Yes. Because I knew how to play the game and avoid his hallucinogenics. It's how he took down my brother."

I arched a brow. "Your brother willingly took drugs?"

"Not willingly, no," he replied. "He dosed him with an air gas while he was asleep in the nest with Savi."

"Shit," I breathed.

"Yeah," he muttered, looking back to Ander. "Do you mean what you said? You'll help kill him?"

"With an appropriate plan, yes," Ander replied, glancing at Elias. "I mean, you were just saying how boring things have become with the Infected. Seems like a good way to shed some blood, yeah?"

Elias's lips quirked up, his dark eyes brightening with excitement. "Abso-fucking-lutely."

Ander nodded. "Good. You and Enrique can chat about schematics and start drawing up a plan. We'll meet in three days to review it. I want at least three tactical options." His gold irises pinned me to the spot. "Meanwhile, you are going to come with me to help solve a dispute."

I frowned. "A dispute?"

"Yeah. Between Jonas and Riley."

That had my eyebrows shooting upward. "How the hell can I help?"

"She wants to bring in help," Ander explained flatly. "An expert who she thinks can fix Kari. Someone she used to work with at the CDC."

"Okay…" I trailed off, waiting for more information. "Not seeing the conflict."

He waited a beat. "She wants to call Kieran O'Callaghan."

My lips parted. "*What?*"

"And now you see the conflict." He turned on his heel, leading the way.

CHAPTER TWENTY-SEVEN

KARI

I woke up with a head full of voices.

They were arguing.

The name *Kieran* kept popping up in conversation, and I couldn't figure out why the name provoked so much anger. But I felt the Alpha energy heightening, the dominance a whiplash to my senses that left me wanting to supplicate on the ground.

Except I couldn't open my eyes.

"I can't fix her on my own," Riley seethed, her high-pitched voice splitting through my skull. "She almost died on my table!"

"And your solution is to call in *Kieran O'Callaghan?*" a deep voice countered. "That will never happen."

"He'll be able to keep her stable while I operate." It sounded like Riley was talking through her clenched jaw. "He's full of healing magic, something I know you're aware of since he *saved your life once.*"

"He did not save my life."

Silence fell, followed by the subtle tap of a shoe against marble.

"Fine," Alpha Jonas muttered. Or I assumed it was Alpha Jonas, anyway. The deep tenor sounded right, and he was the only Alpha I'd heard Riley really speak to in this manner. "He *helped* bring me back, but that doesn't mean I trust him."

"How many times do I have to tell you that he never touched me," Riley said, her change of topic confusing me and making me wonder if I'd missed a link.

"My denial isn't about that."

"It's absolutely about that."

"He's a V-Clan Alpha. And not just any V-Clan Alpha, but the damn Prince of Blood Sector," Alpha Jonas snarled. "*That* is my objection, Omega."

"Oh, don't you 'Omega' me, *Alpha*."

"I will bend you over this fucking table right now and—"

"And what?" she demanded. "Fuck me into submission? Do it. I dare you. Let's see what happens afterward."

He growled.

She growled back.

And someone else cleared a throat. "Sven has something he wants to say," a commanding tone announced.

Alpha Ander, my wolf recognized, whimpering in my mind. While he'd been relatively nice since I'd met him, the male still terrified me. I had no idea how his Omega put up with his dominant air. He was even worse than Alpha Ludvig.

"Why do you want to bring Prince Kieran in?" Sven asked, his voice sending a wave of comfort over my otherwise cold body. He made me feel immediately safe, his presence soothing some of the ache within my mind.

"He has healing abilities that will prove useful in this situation," she explained. "I worked with him during the initial pandemic. He's a friend." The latter was spoken through her teeth, and I suspected she'd shot a look at her Alpha when she'd uttered it.

This Omega is… unique, I marveled, awed by her ability to hold her own in a room full of Alphas. During the few times I'd spoken to her over the last however many weeks, she'd been gentle and soft. Although, she was anything but that when her Alpha came around.

If I couldn't sense her Omega scent, I would call her an Alpha female.

Except, she was dwarfed by Alpha Jonas's size, and I noted that the few times she'd sought comfort from him, he'd jumped at the opportunity to be her primary support.

Which left me really confused by their dynamic. I'd overheard Elias muttering, *Bratty submissive*, at one point. But I hadn't been able to comprehend that concept, let alone understand why it'd seemed to amuse him.

"Define 'healing abilities,'" Sven said, his palm drifting up my arm to my shoulder. Goose bumps pebbled along my flesh in his wake, the warmth of his skin a stark contrast to my cool state. It left me wondering if this was real or not.

I felt awake.

Yet not.

Sort of like I was stuck in a dream state between reality and fiction.

As Riley started talking about enchantments and V-Clan magic, I started to seriously consider the whole dream idea. Because none of what she described sounded possible. Something about him holding me stable while she removed the wires, otherwise I would bleed out on the table again.

"He also might be able to revert the damage done to

her reproductive organs," she continued. "That's not something I can do even if I finish removing all the metal. But he just might be able to aid her shifter energy and rejuvenate her insides."

My lips wanted to curl down but couldn't. *Finish removing all the metal?* Did that mean she had left pieces of the wire inside me? Or was it all still there? Had the surgery failed?

I expected it to.

But I hadn't heard the verdict spoken out loud yet.

What does this mean for me and Sven? It was the question I'd avoided since arrival in this strange sector. *Will he find a better Omega?*

I… I didn't want him to do that. However, I also knew he should. Because if I couldn't give him what he needed, then it wasn't fair for me to keep him. He deserved better than that. After everything he'd done for me, I owed it to him to ensure he found someone of worth. A mate he could truly knot.

Not a wolf like me.

I sank back into my mind, barely hearing the rest of their conversation. All they kept talking about was *Alpha Kieran,* whom Riley called *Prince Kieran.* And his magic. And whether or not to allow him to visit Andorra Sector.

"We don't even know if he'll agree to this," Riley said after several points were debated. "So this is all a moot argument if he refuses to help."

"He'll help," Alpha Jonas snapped.

"You don't know that."

"I do, Riley," he returned. "Because it would be you asking, and we both know that male would move the earth for you if he could."

"*We are just friends.*"

"You might consider him a friend, but he certainly doesn't see you that way," he countered. "And I won't argue this with you anymore. I'm an Alpha. I know when a male has interest in my fucking mate."

The door slammed shortly after that statement, making me jolt inside.

Silence fell.

Then Riley sniffled, showing a softer side. "I… I don't want to upset Jonas, Ander," she whispered. "But Kieran can help. I know he can." Her fingertips drifted over my stomach, causing me to flinch internally.

And just that movement told me everything I needed to know.

This is very much real, and the wires are definitely still there.

"I can't fix her on my own," she added softly. "I need help, and Kieran is the best there is outside of Andorra Sector. It's Kari's only hope. I can't tell you what to do or how to proceed; I can only tell you that without him, I'm at a dead end."

My heart stuttered in my chest, my soul withering beneath the veracity of her words.

All the air just seemed to vacate my being, leaving behind an excruciating wave of pain that tormented me more than the wires inside my abdomen ever could.

It felt like I was… disappearing.

Sinking into a void.

Leaving this world behind for good. But there was no peace in this death. Just hollow misery swallowed whole by a bleak darkness.

I stopped listening. I stopped being. I stopped caring.

And just… accepted my fate. A fate I should have accepted from the beginning. A fate I should never have questioned. Because what was left behind in my spirit was a splinter of agonizing potential—a life of what could have been.

A life with Sven.

A life I would never truly experience.

A life… I needed to say goodbye to.

A life I needed to end.

CHAPTER TWENTY-EIGHT

KARI

Sven's purr reverberated through my being, drawing me into a dreamlike state I longed to live in forever. I forgot about everything and everyone else and focused solely on that sound.

His lips tasted my hair, my temple, my cheek.

I hummed in response, reveling in the warmth only my Alpha could provide.

Until I remembered that he could never be my Alpha.

The surgery had failed. And from what little I remembered, the only solution they had was one that upset several of the Alphas in the room.

The details were foggy, but my resolve was firm.

Sven couldn't be mine. I'd known that from the beginning, but he'd sparked a kindling of hope inside me that had followed me into my dreams, bringing to life a fantasy that would never be.

That fantasy would only worsen over time, providing me with a deeper glimpse into a world that could never be mine.

It wasn't fair to me. And it certainly wasn't fair to him.

I just needed to find a way to make him understand that we had no future together. It would hurt. But it would be worth it in the end.

He would probably send me back to my father. However, a bleak, dark part of me would almost prefer that fate to the eventual destruction Sven would wreak upon my soul when he found a worthier Omega. Just the thought of it was enough to rouse me from the purr-induced comfort, a sharp pang slicing through my chest.

"Kari," Sven murmured, a note of concern in his voice.

Probably because I'd cried out, or maybe whined. I couldn't even say. I was so broken and far removed that I was no longer in charge of myself.

I'd handed over the reins to my wolf weeks ago, or maybe it was months now, and I couldn't seem to claw my way back to the surface. She led based on instincts, her animal mind easier to hide behind.

But I couldn't remain there. Not any longer. Not now that I knew there truly was no hope for me.

"Kari," Sven repeated, his lips at my ear. "I know you're in there. And I need you to come out and talk to me."

My wolf didn't want to talk. She wanted to kiss him, lick him, worship him with her mouth.

I almost gave in to her, wishing to indulge myself one more time before I said goodbye. But my body felt too weak to do what I needed.

"You've been sleeping for two days," he continued softly. "But I can sense that you're waking up, and I want to talk to you."

You are, I thought back at him, confused. *I hear you talking to me right now.*

"I'm not going to let you hide behind your wolf anymore, little wonder. We're going to talk about the future today, and you're going to listen to what I have to say."

My heart skipped a beat at the certainty in his tone.

And then it broke a little as I consumed and interpreted his words.

"Come on, Kari," he said, a hint of dominance underlying those three words.

I swallowed.

And his purr stopped.

"Talk to me." A demand. One underlined in steel. "*Now*, Omega."

I shivered. He'd never used that tone with me. But I recognized it as an Alpha who was out of patience. I slowly opened my eyes, surprised with how easy the action came to me. While I felt sluggish, my body seemed almost rejuvenated. His comment about two days in bed sounded right. And somehow I knew he'd purred the whole time for me.

I'm going to miss that purr, I thought glumly, my wolf whining inside. She wanted out, to take over again, and it would be so easy to let her… to just step aside… to bow… to give her—

"*Kari*," Sven growled, forcing my eyes back to his. Something about his tone made it impossible for me to hide, his dominance a whiplash to my senses that grounded me in the present, forcing me to be here with him.

"I've let this go on for too long." He sounded angry now. "I'll control all access to your wolf, if that's what it takes. Now say something, Omega, so I know you're hearing me."

I winced, not at all liking his tone or the way he called me by my designation instead of my name. I'd also grown rather fond of *little wonder*, too. And I didn't understand why he was suddenly being cruel to me.

"Are you doing this because the surgery failed?" I wondered out loud, my voice raspier than usual. "Are you… are you mad at me?" *Because you've finally realized I'm not the Omega you want?*

His blue irises flickered with an indescribable emotion. It was there and gone in a blink. "I'm doing this because I want to talk to you, Kari. The person. Not your wolf. And I've let you hide behind her to the detriment of our connection. I'm fixing that. Today. Right now."

I stared at him, both alarmed by his ferocity and the words he'd used. Why was he punishing me for relying on my wolf? Didn't he enjoy our time together? "I've done everything to try to please you," I whispered, feeling defeated. "I-I don't understand."

He cupped my cheek, his thumb brushing my jaw. "You do please me, Kari. Very much. But we need to have an important conversation, and I can't do that with your wolf."

"Okay," I breathed, nodding a little.

"No. None of that. No more acquiescence and submission by little nods and placating words. I want a real conversation." His irises flared with power, the authority in his expression making me want to roll over onto my back and do exactly what he was telling me not to do.

"I don't know how else to act," I said honestly. "I'm doing what's natural to me."

"No, sweetheart. You're hiding. You're afraid. And I get that. I know this is terrifying. But what you're doing doesn't help us step into the future together. You're deferring to your wolf and disassociating from the present to protect yourself. And by doing so, you're not healing or growing."

I frowned, not liking his accusations. When we'd first met, I'd barely been able to speak in his presence, let alone lie here naked in a bed and talk to him. "You're wrong."

His eyebrows lifted. "We haven't had a real

conversation in over a month. Hell, it's almost been two months. All you do is rely on your wolf to guide you."

"Because her instincts feel right."

"And they are to an extent," he agreed. "But I need your mind, too, Kari. I need to know your feelings. I need to know your worries and desires and hopes and dreams. I can't battle your fears if I don't know what they are. I can't give you what you want if I don't know what you crave."

He wanted to know my mind? To know my worries and dreams and *hopes*? That final word gave me hives. "I have no hope," I told him sharply. "I don't want to hope. I hate hope. My life *does not allow for hope*."

I wasn't sure where the vehemence came from, but I grabbed it and held on. It breathed fire into my veins, making me feel oddly alive.

"You've never once asked what I want. No one does. I'm a doll. You brought me here to fix me so you can mate an Omega. You chose me. I don't know why. Maybe because I was available. Maybe you like broken females. Maybe because I was a new challenge."

I just kept talking, the words ones I'd thought in my mind at various points but had never voiced. However, he'd asked me to voice them now, so I would. And I'd kill *all this hope* in the process.

I'd destroy it.

Burn it to the ground.

Demand he leave.

And whittle away to nothing in his wake.

Because it was preferable to the alternative. To continue stringing this along when there *was no hope*.

"The surgery failed," I snapped, the raspy quality of my voice long gone beneath my wave of foreign courage. "I'm an unmatable Omega. I'm a slave. I'm *nothing*. I can't give you a child. I can't even be claimed. You can knot me. Fuck me. Use me for your pleasure. *But you can't have me.*"

And I hated it.

I loathed not being able to be his. But that was life. And to hope for an alternative was just wrong. It hurt. It really fucking hurt.

Tears threatened my eyes, the pain inside my heart so much worse than the one in my abdomen.

I don't want to hope. I don't want to feel. I don't want this.

"I can't be your Omega. I don't even want to be yours." Because it meant waiting around until he found someone else. Someone worthier. And having to watch him walk away.

"You're a young Alpha," I added in a whisper. "Don't you understand what that means? You have so many years ahead of you."

So many years to find another Omega. A better fit. Someone who could give him everything he wants.

"You asked what I wanted, and it's not this. It's not you. It's not…" *This endless, painful hope!* I thought, unable to voice my words. "I don't want…" *I don't want to hurt…* "*You.*"

I wasn't even making sense anymore, the words in my mind not matching the ones out loud. It was like I'd spent my entire lifetime mute only to just now learn how to speak. And I wasn't explaining any of this right—as evidenced by the furious look on his face.

He definitely wouldn't be purring for me again.

He looked like he wanted to kill me instead.

And I couldn't even blame him.

"Do you have any idea why I've been helping you these last two months?" he demanded.

I nodded. "To claim me."

LEXI C. FOSS

"No, Kari. I claimed you when I pulled you from that cage. I've been helping you because *you are mine.*"

"But I'm not yours," I replied. *Not really.* "And you're not mine." Which was why I had to let him go, to find a better Omega, one who could give him what he wanted and needed.

My chest ripped open, my sternum cracking into a million pieces. Because this was the hardest thing I'd ever had to do. It hurt more than a thousand nights in my slave cage combined.

I've fallen in love with him, I realized. My wolf had come to rely on him, and in the process, I'd given him my heart. Such a foolish thing to do. But at least I had the memory of him.

"You need to find another Omega," I whispered brokenly. *Someone more worthy.* "Someone who can accept your claim." Because I couldn't.

I would dream of him forever, the Alpha who was kind and stole my heart. And maybe if I was lucky, he'd think of me sometimes, too.

But I doubted it.

Once he mated with a proper Omega, he'd forget all about me.

"You can go now," I told him. "I would prefer that, please." Because if he stayed for another minute, I'd crumble into tears at his feet and beg him to stay. "Please go."

"You want me to leave?" Incredulity colored his tone, his expression aghast.

"Yes," I whispered. "That's what I want." A lie, but there was no other choice. He had to move on. And I had to… exist. "But I do have one request."

His expression shuttered as he stared at me. "Which is?"

242

"May I stay in Andorra Sector?" I asked, my voice small.

I didn't really want to stay here; I wanted to go with him. But I wasn't strong enough to watch him move on with another Omega. It would destroy me completely. At least I would be safer here. From what I'd observed, they didn't have a slave camp like Bariloche Sector.

"You… you want to stay here in Andorra Sector? And for me to leave?"

I nodded stiffly. "Please."

He studied me for a long moment, his expression turning solemn. "All right, Kari. If that's what you want." He didn't say anything else, just rolled off the bed and went to find his clothes.

I watched him as prey might eye a predator, terrified that he might turn on me, but also longing for him to pull me into his arms and demand I obey.

It was a mental complex that I didn't understand.

But the pain inside told me this was right. I couldn't keep living in this fairy tale. I needed reality, and my reality didn't include Alpha Sven.

He finished dressing, then stood in all his Alpha glory beside the bed. His lips parted as though he wanted to say something. But it ended with him just shaking his head. "Good night, Kari."

His words stayed with me long after he left. There was a strange sort of hope lingering in his wake because he hadn't said *goodbye*, just *good night*.

But as the night hours rolled on until dawn, I started to wonder if I'd misheard him.

And then our entire conversation played through my mind, and I began to wonder if I'd misunderstood a lot of things.

My wolf remained cold inside me, refusing to offer me

any comfort. She hated my decision. And the more I thought about it, the more I hated it, too.

It was as the sun began to set again several hours later that my true reality began to seep in. I'd stayed in bed all day. Not crying. Not really feeling anything at all. Because all my emotions had fled. Sven had sucked them into him and walked away.

Which was when the truth of it all finally hit me.

This had never been about the emotions or the desire to free myself from the pain of a fantasy life. Because those feelings had never been mine to own. I was nothing. Just a shell of a being. A female shattered from years of endless torment.

And I'd been drowning in a pool of death until Sven had come along and offered me a lifeline.

In the form of a dream come true.

Because Sven is my hope.

And I'd just sent him away. For good.

CHAPTER TWENTY-NINE

KARI

I DIDN'T WANT to eat.

There was no point.

I didn't want to speak.

There was no point.

But Riley insisted otherwise. She showed up with food, saying I needed my strength. So I ate to appease her. Then she tried to talk to me.

My hope is finally gone.

My Sven left.

He's never coming back.

What have I done?

The words rolled around in my head, causing me to sink deeper into a pit of despair. I'd chased away my light. Everything felt so dark without him. So cold. So bleak.

I wasn't sure how much time passed. I didn't pay attention to the windows or the sun or the moon. I barely acknowledged Riley when she visited.

My wolf refused to help me, her spirit fractured from my mistake.

"Mistake," I mumbled to myself, repeating the word. Because that was exactly what this all had been. *A mistake.*

But I wasn't sure which part bothered me most—the fact that I'd allowed myself to fall for Sven so completely or the realization that I'd turned my back on the first glimpse of hope I'd experienced in a very long time.

I paced the suite, wishing for him to return.

He didn't.

I started thinking about what I'd done wrong, replaying our conversation over and over again in my mind. I'd told him I didn't want him. I'd told him he should find another Omega. I'd begged him to leave.

And he'd listened.

My hands tightened into fists at my sides.

How dare he actually leave.

Except, how dare *I* tell him to.

I growled at him and then at myself for the entire confusing situation. I… I shouldn't have told him to leave. But what choice did I have? He needed someone better, someone worthier.

And yet…

And yet, I think he should be mine.

I collapsed to the floor beneath a wave of sadness, my heart breaking even more than it had when I'd demanded he go.

How could he listen to me? Why did I push him? Why am I like this?

Tears rolled down my face, the sadness I'd kept at bay exploding from me on a low, keening whine. I wanted him back. I wanted our future. I wanted a different life. I wanted to breathe. I wanted his purr. I wanted *him*. I wanted my Sven.

I told him he wasn't mine. That I wasn't his. That I didn't want him.

What the hell is wrong with me?

Oh, but I knew the answer to that. There was so much wrong with me, my body shattered beyond recognition. However, Sven had still chosen me despite all my flaws.

And I'd rewarded him by sending him away.

He'd demanded I talk. He'd mentioned hope. And I'd... I'd chosen the dark path. The wrong direction. I'd chosen *pain* under the guise of protecting myself.

I curled my knees to my chest, my limbs shaking with the ache pouring out of me. I couldn't see, my vision painted in a river of sadness. I could barely even breathe, my lungs choking on the tears of my self-demise.

It hurt.

But it reminded me that I was alive.

It told me I was capable of more. Because I could still feel. Which meant I could *heal*.

I clung to that realization, my heart slowly piecing itself back together into an organ that understood *hope*.

Sven.

I needed him. I wanted him. I'd *claimed* him.

Maybe not completely. Maybe not even correctly. But I'd marked him with my soul. I'd created nests with him. My wolf had worshipped and loved him.

Now it was time for me, *the person*, to do the same.

But how? I wondered, that hint of despair threatening to overwhelm me once more. *How can I accept him when I'm incapable of mating?*

I pondered over that question for hours, swimming through a sea of *what-ifs*, until finally I understood.

It wasn't about the knot or my inability to mate. It was about trusting him to want me despite all that. It was about knowing his heart lay with me even without the claiming bite. It was about putting all my faith in my life partner to protect me, cherish me, and adore me for who I was now, not who I could be.

Sven had been all those things.

He'd stood by me, made me feel safe—all the while promising to help me, to nurture me, to heal me, to court me when I was ready—and had never once given up hope for us.

He was the light I needed to guide me from the shadows. The sun to my moon. The Alpha my wolf desired, and the man my heart needed.

He's mine.

The words settled over me with purpose, my soul rejoicing at the finality of my decision. Alpha Sven had taught me how to breathe. He'd shown me that life in Bariloche Sector wasn't the only way to exist. He'd turned me into a true Omega, not a slave, helping me see that, despite my broken state, I deserved more.

I deserved *him*.

Perhaps not now that I'd treated him so poorly, but I was someone he could love, flaws and all.

I stood, my legs stronger than I expected, my wolf fortifying my strength and demanding I act.

Shower.

Dress.

Eat.

Those were my orders, and I completed each one in silence, my mind focused and ready. I just needed to find Sven.

Is he even still here? Has he left Andorra Sector?

I wasn't sure how many hours or days had passed. Maybe only a handful. Or maybe several. Time was a concept I'd never mastered because it didn't matter.

But Sven did.

He mattered.

He's mine.

I was still repeating those words to myself when Riley arrived. She carried a tray of food with her, only to widen her eyes at seeing me already seated at the little two-person table with a reheated plate in front of me. I'd found it in the fridge and had warmed it using the contraption Sven had taught me to use. Some sort of instant heater with red lights.

"Oh." She set the tray aside on the counter and took the chair opposite me. "It's good to see you eating."

"Where's Sven?" I asked, not wanting to chitchat today. She usually asked me how I was feeling, requested to take vitals from me, and wanted to know the last time I'd shifted. None of that mattered right now.

Only Sven.

"Is he still in Andorra Sector?" I pressed, impatience riding me hard. *I need him. I need him right now.* Not because of his purr or his light, but so I could tell him how I felt. That he was mine. That I wanted him. That I believed in him. That I trusted him to keep me. To help me. To protect me. To be mine.

And I wanted to be his. I'd do whatever he wanted, whatever he *needed*, just to be in his warm presence once more.

"I…" She trailed off, her vibrant blue eyes flicking downward as her matching hair fell in her face. It was an unnatural sapphire color that I suspected she dyed. But that wasn't important right now. "He's been staying in his old quarters," she continued softly. "But I saw him heading toward the airfield on my way here."

I jumped out of my seat. "He's leaving?"

She swallowed. "I don't know. Maybe."

"I need to talk to him. I need him to understand… I… I have to apologize. I have to… Riley, I can't let him leave." It was exactly what I'd told him to do, but it was the opposite of what I truly wanted. "Can you help me stop him? Can you at least take me to him so I can… I can…" *Do what?* I thought, blinking. *Stop him?* "I just… I just need to tell him…" I wasn't sure what yet.

Something.

Anything.

That I wanted him. That I desired him. That I was wrong before.

It might be too late, but I wouldn't know unless I tried. And it would definitely be too late if I let him leave.

"Please, Riley. Can you get me to him?" I'd figure out what to say when I saw him. I just… I just needed to try.

Riley must have seen the desperation in my features because she nodded slowly, pulling up some sort of surveillance footage on her wristwatch. It was just like Sven's, blending into her skin, but full of high-tech controls. When she pulled up the footage of him outside on the airfield, my heart skipped a beat.

He looked determined.

And angry.

I swallowed. *He's mine. I have to tell him he's mine.*

The resolve settled heavily in my gut, driving me forward. This was so much different from when I let my wolf take over. This was all me. My mind. My body. My heart. And I was following my instincts the way I should have from the beginning. But I'd been scared, hurt, and unable to believe Sven's intentions beneath the wave of my conditioning.

However, I understood him now.

At least mostly.

There was still a huge amount of hesitation inside me, a terror that I could be setting myself up for inexplicable heartache, but my desire to see this through outweighed the intimidated part of me.

Sven had awoken this within me, had provided me with a path to walk down that I'd never known existed.

I wanted to follow it to the end, to throw myself at his feet and beg him to stay.

"Okay," Riley said slowly. "You'll need to be very quiet and follow me."

I nodded, agreeing to her terms. Quiet I could do.

I slipped on a pair of boots over my jeans, pulled my damp hair up into a ponytail, and stretched the sleeves of my black sweater down over my hands. I didn't have a coat or gloves, so this would have to do. Fortunately, shifters naturally ran hot. And from what I'd seen through the windows, a lot of the snow had started to let up, suggesting it was spring in this area of the world.

Riley wore an outfit similar to mine, only she had on sneakers instead of boots, and her hair hung over her slender shoulders in a curtain of blue silk. She would be easily recognizable, which made it fortunate that we didn't run into anyone on our way out. I suspected that was a result of her checking her surveillance every few seconds as we moved.

She keyed a code into the elevator, whisking us to a floor I hadn't been on before. It was different from the entrance area with the huge windows and white walls that I'd seen upon arrival. This one was stark and almost bleak, the concrete walls reminding me of my prison back home.

A shiver tickled my spine, the first hint that I'd trusted the wrong wolf settling in my spirit.

She's my doctor, I chided myself. *And she's an Omega. She's not going to hurt me.*

It was just my ingrained inclination to not trust anyone. But I shoved that aside now, choosing to put my faith in the female who had been trying to treat my condition these last however many weeks or months.

She paused to check her watch again, using a finger to hold me at bay.

Then she nodded and stepped through a steel door that took us outside. I crept out with her, staying to the side of the building like she did, until we found the edge of the airfield lurking beyond.

She peeked around the corner and I followed suit, my heart thudding rapidly in my chest at the sight of Sven walking toward a plane several yards out. Jonas, Elias, Enrique, and Ander were all with him.

My wolf whined at the sight, demanding I shift and run to him.

No. I needed to do this as me, not her.

So I told her to heel. It was a weird sort of sensation—putting a part of me in time-out to remain in charge—but it felt oddly right. Like I was supposed to always be in charge. Not her. I'd spent most of my life cut off from my wolf, so it'd felt only natural to allow her to take over.

However, a growing part of me began to understand that it should be a combined effort, not a this or that. She could still exist within me, still urge me to do things, but it was up to me—the person—to accept her choices.

And right now, I chose to ignore her decision.

Let me do this, I told her.

She didn't fight me. She merely nodded and sat down inside my mind, waiting and watching and promising to be there when I needed her.

It was a dizzying experience, but it felt right, and it oddly bolstered my confidence.

Riley trembled, her expression telling me she wasn't sure she'd made the right decision here upon seeing her own Alpha with mine.

But I knew this was where I needed to be. I felt it within my bones. *That's my Alpha out there, and he needs to know I want him.*

I took off at a sprint before she could stop me, my soul rejoicing at the sight of Sven turning toward me.

Only to freeze at the fury crossing his features as he caught sight of me.

Oh… My feet tripped beneath me at the abrupt halt to my forward motion, sending me to the ground a dozen or so steps away from him.

My knees protested as I hit the pavement, and a roar of growls sounded in my ears.

"*Riley*." Alpha Jonas's voice sent terror through my heart.

But it was Sven's ferocious snarl that stole the air from my lungs.

The sound reminded me of home. Of my cell. Of my former existence.

I'm not that Omega anymore. I'm… I'm… I didn't know how to finish the thought, nor was I given a moment to try.

Rough hands gripped my shoulders, yanking me up off the ground.

Only, they didn't belong to Sven.

They belonged to a dark-eyed Alpha with sharp, tan features and thick black hair. He released a low rumble in his chest, one that was almost like a purr but underlined in fierce intent.

I wasn't sure where he'd come from or why, but as I looked over his shoulder to Sven, it was to find a flicker of irritated menace in his features. Like he'd given up all rights to me and couldn't stand the sight of me.

And now he was leaving me to face my new fate.

Alone.

CHAPTER THIRTY

SVEN

"WHAT IS this I hear about you heading off to Bariloche Sector to kill Carlos?" my father asked as I answered his call.

I rolled my eyes. "Kaz is such a tattletale." I'd called him last night as I'd paced the walls of Andorra Sector, telling him about my plans to head to Bariloche Sector and kill the son of a bitch who had broken my intended mate.

Oh, she might not think she wanted me.

But I knew better.

Which was why I'd given her some time alone to think it all through. She'd claimed I was young and that she didn't want me, so I'd prove my worth to her by bringing her father's head back on a silver platter. Then I'd force her to accept me, regardless of her situation.

So I couldn't knot her. Someday, that would change. And I was willing to wait as long as it took to be able to formally claim her. Sooner or later, she'd understand that.

"What's the plan?" my father pressed as I strolled down the corridor toward the building's exit. "And I assume your brother is going with you?"

"He was," I said. "But not anymore."

254

His eyebrows rose on the screen. "You're going alone?"

"I'm not going at all. Not now, anyway."

My father frowned. "What changed?"

I glanced at a silent Jonas beside me. "Another plan fell into place first." After Kari's little tantrum, I'd gone to Jonas and demanded he make the call to Blood Sector. I understood he had certain reservations about inviting a V-Clan Alpha out to play, but if Riley thought he could help, then I wanted to pursue the possibility.

My Omega might have given up hope, but I hadn't. I never would. And I would continue to be her hope even in her darkest hours.

"We're heading out to meet Alpha Kieran O'Callaghan," I continued, pushing through the door to the cool air outside. The sun was warm enough to melt some snow, but only barely. "Riley thinks he can help Kari. And he's set to arrive any minute now."

My father was quiet for a moment before nodding. "Tell K I said hello." He hung up before I could respond to that.

Jonas and I shared a look. "Your father knows Alpha Kieran?"

"Apparently," I muttered. My dad was full of secrets, which I supposed he'd earned the rights to over his five-hundred-plus years of existence. From what I understood, Alpha Kieran was even older, the rumors painting him to be at least a thousand years old.

Yet he didn't have a mate.

Or he had an intended one, but she was missing. That was the story I'd heard, anyway. She'd supposedly disappeared during the Infected era, running away from her fate by his side, and he'd been searching for her ever since.

LEXI C. FOSS

I understood that kind of determination because I'd do the same for Kari.

Enrique, Elias, and my brother met us out on the tarmac, all of us similarly dressed in sweaters and jeans. We weren't sure what to expect from Kieran's arrival, as the V-Clan Alphas were notoriously unpredictable. Their technology rivaled that of Andorra Sector as well, their stealth jets renowned for appearing and disappearing beneath waves of magic clouds.

They were wolves that acted more like panthers with their silky midnight fur and catlike reflexes. Spring was their mating season, with the summer months being spent indoors in states similar to hibernation while the babies grew.

Sunshine was their nemesis, hence our shared surprise at Kieran choosing to arrive during daylight. He hadn't provided any notice, just sent Jonas a message informing him that he was on his way here about an hour ago.

"He just radioed the tower," Ander informed us as he stepped up beside me. "He's here."

Jonas grumbled, his irritation palpable.

It wouldn't help to thank him, so I didn't. He clearly had history with the V-Clan Alpha, and that history seemed to involve Kieran's friendship with Riley.

This had better work, I thought, gritting my teeth.

The others seemed to share my sentiment as we formed a dominant welcoming party of sorts at the edge of the landing strip.

Definitely high-tech, I mused as I admired the sleek design and nearly silent approach of the incoming jet. It landed with a gracefulness I couldn't help admiring, my pilot heart itching for an opportunity to take the beauty for a spin.

But I didn't let my interest show.

Instead, I painted my features beneath a mask of

indifference. I didn't know this Alpha. Therefore, I didn't trust him.

Jonas stiffened beside me, his wolf lurking in his gaze.

Then a familiar scent caught my own animal's focus. *Kari.* Her sweet perfume beckoned me to turn, causing me to nearly freeze at the sight of her *running toward me*.

What the fuck? I thought, furious to find her unprotected out here and in the presence of an unknown Alpha approaching. I took a step forward, ready to intercept her and shove her behind me, when her eyes lifted to mine in fright and she tripped over her own feet.

I shook my head, confused by the visual of her on the ground and *outside*.

She was supposed to be safe in her room, recovering from her episode, while I made the deal with Kieran to help her.

A shadowy energy appeared in my peripheral vision, making me growl low and menacing as the smoke turned corporeal in the form of an Alpha male. He ignored all of us, going straight for Kari as Jonas snarled out, "*Riley,*" in a furious tone.

I glanced at the stumbling Omega, her eyes rounded in shock at the sight of the V-Clan Alpha, then dropping to the ground upon hearing her own Alpha bark out her name. He grabbed her in the next instant, pulling her roughly behind him and momentarily distracting me from the scene at hand.

Much to my surprise and irritation, the V-Clan Alpha had picked up Kari, his entire focus on my trembling intended. Her eyes met mine, stark terror and sadness pouring off her as she begged me with her eyes to do something.

I took a calming breath, the desire to rip Kari from the

257

other Alpha's hands flooding my veins with so much aggression that I almost acted on instinct alone.

But I sensed his dominance as superior to mine. Old, archaic, royalty.

Kieran O'Callaghan.

I could challenge him, but he'd win. Even with my desperation to reclaim my mate, he'd destroy me beneath a wave of calculated magic. I could feel it in my veins, sense it in my mind, and almost see the visual playing out before me.

It was… humbling. And infuriating.

And wrong, I realized in my next breath. "Get the fuck out of my head," I snapped, my wolf standing up and shaking off whatever daze this enchanted being had just cast over me. "*Now.*"

A chuckle sounded in my mind, followed by a smooth voice saying, "What the hell have you done to this poor Omega?"

The scene began to pick up around me, reality slowly seeping through the cloud of whatever spell had been woven through my spirit.

This being is very *powerful*, I realized, blinking as I took in Kieran holding my mate once more.

Time was elusive. He'd held me suspended in some sort of fog, tricking my wolf into submitting without even lifting a hand to challenge me.

From the fury radiating off Ander, Elias, and Enrique, he'd done the same to them.

Only Jonas appeared to have his wits about him, perhaps because he held Riley, and it was clear with a single glance that Kieran had a soft spot for her. And it seemed he was already developing one for my Omega, too, because he was holding her face with the care of a nurturing Alpha, not a hungry one.

"So much pain," he whispered, staring into her eyes. "Shh, it's okay, little one," he cooed, causing her eyes to droop in response. "I'll help you, just as soon as these Alphas tell me what they've done."

"We didn't do anything," Jonas snapped at him. "Bariloche Sector did this."

Kieran blinked his midnight gaze once, then looked at Jonas. "Alpha Carlos?"

"She's his daughter," I interjected. "And my intended mate."

The V-Clan Alpha took my measure, then glanced at the trembling female in his hands. "Is this true, little one? Do you belong to him?"

I groaned inside, aware of what she would say next. It was on the tip of my tongue to explain her mental state when she replied, "Y-yes. Alpha Sven is mine."

Shock blasted all my thoughts away. Because that'd been Kari speaking, not her wolf.

It caused my inner beast to rumble in approval, his internal voice saying something along the lines of, *Too fucking right, I'm yours.* But my mouth couldn't voice the words because I was too stunned by her open declaration.

I'd expected a fight, to have to declare her mentally unstable, but she'd uttered the words with a confidence I felt to my soul. The stammer at the beginning had disappeared by the end, her statement sound and grounded in force.

She knows I'm hers.

"I see." Kieran gently released her and guided her into my waiting arms. "I'm not sure how you treat Omegas here, but we don't allow ours to crawl on the ground when in the presence of others. That behavior is reserved for our bedrooms only."

Kari trembled against my chest, causing me to purr for

her. I kissed the top of her head, thanking her without words for claiming me in front of the others. Part of me was still stunned, wondering where this female had come from, because the one I'd left the other day had clearly held the opposite conviction. Hell, she'd acted as though she'd hated me.

But this version of her curled right into me, relaxing the moment my purr met her ear.

Mine, I thought, grinning against her head. I couldn't even be mad that she'd run out here unprotected now. Because she knew her place, and she was officially safe in my arms.

Well, minus the clear predator in our midst.

His mind game had proven him to be Alpha over us all, something that left everyone unsettled except for Kieran. Even Jonas appeared disgruntled, probably because he knew there was nothing he could do to protect his Sector Alpha from Kieran's mindfuck.

"You called him," Riley whispered. "Why didn't you tell me that you called him?"

"It was meant to be a surprise," Jonas replied, his tone curt. "I also didn't know if he would show up, and I certainly didn't anticipate you being out here to greet him."

"Yes, what are you doing out here, Omega?" Ander demanded. "Your charge was to keep Omega Kari company inside, not *let her loose in my sector*."

Kari quivered in response to his obvious ire, and Riley whimpered behind Jonas. "I-I… Kari wanted to see Alpha Sven…"

"And you agreed?" Ander's expression morphed into tight lines of fury. "She's an *unmated Omega* without a protective escort. What would have happened if we weren't out here? Did you consider that? Did you consider anything at all?"

"I-I'm sorry," she stammered. "I just… I just wanted to help…"

"By putting her in a dangerous situation that could have gotten her injured or worse?" Ander sounded incredulous, in addition to pissed off. "You will deal with this, Jonas, or I will. And you won't like how I choose to do it."

"Oh, trust me, I will be handling this," Jonas replied, his tone equally furious and drawing a whine from the Omega behind him. "Quiet," he snapped before focusing on Kieran. "This was not how we intended introductions to go today. I apologize for the theatrics." He spoke through gritted teeth, the apology sounding almost painful.

"As I'm not one for wasting time, no apologies are needed. I've already performed the needed evaluation, and the answer is yes, I can help your Omega."

My eyebrows lifted. *He already completed his exam? How?* I'd never met a V-Clan wolf, so I knew nothing about their magic. But to conclude all of this so quickly seemed… impossible. And yet he stood before us with a confident air, his Alpha status evident in his regal stature.

"That said, I'll need Riley's sturdy hands to help assist me. And I won't be waiting around to operate just because she's too sore from whatever punishment you intend to give her." He checked his wrist, a screen appearing above his skin. "I work best at night, and the sun falls in three hours." He shifted his attention to Ander. "I require a meal and a bed to rest. This will cost me a great deal of energy."

"Done," Ander said without missing a beat.

Kieran nodded, his dark eyes meeting mine. "From what I can sense of her organs, she's not experienced estrus in several years. It is very likely that she will immediately go into heat when we're done here. As she says she is yours, it's your responsibility to be ready to handle it."

"I don't need you to tell me how to take care of my Omega."

He glanced between Riley and Kari, his eyebrow inching up. "I'm very much unconvinced of that." Then he looked at Ander expectantly.

"Elias, show Kieran to his quarters," my brother said without looking at his Second. "Try not to challenge him along the way."

Elias snorted. "After that mental mindfuck? No promises."

Kieran merely smiled. "Lead the way, *Second*."

I watched as they walked, my mind reeling from the unexpected twist of events today. We'd anticipated him having to thoroughly examine Kari before naming his terms, but it appeared he already knew exactly what was needed. And all he'd required was a bed and food.

"There has to be a catch," I said as he disappeared into the building with Elias. "He can't possibly be doing this basically for free."

"V-Clan wolves are known for cherishing their Omegas even more than we do," my brother murmured. "I suspect just feeling her pain was enough to push him to help."

"Something you anticipated," Enrique interjected. "You weren't surprised at all that he agreed to this."

"No, I wasn't," Ander replied. "Because Omega Kari isn't the first one I've seen him take care of." He flicked a gaze back at Jonas and Riley. "He holds Omegas in high regard, even to the point of saving an Alpha mate just to ensure an Omega's healthy mental state."

Jonas grunted. "He did not save my life."

"He did," Ander replied softly. "In more ways than

one." Then his golden irises flared as he locked them on Riley. "Given Alpha Kieran's requirements, your Omega's punishment will need to happen after the surgery."

"Yes," Jonas agreed gruffly. "Fortunately, that'll suit her better because she'll have to survive the night, all the while anticipating what I'll do to her when she's done."

"It-it's my fault," Kari stammered softly, interrupting the discussion. "I asked her to help me. I-I should take the punishment, not her."

"No," my brother said before I could say a word. "You're not one of my wolves. But Omega Riley is. And as my wolf, she knew the risks of taking you from the building without proper protection. Isn't that right, Omega?"

Riley tried to clutch on to Jonas, but he stepped away from her, letting her face the wrath of their Sector Alpha on her own. It had to be killing him to do it, but what she'd done had been reckless. My brother was right—she'd put Kari at unnecessary risk. Since it had been me they'd been trying to find, she should have just called Jonas and told him what they wanted. Instead, she'd chosen to sneak Kari outside, and while I appreciated that she'd been taking her to me, it'd been the wrong action on her part.

What if Kieran had brought others with him?

What if Kieran had meant to harm us?

What if it hadn't been Kieran who came through the dome walls, but someone we weren't expecting?

There were so many situations that led to potential harm not just for Kari but for Riley, too. While the latter might be able to take care of herself, Kari was very vulnerable to pain.

She was also unmated.

And she had a propensity for submitting immediately.

I agreed with my brother and Jonas on this one—Riley needed to be punished for her actions. Forcing her to wait for that punishment would serve as a reprimand in itself, especially if Jonas didn't stand behind her as a collective unit.

He was showing her what it would be like on her own.

Which was what would have happened had he not been outside when she'd emerged with Kari.

Face your consequences, his stance said now. *And you'll face them alone since you chose not to maintain a united front with me as your Alpha.*

"I'm sorry, Alpha," Riley whispered. "We thought Alpha Sven was leaving. We were trying to stop him."

My eyes widened in surprise at her confession. *Kari thought I was leaving her? She expected me to give up that easily, after one little tantrum?*

"Then you should have called your Alpha to have him help, rather than put a vulnerable Omega at risk by doing it yourself," Ander replied curtly before looking at me. "Get Kari back inside. She'll need to be calm and ready for the surgery tonight."

She trembled against me, driving home his point. She couldn't remain out here to listen to the Alphas reprimand Riley. They wouldn't hurt her. Not even after the surgery. But they would guarantee that she never did something that foolish again.

I just hoped she was able to perform the surgery without too much emotion clouding her judgment.

But a glance at Jonas told me he had that well in hand. He'd make certain that she had what she needed to succeed, while also maintaining a punishing air. Their relationship went back a century, meaning they knew exactly how to handle each other. And from what I'd witnessed, they worked well together.

And now it was time to ensure Kari and I developed the same type of relationship.

I'd prepare her for tonight, too.

While also reminding her whom she belonged to. Because she couldn't go into this with any more doubt. No matter what happened, she was mine. And it was time for me to make sure she understood exactly what that meant.

CHAPTER THIRTY-ONE

KARI

SVEN LED me back up to our suite and straight to the bedroom. "Strip," he said, his voice holding a demand that sent a quiver down my spine. "Now."

My lips parted. "Sven—"

"*Now*," he repeated.

I shivered beneath his dominance, but my wolf sighed in my mind. She wanted him with a ferocity I felt humming through my veins. We'd disobeyed him. We'd hurt him. And now we'd be reprimanded by him.

She was looking forward to it.

Meanwhile, I wasn't sure how to feel yet.

I tugged off my boots beside the bed, then pulled off my sweater and jeans, revealing that I wore nothing beneath. Something about that made him growl. "That's all you wore on your little jaunt outside?"

I swallowed. "I was going to you, to stop you from leaving."

"I wasn't fucking leaving, Kari. I was welcoming Alpha Kieran to Andorra Sector. We were meeting to begin negotiations on him helping you."

My lips formed a little O as I blinked up at him. "But you said *goodbye*."

"No, I said *good night*," he replied as he yanked off his

sweater. "And then I spent two days with Enrique and Elias, helping them to plot an attack against Bariloche Sector while Jonas called Kieran. We were going to leave later today, but Kieran contacted us an hour ago to say he was en route."

"You were going to Bariloche Sector?" I repeated on a whisper, my heart in my throat. *For the other Omegas?*

"Yes. To kill your father for what he's done to you."

I startled at the vehemence in his words. "To kill my…? Not for the Omegas?"

"We intend to save them, but his head is what I'm after. I'm going to kill him for you. Brutally. He will pay for what he's done to my Omega." He kicked off his shoes and started undoing his belt. "Sit on the edge of the bed. Legs spread so I can see the heart of you. Toes angled toward the floor."

I did what he commanded, scooting to the end of the mattress, while considering everything he'd said. *He was going to Bariloche Sector to avenge me.*

The realization warmed my heart, even while that treacherous voice whispered that he had an ulterior motive to find a better Omega.

I swallowed that insecurity, forcing it out of my mind. He had spoken about saving the Omegas like it was a secondary objective, not the primary one.

"Do you still plan to go?" I asked as he pulled the zipper of his jeans down. "T-to Bariloche Sector?" It was becoming more difficult to focus on our conversation, my gaze automatically dropping to his groin.

He tugged his pants down, allowing them to drop to the ground. I shivered at the sight of him, his cock angry with arousal and pulsating with need through the thin barrier of his boxer shorts.

Mine, I thought, slick gathering at my center in

267

preparation to take him. It didn't matter that this would hurt. I just wanted to feel him inside me. To take his knot the way I should.

Only, I couldn't.

Not really.

And that realization had me glancing upward into his hungry eyes. *What is he going to do to me?*

"Yes, Kari. I still plan to go to Bariloche Sector. Not for a replacement Omega, but to kill your father." He tugged off his boxers, leaving him as naked as me. "That's what you still don't understand. You're mine."

"I-I know," I started, trying to recall everything I wanted to tell him.

But he wasn't done speaking.

"No, Kari. You don't. You thought a few words could send me running from you? Back to Norse Sector with my tail between my legs?" He sounded angered by the suggestion, making me flinch a little. "I'm never fucking leaving you, Kari. *That* is what you don't seem to understand. You think all this is about fixing you so I can knot you."

He stepped forward between my spread legs, his thighs hot against my cooler skin. His fingers drifted up my sternum to my throat, then higher into my hair as he grabbed hold of my ponytail and tilted my head back to meet my gaze.

"I'm not doing this for me, Kari," he continued, his voice soft yet underlined with a hint of savagery. I swallowed, the tone speaking to my soul and demanding I listen. Hear him. Believe him. *Embrace* him. "I'm doing this for *us*."

His opposite hand drifted to my face, his knuckles brushing my cheek.

"Part those pretty lips for me," he whispered, his

dominance wrapping around me and forcing me to obey.

My mouth parted.

"Good girl," he praised, stepping even closer and wrapping his fingers around the base of his shaft. "Stay just like that."

I did.

"Don't swallow," he added. "Not yet."

It took conscious effort to follow his command, to not allow my throat to work as saliva built in my mouth. I wanted him with a ferocity I felt to my core.

My body dampened even more, my slick practically pooling out of me.

And my mouth panted, my need to taste him driving me mad with desire.

Alpha, I nearly said, but a warning look from him kept me completely still.

He traced his thumb along my bottom lip, then dipped inside to gather some of my moisture, and drew a circle around the head of his cock with it.

Oh... My thighs threatened to close, the need for friction a yearning I couldn't fight, but his legs prevented me from moving.

And his eyes kept my mouth open for him.

I panted.

And he repeated the action of stroking my lip, dipping inside, and using my essence to decorate his beautiful shaft.

When his fingers closed around his knot, I groaned, my own hands trembling with the craving to touch him. *Please, Alpha,* I begged with my eyes.

He still had hold of my hair, forcing me to watch his face as he pleasured himself before me.

"I'm not doing this for me," he repeated gruffly. "I'm doing this for *us.* I already own you, Kari. You're already mine, just as much as I'm yours. The knotting, the bite, it's all secondary to me. *You* are what matters most. And I've never doubted for a moment that I won't be able to help *us* because I've known from the first time I saw you that you were meant to be mine."

Another swipe of my lips.

More saliva.

And a firm stroke along his hard steel.

A whine built in my throat. *I want that. I want him. I need him.*

"Shh," he hushed, my internal complaint escaping through my parted lips. "I'm going to give you everything you want and more. But I'm in charge now, Kari. I'm going to show you what it means to be mine by controlling how much you take, how much you swallow, and how much seed I release. You're mine to cherish and protect, mine to punish, mine to possess, and mine to knot however the fuck I want."

A tremble tickled my spine, just a tiny glimpse of fear that had his jaw hardening.

"And that right there is why we're doing this," he added, his voice a low hiss of sound that caused my stomach to twist. "Mates trust each other, Kari. You might not wear my bite, but that doesn't make you any less mine. And I'm going to make sure you understand that by the time I'm done. Now widen your mouth."

My jaw slackened, my body his to command.

He skimmed my cheek with his knuckles again, his approval evident in that tender touch, then he brought his cock to my lips.

I reached for him on instinct, but he caught my wrist and lowered my palm to my thigh. "I'm in charge," he said again. "You'll take what I give you. And you'll trust me not to go too far."

I shivered, my insides doing flips at the air of control

surrounding him. It threatened to take me under, to pull out my wolf and allow her to submit on my behalf.

But I sensed the importance of remaining here with him, of listening to him, of learning to be what he needed as a *shifter*, not an *animal*.

I swallowed as he hit the back of my throat, then forced myself to relax as he pushed just a little further, making me take him.

"So good," he praised, his fingers tightening subtly in my hair. "Eyes on me, little wonder," he said. "I want to see *you*."

Not my wolf, I translated. He was testing me, guaranteeing that I remained present while he took me. That knowledge made me feel safe and desired at the same time.

He was ensuring my comfort, while also guaranteeing I couldn't hide.

I stroked my tongue along the velvety skin in my mouth, reveling in his taste and moaning as my thighs slickened even more with my need. I'd craved Alpha cock before, my body primed and trained to yearn for the knot, but I'd never been more turned on than I was right now.

His heat ignited a flame inside me that burned just for him. It shot sparks through my veins, causing my nerve endings to tingle.

"Deeper," he growled, tilting my head at an angle that widened my throat for him.

I groaned as he slid inside, then stilled when he cut off my ability to breathe.

He stayed there for a beat, his hand an iron fist in my hair and forcing me to take him.

I didn't fight.

I waited.

I trusted him to release me.

And as he did, he praised me for the effort, his free hand brushing my cheek once more before he returned his fingers to his knot.

"You're going to swallow as much as you can," he murmured. "And then you're going to swallow some more."

I nodded, eager to comply. His seed inside me made me feel closer to him, like we were joined in a way no one could take from us.

"Mmm," he hummed, approval evident in that sound. "Eyes on me, little wonder. No matter what."

I blinked up at him, only then realizing that I'd closed my eyes in anticipation. Twin pools of deep blue stared down at me, the Alpha losing himself to his lust.

I'd seen that look so many times before.

It usually terrified me.

But not on Sven. I knew he wouldn't hurt me, even as he began to pump harshly into my mouth, his cock hitting the back of my throat. And yet, with each vicious gyration, I trusted him to keep me safe.

I opened even deeper for him, allowing him to use my throat.

And as he started to come, I swallowed for him, just like he'd said I would.

His pupils went full black, engulfing his irises as he watched me work to take as much as I could.

There was no air.

Just his seed.

I took... and took... and took...

Panic flared at the vestiges of my consciousness, just a little voice telling me I could drown like this, but I shoved it away and held his gaze. *I trust you.*

Pride flickered in his expression as he watched me, his fingers working his knot and forcing me to consume even more. Black dots danced before my eyes, but I refused to give in to the urge to yelp or move away.

He won't hurt me.

He's my Alpha. My Sven. My hope.

His lips curled, and his grasp in my hair tugged as he pulled my mouth off of him. But he didn't stop coming. He continued to empty his seed all over my neck and chest while holding my gaze the whole time.

"Rub it into your skin," he demanded.

I lifted my fingers, complying without question.

His gaze left mine to watch, his nostrils flaring at the sight.

"Now move back to lie on the bed and keep your legs spread," he said darkly.

He's going to knot me, I realized, my mind blanking for just a moment before another thought hit me. *No, he's not. He won't hurt me like that.*

I knew he wouldn't because we'd spent countless hours in bed together and not once had he taken me.

It didn't matter how angry I'd made him; he would never harm me.

The knowledge settled somewhere deep inside me as I moved to the center of the mattress and spread my legs for him, just as he'd requested.

I trusted him unequivocally, and I let him see that in my eyes as I met his gaze once more.

"There's my mate," he said, crawling onto the bed to settle between my thighs. The length of him slickened through my folds as he rubbed himself against me, gathering all my fluid before entering me in a thrust that had me seeing stars.

I froze, shocked by the intrusion.

But he hushed me in the next moment, his cock slipping right back out of me.

I swallowed, panting beneath him. "Just making sure you know you're mine," he whispered against my ear. "And that I have more than enough control to keep myself from knotting you."

He punctuated his point by reaching between us to take hold of himself and releasing even more of his cum, directly into my entrance.

"You're mine, Kari," he said, his lips ghosting over my cheek before reaching the edge of my mouth. "And my seed in your cunt proves it." His eyes held mine as he continued to spill himself inside me without thrusting home again. Just his head, right there, kissing me intimately, while he came… and came… and came.

My body was on fire, my insides screaming for him to complete me, but I knew he wouldn't. Not to torture me. Not because he wanted me to beg. No, he was doing this to prove his own control. To show me that he was my Alpha. My protector. My mate. And he would *never* do something to purposely injure me.

I lifted my hand to his cheek, utterly lost to his show of strength and prowess.

And I nodded.

Because he was right.

"I'm yours," I breathed. "And you're mine."

He smiled. "I am very much yours," he agreed, his lips ghosting over mine. "No matter what happens tonight, I'll still be yours. Forever, Kari."

I believed him, something I told him with my eyes and with my mouth as I kissed him.

"If this doesn't work," he said after a few minutes of sensual silence, "I'm not giving up. I'll find a way, Kari. I vow it. You're my little wonder, and I'll do whatever it takes to heal you. Not for me, but for us. And for you." He took my mouth once more, his tongue weaving a benediction through my soul. "I would move the world for you, Kari," he whispered. "And I will. You'll see."

I melted beneath him, believing every word.

Sven was my hope. My love. *My Alpha.*

CHAPTER THIRTY-TWO

SVEN

THIS PRISTINE WHITE corridor was becoming my second home.

I'd paced this line after Kari's failed surgery, and then again when I'd made the call to Kaz about going to Bariloche Sector.

And now, I walked the exact same path while I waited for the outcome of Kari's current operation.

I palmed the back of my neck and blew out a breath as I replayed Kieran's last statement through my mind. *This is going to work. But I need to focus, and I can't do that with all your possessive energy wafting around. So fuck off and let me do my job.*

I'd wanted to punch the arrogant prick in the face. However, I couldn't. Not when he started his statement with, *This is going to work.*

It's going to work, I agreed. *It's abso-fucking-lutely going to work.*

I could feel the rightness of it in my gut, my wolf smug in his confident stance as he hummed in approval at freeing our mate from the last of her slave bonds.

"Want to pace all night or do something useful?" My brother's voice echoed down the hall as he turned a corner with Elias and Enrique right behind him.

"We have another war plan to review, if you're up for

it," Elias added. "Figured we might as well create a third backup since we're not going tonight. Can never be too prepared and all that."

We already had a pretty solid idea, but I didn't mind having something else to focus on. "Can it be done here?" Because I wasn't leaving Kari. Just being out of the room was painful enough.

"Yep." Elias flicked his wrist, pulling up schematics to showcase over the white wall.

My lips twitched because they'd clearly anticipated my agreement, or they wouldn't have been so ready to review the plans.

Thank you, I said with my eyes to my brother, appreciating him more than I could ever say. I knew this had been his idea more than theirs.

He gave a nod as though to reply, *What's family for?*

Elias dove right into a tactical discussion to review the original plan we'd discussed on how we were going to take down Bariloche Sector's Alphas.

The first part involved an anti-hallucinogen, something Enrique had suggested to help wake up the Alphas who might want to pick a bone with Carlos.

The second part moved into the assault plan. With Enrique's guidance, we had a full layout of Bariloche Sector, a complete list of potential weapons, and the identities of those who were die-hard Carlos supporters. He'd also told us where the Omegas were being held, outlined the torture pits—which were the ones Kari had mentioned to me that were filled with Infected—and pointed to a highlighted area that was known to Carlos only.

The latter was the focus of tonight's discussion. With the extra time on our end, my brother had sent in a drone to capture imagery from Carlos's private area. "We don't have the information back yet, but we will soon," he said, pulling up the live feed of his toy. "Should hit Bariloche Sector airspace in the next five minutes."

"Ah, so that's the real point of all this."

"Yeah, we had thirty minutes to burn, so we figured it couldn't hurt anything to go through the plan again," Elias said, shrugging. "Distracted you, right?"

I snorted. "A bit." But not entirely. My ears were tuned into the room just a few paces down, waiting for any sign of a complication. Fortunately, it was quiet and calm.

Enrique leaned against the wall while we waited, but I sensed a hint of his nervous energy. "You think your brother might be in there."

"It's one of the only spaces I've never been able to check," he replied. "So yes."

I nodded, understanding. He'd told Ander and Elias about his twin and how he suspected he was alive. They'd demanded to know what was in all this for him, and he'd bluntly voiced the truth.

From what I'd seen, he and Elias had become fast friends. They both shared a penchant for sparring and weaponry. With Elias being Ander's Second, he had access to all the fun toys, something Enrique had been very eager to learn more about.

A beep sounded from Ander's wrist, alerting us to the drone's approach.

Then we watched as it crept along through the blue sky —it was still light in that part of the world—but equally covered in snow. I'd never been to the Patagonia region, but I'd seen photos. Trees, ice, snow, mountains, and startling blue lakes.

The drone sailed over one of those now, keeping low to the ground.

"You sent a stealth one in?" I guessed, recognizing the

camouflaging tech. It would turn the machine a brilliant blue to blend with the water below it.

"Yeah," my brother confirmed, his eyes on the screen. "Enrique programmed the coordinates this morning after Kieran's call."

Sounded about right.

We continued watching, the drone doing a sweep of the land to prove Enrique's intel correct. Then it slowly entered the heart of Bariloche Sector, and we all surveyed the results with gritted teeth.

It was worse than I'd imagined.

Slaves of all kinds.

Blood.

Cruelty.

Pits that went beyond just Infected torture, but other types as well.

Omegas being fucked almost to death out in the daylight, like it was perfectly fucking normal.

Chained Betas.

Drugged-out Alphas.

Everything Enrique and Kari had said was true. I hadn't exactly doubted them, just hoped some of it had been an exaggeration. But no. It was even worse than what they'd described.

However, when the drone snuck over a wall into Carlos's private sanctuary, the air of death and savagery turned into an oasis. There were a handful of Betas walking around, all of them clearly slaves, as evidenced by the collars around their necks, but the opulence of the palatial estate suggested wealth and elegance.

There were gardens, white walls, pristine rooms, and gold furnishings.

"Doesn't look like a prison," Elias grumbled.

"No," Enrique agreed, sounding frustrated.

"Send it below ground," a new voice suggested, causing us all to turn toward the unexpected presence.

Kieran stood leaning against the wall, arms crossed casually, as he studied the footage. He glanced at us all innocently, like he hadn't just appeared out of thin air to lurk and watch the show.

"What?" he asked, sounding less than contrite. "If I were keeping hostages, I'd put them underground, not in my home." His gaze bounced between us. "I mean, that is what we're looking for, right? Hostages?"

"*We* were not doing anything," Ander replied.

Kieran merely smiled. "Ah, well, I do have a question before I respond to that." His focus went to me. "Has Kari mentioned anything about a V-Clan wolf? A healer, perhaps?"

"What are you doing out here?" I demanded. "Shouldn't you be in there?" I gestured pointedly at Kari's operation room.

"Oh, yes, we're done."

"Done?" I repeated.

"That is what I said, yes," he murmured. "It was successful, in case you were wondering."

"Of course I'm fucking wondering," I snapped, stepping forward.

He pressed a palm to my chest, his magic freezing me in place. "She's still sleeping, Sven, but she should wake up within the hour. So you'll need to be prepared, as I could sense her estrus is already taking over."

"Then let me see her," I said through gritted teeth, highly irritated by his enchantment.

"I just underwent a substantial sacrifice of power on behalf of your Omega to ensure she survived the surgery with no scars or lifelong side effects. It's also worth noting that without me, she would have likely died," he said calmly, his midnight gaze flickering with obvious warning. "So please do me the honor of telling me if your Omega has mentioned anything about a healer."

My wolf wanted to shove him out of our way and be done with this.

But the man in me heard what he'd just said about helping my Omega, and I couldn't help but give him the courtesy of a reply. Because I owed him. And if all he wanted from me was an answer, I'd give it to him.

"She said one of the Omegas in Carlos's camp can heal. She also said Carlos is a collector and not all his Omegas are X-Clan wolves."

"Interesting," he murmured thoughtfully, glancing at Ander. "I will need to remain here for a few more days until Omega Kari is within her right mind to tell me more about this healer. Can this be arranged?"

"If you'll stop using your enchantments on us, then yes," my brother replied on a subtle hiss of warning.

Kieran smiled. "But of course."

I almost stumbled forward, his magic releasing me instantly. His palm against my chest kept me from falling into him. "She's going to be almost inconsolable in her need. Good luck." With that, he faced Ander as the drone's footage disappeared. "I suggest infrared for your next drone."

My brother smirked and brought back up the screen, doing exactly that.

I left them to discuss their toys, Bariloche Sector, and sleeping arrangements.

I had an Omega to tend to.

And I really hoped Riley would be a little more forthcoming about the details on Kari's physical state. Because something told me I wasn't getting any other details from Kieran.

"So you removed all the wire?" I asked, recapping what Riley had just told me.

She nodded. "Yes. I was able to remove it all while Kieran rapid-healed her organs. It was slow and took some careful maneuvering, but we were able to remove everything inside her that kept her reproductive system from being able to heal on her own. Then he took care of the scarring and stitched her up with magic."

I blinked. "Stitched her up with magic?"

She pulled up Kari's shirt to reveal smooth skin. "No real stitches. He… he mended her skin cells with his mind." Her blue eyes skipped over to Jonas as she swallowed.

He remained stoic in the corner of the room, arms crossed, expression emotionless. He'd been like that when the surgery had started, and hadn't moved an inch from his post by the door since.

"So you think she'll make a full recovery?" I pressed, refocusing on Riley.

"Yeah. Kieran said he could sense her heat already blooming," she replied, swallowing. "He warned it'll be violent since she's gone without estrus for several years. And he also said the chances of pregnancy are unlikely, given how young and raw her organs are right now."

"But the knot won't hurt her?" I pressed, needing to know before I helped handle the heat part of the equation.

She shook her head. "It… it hurt before because of the wires." The words came out in a whisper, her eyes filling with unshed tears. "The wires were purposefully placed to ensure the knot would be agonizing for her. There's no way the twists at that point inside her were accidental." She swallowed. "H-her father wanted it to hurt."

My jaw clenched. I would see to him once I made sure my mate was fully healed.

With a tight bob of my head, I managed to say, "Thank you, Riley."

"You're welcome," she whispered, swallowing thickly. "And I… I'm sorry I endangered her earlier."

I met Jonas's stony gaze, then looked at Riley and nodded again. I wouldn't forgive her. That wasn't my place. Her Alpha needed to reprimand her in the way he desired, and any words from me would undermine his authority on the topic.

She bit her lip and stepped back. "It's safe to move her upstairs, but I would do it quickly. Once she goes into estrus, the whole building will know it."

I ran my hands over Kari's body, checking for any signs of bruises or swelling, but she was all smooth, curvy female beneath my palms. So I picked her up and cradled her to my chest with a purr.

Jonas watched my approach and opened the door without a word.

As soon as I cleared the threshold, it closed and locked behind me.

"Here?" I heard Riley ask in a low voice.

I didn't stay to find out what Jonas had in mind. Instead, I headed toward the elevator bay and noted the vacant hallway.

Ander must have finished his show-and-tell and taken Kieran to his quarters.

I'd have to ask the V-Clan Alpha later how he knew about the healer Omega. It was something that had crossed my mind after I'd checked on Kari and found her recovering, just like he'd said.

She remained unconscious in my arms as I took her

back to our suite, her petite frame the perfect weight for me to carry.

When we returned, I took her to the bathroom to bathe her to the best of my ability. Then I laid her on the bed as I went about finding all the supplies we would need.

After Kieran's warning earlier, I'd ordered a few items —all of which had been delivered.

Water.

Sheets.

Food.

The bare essentials for an Omega in heat.

I'd never seen one through estrus before, but I understood the dynamics and what would be required of me and my body. And I was more than ready to perform for her.

I stripped out of my clothes, setting them beside the sheets in case she wanted them for her nest, and slid into the bed beside her to wait.

CHAPTER THIRTY-THREE

KARI

WARM. Safe. Alpha.

I moaned, the trifecta of perfection humming wildly through my veins. Every inhale brought me Sven's masculine scent, that woodsy concoction an aphrodisiac that set my soul on fire.

I wanted more.

He rumbled behind me, the low growl a sound that used to terrify me with other Alphas. But not Sven. I welcomed his dominance and protection and rolled toward him, needing more of his intoxicating cologne.

"Kari," he murmured, his fingers combing through my hair as I nuzzled his bare chest.

Naked, I marveled, my thigh sliding between his muscular legs. *Gloriously, amazingly naked.*

He felt so good. So right. So exquisite. I wanted to become a part of him, to glue our bodies together and become one.

It was an intrinsic desire, one that caused my stomach to twist painfully with *need.*

Which had me freezing against him.

My abdomen... I pressed my palm to my lower belly. *I feel... I feel free.*

And yet, there was a subtle ache growing inside me, one that demanded gratification.

My mind spun as I tried to understand what it all meant. Everything was so foggy, lost beneath a cloud of instincts. My wolf fought for control, demanding I just give in, but I forced her to heel, my need to understand too strong for her to battle.

"Sven," I breathed, my eyelids heavy as I forced them open. "Where are we?" I felt clean. Rested. *Excited.*

I didn't understand.

Again I tried to remember, to figure out what had happened.

"In our guest suite in Andorra Sector," he replied. "You're waking up from surgery. And you're going into estrus."

I frowned. "Not possible." I hadn't gone into heat in more years than I could count.

Except… A shadowed memory lurked just outside my reach, something about a warning. A male saying I would go into heat after the operation.

I blinked, the world spinning as my abdomen tightened painfully once more. But it wasn't the ache I usually experienced. This one was new. Hotter. One that caused a fresh wave of slick to coat my inner thighs.

Moaning, I arched into my Alpha and felt his cock throb against my lower belly.

Mmm, yes, I want that inside me. I want him to knot… wait… I blinked again, confused. Why would I crave that? Knots hurt.

"You're going into estrus," Sven had said.

"How is that possible?" I asked, oblivious to whatever else he'd just said. Time and space were moving awkwardly around me, my instincts focused on my body alone. But I strove to hear his reply now, to understand my current state.

"The surgery was successful, Kari," he said, his fingers knotting in my hair as he gave a little tug that grounded me in the present. "Riley was able to remove all the wires. And Kieran healed you."

Kieran, I repeated, recalling the handsome V-Clan Alpha. He was the one who'd warned I would go into heat. He'd told Sven to take care of me. Or had he told me that?

I frowned, recalling a whispered promise in my ear about how Sven would be there soon to see to my needs. *You're in good hands, little one. Rely on your Alpha to see you through this.*

Why had he said that?

No, *when* had he said that?

I could feel his residual energy inside me, renewing me with life. It was unlike anything I'd ever experienced. Not even Omega Quinn had ever been able to make me feel that good after an abusive rut back home.

"Kari." Sven uttered my name with a hint of command. "How do you feel?"

"Alive," I replied dreamily. "Warm. Safe. Ready." The last word gave me pause. Was I truly ready?

Knotting had always hurt in the past. But this felt different. I wasn't desperate for his knot because he'd tormented me with sensors or drugs. I wanted him inside me to complete me. To make me whole. To… to *claim* me.

I was already his, but I wanted his stamp inside me. Just thinking about it had me arching into him again on a whine, my veins lighting up with a flame only my Alpha could temper.

"*Sven…*" I swallowed, the need for him mounting with every passing breath. "Take me. Please. While I remember. While I'm still *me*." It was a dire request, one I hadn't meant to voice but now needed more than anything else in the world.

Estrus would take me to another plane of existence, one driven by animal instincts and the need to procreate. I would lose complete control, be unable to truly experience our bond outside my urges.

And I desperately wanted to fully experience him inside me for our first time.

"Please, Sven. I have to feel you knot me. Right now. So I remember. So I choose. So I truly *believe*." I wrapped my palm around the back of his neck. "Be my hope. Show me what it's like to live in a real dream. Be mine as you were meant to be."

He whispered my name against my lips, the adoration and promise in his tone going straight to my soul. His mouth claimed mine in the next breath, his kiss a benediction filled with hot intent. I gave everything to him, submitting and telling him with my tongue that I was his.

He tugged on my hair, guiding me to my back and rolling on top of me to press me into the bed. His muscular weight felt heavy and right, his air of control exactly what I needed and craved.

More slick spilled out of me, beckoning my mate, *my Sven*, to take what was already his. It almost hurt, my body demanding he act and slide inside. But instead, he drew his hot length through my folds, teasing and taunting and drawing a begging mewl from my throat. "*Sven…*"

I was so close to losing my mind. So close to falling into a state of being I'd never expected to feel again. And while I longed to experience pleasure, to embrace my true nature, I needed him more.

His teeth skimmed my lower lip, nibbling gently as though to prolong the moment—a moment we didn't have.

I gripped his shoulders, then drew my nails down his

back, demanding my Alpha do what I needed, take me to new heights, knot me with his—

"Oh!" I cried out as he entered me without warning, his length pulsing inside me as he filled me to completion in a single harsh thrust.

Tears blanketed my vision, but they weren't born of pain so much as joy.

Because it felt *right*, like my Alpha had finally joined me the way he should.

My insides ached at the penetration, simultaneously complaining and rejoicing at his abundant size.

And then he began to move.

Not fast, but slow, forcing me to feel every inch of his length as he slid through my slick to enter me deep and almost pull out again.

It was torture of the best kind, causing me to bow up off the bed as I demanded *more*. I screamed for him, his name a curse and a blessing on my tongue, until his mouth swallowed the sounds and his tongue dueled me for dominance.

Each stroke reminded me who was in charge.

Each pump of his hips told me whom I belonged to.

Each harsh punch forward ensured no one would ever enter me except Sven.

"Mine," he growled against my lips, his possession warming me from my head to my toes. He was falling into the rut, his need to accentuate his claim demonstrated with his increasing pace.

It hurt in the best way, erasing all those who had come before him, and forcing me to only think of him, my mate, my Sven.

I panted, the inferno inside me reaching a sizzling point, the cusp of madness threatening my thoughts, but I held on to my sanity with a tight grasp, needing just a few more minutes.

Let me feel. Please let me feel!

"Knot me," I begged. "Oh, Sven, please… I *need*…" It came out on a mewl of sound, my voice high-pitched and breathy and completely foreign to my ears. I'd never experienced anything like this, the intensity of our friction searing my very soul and grounding me in this moment forever with him.

He kissed me once more, his tongue whispering promises of forever against my own, his body marking me as his with every excruciatingly perfect thrust.

He could break me right now, and I wouldn't care.

He could knot me to oblivion, and I would merely sigh his name.

He owned me so completely that my heart was his to cherish and possess and my body was no longer my own.

"I'm yours," I whispered against his mouth. "Always yours."

The words seemed to spur him on, his muscles clenching around me creating a masculine blanket of warmth and ferocity that sizzled through every ounce of my being. I wrapped my thighs around his hips, receiving him deeper and drawing a deliciously dark sound from his lips.

"Fuck, Kari," he murmured, his eyes opening to find mine. "You feel so fucking amazing. So tight. So perfect. So *mine*."

"Yours," I repeated, arching up into him and begging for more.

But he slowed his pace, his blue irises holding mine as he forced me to experience every inch of him once again.

I squeezed him with my walls, my lower belly twisting with a fierce desire that spasmed along my arms and legs.

"Please," I begged, not sure what exactly I needed. But his expression told me he knew.

He caught my wrists and stretched my arms out over my head, where he interlocked our fingers. And he stared deeply into my eyes as he controlled our pace.

Agony rippled through me, my insides demanding he go harder and faster, but he tortured me with slow, purposeful movements while holding me down beneath him. Then ever so slowly, he kissed me once more.

Something about this was tender, beautiful, a moment I would forever cherish.

My big, strong Alpha was making love to me. Not fucking, not taking, but showing me with his strength and control just how well he could master me.

And that knowledge caused my heart to open up inside me, blooming with a force that stole all the air from my lungs.

"Sven," I said on an exhale, my thighs shaking around his hips.

He licked my bottom lip, then kissed a path to my ear. "I love you, Kari," he whispered, nibbling softly. "And I'm going to show you how much now."

He didn't give me a chance to reply, his mouth moving down to my breast as he punched his hips forward on a thrust that had me seeing stars.

His knot, I realized with wonder as he exploded inside me. I felt it shoot up from his base as his teeth sliced into my flesh.

The power consumed me, his claim an anticipated and stunning sensation that rendered me speechless beneath him.

And then I was screaming in a beautiful pain unlike anything of my previous experience. It erupted from deep within, shooting heat and spikes of ecstasy through my limbs and leaving a fiery trail in its wake.

Oh...

I tumbled off a cliff into a rapture that swallowed every inch of my soul, leaving me a quaking mess on the bed of slick and seed and blood.

I felt complete.

Alive.

Utterly owned.

He claimed me, I marveled, feeling his tongue laving the wound above my nipple. *He truly claimed me.*

And still his knot pulsed, his cock thrumming wildly in my tight heat, filling me with his essence in hot waves of pleasure.

I couldn't stop coming. It felt like all the orgasms from my entire life were stuffed into one, and my body didn't know how to cease this unbelievable vibration.

I moaned.

I cried.

I begged for more.

It was the strangest combination of reactions, all grounded in desire and love and exquisite agony.

Sven cooed and hushed me, his lips ghosting up my neck to my ear, where he murmured praise and adoring thoughts. He told me I was beautiful. He called me perfect. He thanked me for being his and for believing in him. He expressed gratitude over letting him knot me. And he promised a whole list of dirty, wicked things next.

I moaned again, arching into him, wanting to experience every item on his very long and thorough list.

But he brought his fingers to my mouth instead, allowing me to taste the union between our bodies.

I shivered, the decadent flavor sending me into yet another climax around his thick shaft. He was no longer knotting me, but he was hard again, ready for another round. And I urged him to fuck me hard this time, my legs wrapping around him in a vise that demanded he give me his power and strength.

He didn't disappoint, driving into me with an abandon that satisfied my spirit.

And again we were coming, writhing, our beasts entirely in control.

My mind rejoiced, my heart pounded, and my body melted for my Alpha.

He kissed his mark once more, freeing my hands and letting me roam his big, muscular form. *All mine*, I marveled, kissing and licking and nipping. Somehow I was on top of him now, his cock lodged deep within me as I rode him the way I desired, taking from him what I needed and demanding he knot me for hours and days.

Sven kept up with my demands, giving me exactly what I required and taking me to the stars over and over again.

His list was ongoing.

He took my mouth, pumping into me and drowning me in seed.

He took me from behind, my slick providing all the lubricant he needed to claim my final hole.

He bathed me, washing the fluids from our skin, then took me against the shower wall and carried me back to the bed while his knot continued to pulsate inside me.

We didn't sleep, our beasts too hungry for each other to dare waste time with such frivolous needs.

I was under him, on him, beside him, over the bed, against various furniture, the window, and so many other places that the experiences blended together in my mind and blanketed me with a serenity that kissed my spirit.

It felt like a dream.

But I knew it was real.

I would be sore when we finished, Sven's body much larger and stronger than my own, but all of this was worth the sweet pain that would follow.

Because I was finally complete.

Possessed.

And claimed.

And *loved*.

CHAPTER THIRTY-FOUR

SVEN

DAY twelve and Kari showed no signs of exiting her estrus.

She was an insatiable little thing, demanding I fuck her through all hours of the day. It was a miracle I could even make her sleep.

I purred for her now as she lay beneath me, her pupils blown wide with pleasure and stark need. She wanted me to take her harder, but I forced her to endure my languid pace. Her little claws scraped down my back in protest as she arched into me in a subtle demand.

"You can't top from the bottom with me, little wonder," I told her, amused by her antics.

She growled.

I rumbled back at her, drawing a moan from her throat. Her voice was hoarse from all the screaming, her body fracturing from the nonstop sex. But she was resilient, her wolf genetics healing her with a grace my own beast admired.

Soon, she would have her voice back, and I knew exactly what she'd tell me.

Harder. Faster. More, Alpha, more.

I kissed a path down her neck to the bite mark above her breast. It was fully healed, apart from the subtle scar that defined her as mine. She'd asked me to reclaim her several times, her wolf liking the feeling of my teeth embedded in her skin.

And she'd marked me back in kind with little crescent stamps all along my torso. Those had healed entirely, not leaving a scar behind—something that seemed to agitate her immensely. Which was why she kept biting me, her wolf snarling, "*My Alpha*," every time.

I loved her possessive energy and her insatiability. But I was beginning to worry about her prolonged heat.

I'd messaged Riley the other night, and she'd put me in touch with Kieran. The V-Clan Alpha had ventured back to Blood Sector, saying to call him when we emerged from our nest. So he'd picked up on the first ring, expecting me to have Kari ready to talk to him. He'd quickly realized that wasn't the case and had smirked when I'd told him she was still in estrus.

"Better keep up, Sven," he'd drawled, hanging up before I could express my concern.

I'd sent him another note this morning, saying she still wasn't finished and asking if I should be worried.

He'd replied by saying, *It's a good thing you're not a V-Clan wolf. Our mates go into estrus for weeks.*

I'd idly wondered if his healing energy was the cause of her prolonged heat. Then she'd demanded I come back to bed, and I'd been here—inside her—ever since.

Her slick walls clenched around me, begging me to knot her again.

But I held back, sliding in and out of her in a rhythmic caress that left her mewling beneath me.

"I love that sound," I murmured, purring as she whimpered. "It's fucking hot, little wonder." I drew my teeth along her bottom lip, nibbling softly. "Mmm." I slid all the way inside her again, drawing out another whine. I smiled, loving her like this, so trusting and needy.

She'd let me take her in every way imaginable, telling me her favorite positions along the way and going as far as to demand repeat performances. I obliged some and improved others.

"You're like a little sex beast," I said, amused, as she squeezed me with her thighs. "You're insatiable and I love it."

"Fuck me," she rasped.

"I am."

"*Harder.*"

"Mmm…" I slammed into her, drawing a delicious sound from her throat. "Like that?"

"Yesss," she hissed, her nails biting into my neck.

I kissed her, loving her with my tongue, and took her with the ferocity she craved once more. She panted beneath me, her nipples hard little peaks against my chest as I took her over the edge into an orgasm that had her screaming soundlessly.

My knot pulsed, the sensation so fucking good that I couldn't stop my own groan of approval as I released myself inside her, bathing her with my seed and staking my claim in the most traditional of ways.

She mewled a little, content with my offering, and nuzzled my cheek as I purred.

Her small mouth opened on a yawn, and her eyes drooped closed even while her body continued to spasm around me. I chuckled, adoring her contentment.

"You're perfect," I whispered, drawing my lips to her ear. "So incredible and beautiful, Kari. I'm so fortunate to have you, to call you mine. Thank you, little wonder. Thank you for finding me."

She yawned again, but her lips curled into a smile. She enjoyed my comments, or maybe it was just my voice that satisfied her. As she wasn't really speaking in words, I couldn't say. But I continued to express my gratitude and compliments as she fell asleep beneath me again.

My muscles ached from the exertion of taking her on repeat for almost two weeks. Kieran's commentary taunted my thoughts once more: *Good thing you're not a V-Clan wolf.*

I snorted.

I could do this for weeks. I just wanted to make sure this was acceptable and normal and *okay*. Because Kari had barely eaten. It was a struggle to make her even drink water. I'd found that the trick was taking her into the shower and fucking her beneath the shower spray. She'd opened her mouth and swallowed like it was my seed pouring down her throat.

An erotic sight, one I'd enjoyed almost daily recently.

But I needed to know she would eventually come out of this state. As much as I relished her turning into a sex-starved Omega, I missed my Kari. I missed her voice. I missed her tentative glances, small smiles, and big blue eyes.

I kissed a path down her throat to her breast, my tongue tracing my mark as my shaft slipped from her heat. Then I continued downward to lick her clean, drawing another orgasm from her while she slept in the hope of pacifying her for a few minutes longer.

She mumbled something unintelligible, her limbs relaxed and her mouth parting on a happy little sigh.

I smiled and kissed her inner thigh, then slipped away to call Riley once more.

She answered on the first ring, her blue hair tangled and hanging in frizzy ringlets around her flushed face. "Still going?"

"Yes," I replied. "And Kieran isn't being helpful."

"Shocking," Jonas drawled from the background.

Given Riley's mussed appearance, I could only guess

what they'd been doing. I supposed that meant her punishment was over, and considering her healthy glow, she was satisfied with that development.

"I'll call him," Riley murmured.

"No, I'll call him," Jonas interjected. "Take care of your mate, Sven. We'll see what Kieran has to say." The line disconnected, the Alpha taking over.

I nodded my approval and went back to the bed to watch Kari sleep. When she woke, we took another shower. Then I tried to feed her. She only accepted items flavored with my seed, her pupils flaring as she indulged in the taste.

We went three more days before Jonas finally reached back out. And by then, I could already see glimpses of my Kari returning to her normal state.

He says it's perfectly natural for her to experience a long estrus after going so many years without one. He anticipates she'll fall into another one quicker than usual as well—one where pregnancy will be more viable—so he suggests you work on your stamina.

I snorted, typing back, *Nothing wrong with my stamina.* A single glance at my female would prove that. She was blissed out yet again, reveling in her post-orgasmic glow. But the thought of making her pregnant did make me smile. She hadn't conceived in this heat cycle, just like Kieran had predicted. A part of me had hoped he would be wrong. Another part of me fully realized that neither of us was ready for that next step yet.

Just relaying his commentary, Jonas replied. *He estimates she'll be done in the next day or so.*

I drew my fingers through her silky hair, purring as she nuzzled deeper into my chest. She was sleeping more now, her body healing from our physical exertions.

A little moan parted her lips as she snuggled even closer, her wolf seeking comfort as she recovered.

I held her firmly, purring and keeping her warm as she slept.

Then I knotted her again when she woke up and carried her to the shower once more.

It was an intimate dance that suited us. But this time, she guzzled the water like a lifeline. And then she promptly ate a real meal afterward.

Before dragging me back to her nest for another round of fucking.

She'd gone through all our sheets, pulling out dirty clothes, fresh linens, and towels to create her safe haven. It smelled like our combined fluids, drawing out my predatory instincts and demanding I claim her over and over again on repeat.

But I remained in control the whole time, giving her what she needed without commanding too much from her.

And when she woke the next morning, her blue irises had returned to ring her black pupils. She smiled sleepily at me and stretched before stroking the mark on her breast.

We kissed.

We petted.

We made love, slowly, thoroughly, and she bit me again —on the neck this time. When I growled, she smiled, her expression adorable and tinged with shyness. "Mine," she whispered.

I returned her grin, pleased to hear her speaking normally, even if it was just one word. At least she'd chosen the perfect thing to say. I palmed her breast, giving it a squeeze, then echoed the sentiment back to her.

She hummed in approval and curled into me to sleep more.

Her senses completely returned later that night, her moan of discomfort arriving with the rising sun. I ran my palms over her, kneading her stiff muscles and doing what I could to heal her with my touch.

When I cupped her between the legs, her thighs clenched and she groaned a little in protest. "Sore?" I asked her.

She nodded, biting her lip.

I licked a path downward to heal her with my tongue.

She mewled as she came, her clit throbbing in my mouth.

And then she fell asleep once more.

By the time noon rolled around, she was awake and clearly feeling better, because she asked for something to eat. I left her in the nest and prepared a feast for her, then carried her into the living area—naked—and fed her while she sat on my lap at the table. Her small frame fit perfectly against me, and not once did she complain about my manhandling. Her wolf needed it, as did she.

She thanked me a few times, nuzzled me and licked me, and smiled genuinely all afternoon.

By evening, she was talking more, telling me what she remembered of her estrus. It was a lot more than I'd expected her to know, as most Omegas fell into the blissed-out state and just existed while their bodies did all the work for them. But Kari's mind had remained with her the whole time, proof of her disconnect from her wolf.

I suspected that would mend with time. She'd already shown admirable improvement, but she had a lot to mentally recover from.

Which led me to a conversation I didn't want to have, but one that needed to happen nonetheless.

I told her about our intentions for Bariloche Sector, how Enrique had mapped out an entire plan with Elias—a plan they'd perfected over the last few weeks using my brother's drones. It turned out that Kieran was right about the underground.

And Enrique's brother was in fact alive.

"We're going to burn it to the ground," I promised her. "The sector doesn't deserve to exist."

"What about those who didn't have a choice?" she whispered, her eyes round from the information I'd given her.

"The innocent will be relocated. The others who survive will have to find a sector on their own and beg to be let inside." That part had been my decision, one my father and brother both had agreed with. They'd asked if I wanted to take Bariloche Sector for myself, but I'd declined. I wasn't ready to lead yet, and I'd bluntly admitted that to both Ander and my dad just the other night during one of Kari's naps. They hadn't disagreed or agreed, just nodded in acceptance of my decision.

"They've been waiting for you to come out of your estrus," I continued. "And now that you have, they're going to want to act as soon as possible." And by that, I meant *tomorrow*. At least, that was what the last communication I'd received from Ander had indicated.

Given what Kieran had said about Kari's likelihood to go back into heat quicker than usual, I agreed with the decision to move immediately. I didn't want to risk being gone when she needed me.

"He doesn't fight fair," she whispered, her fear trickling over us as I carried her back to our nest. "You don't know him like I do."

"Yes," I agreed. "But Enrique is going with us." I met her gaze. "His brother is alive."

Her eyes widened. "Alpha Joseph?"

I nodded. "And your sister is still alive, too. He's going to save them."

"By… by challenging Alpha Carlos?"

"There won't be a challenge," I told her. "We're going to kill him without trial. Just like he's done to countless others. And all his supporters are going to die, too. Bariloche Sector will be completely destroyed."

"Oh," she breathed, blinking at me. "You're certain you'll be okay?"

I smiled. "Absolutely certain. There's nothing he can do to stop us. Our tech outmatches his, and we've developed a toxin to counter his hallucinogens. He'll be completely out of his realm of reason." I laid her on her back and crawled in beside her. We were both still naked, but I needed her covered for this next part, so I pulled up one of her blankets.

She frowned at it like she wanted to put it right back in place, but she didn't reprimand me for it.

"Kieran asked that we call him when you were better, too," I added. "He has some questions for you about the Omegas in Bariloche Sector."

Part of me wanted to ignore his request and not follow through, particularly as he hadn't been all that helpful during Kari's estrus.

But he'd cured my mate, while likely saving her life in the process, and that was a debt I could never fully repay. So I'd start by honoring his wishes.

"Are you okay with me calling him now?" I asked her.

"Here?" she whispered, glancing around our nest.

"Is he not allowed to see it?" I wondered out loud, frowning. Because my wolf absolutely wanted the Alpha to see it and to know that Kari was mine. That he couldn't have her. That she would forever belong to me. But if my Omega didn't want to share our safe place, I would abide by her wishes.

"N-no, it's just…" She trailed off, her cheeks reddening and making me smile.

"Ah, yes, that's *exactly* why I want him to see it," I replied with a low rumble. "Consider it your way of showing that his magic worked."

Her cheeks darkened even more, but she nodded. "Okay."

"*Really* okay, or *wolf* okay?" I asked her, needing to know.

"Me… Kari… okay," she said, a smile in her eyes. "I would like to thank him for… everything."

And that gave me another reason to make this call— my mate wanted to express her gratitude. I would never deny her that opportunity. Kissing her temple, I called up Kieran with my wristwatch.

His face appeared seconds later, his gaze knowing as he studied me. "My record is twenty-nine days," he said by way of greeting. "Better luck next time."

I rolled my eyes. "Do you want to talk to my Omega or not?"

"Oh, I very much do," he murmured, his expression turning serious.

I used my fingers to rotate the screen toward Kari. She cuddled into me more, like she was seeking my strength to face the Alpha on the screen. "Thank you, Alpha Kieran," she whispered. "Thank you for fixing me."

"It was never about fixing you, little one. It was about curing you of a burden that should never have been inflicted upon you," he replied softly. "And all the gratitude I need is seeing that pretty blush on your face right now."

My teeth clenched, his flirtatious tone irritating my wolf. "I'm beginning to understand why Jonas isn't your biggest fan." The suave, smooth-talking V-Clan Alpha clearly had a soft spot for Omegas. And he ensured the entire world knew it, too.

Kieran grinned, his midnight irises returning to me. "Jonas's reasoning has nothing to do with Riley and everything to do with his wounded pride." He didn't give me a chance to reply, his focus already switching back to my Omega. "I'll be quick, as I imagine you have other activities on your mind now that you're properly mated."

My wolf hummed in approval at the statement, my desire to kiss her mark riding me hard. But that would require exposing her breast, and I didn't want to do that with another Alpha watching.

Undressing to shift was one thing.

Undressing in the nest was entirely another.

"When I was healing some of your scars, I sensed a residual energy from one of my own. I would like to ask you about it."

"You mean Omega Quinn," she murmured, her expression sheltering. "Alpha Carlos doesn't know what she can do."

"And by 'what she can do,' you mean heal, yes?"

She nodded slowly. "Similar to you, but not as powerful."

His lips curled. "My touch has been perfected over time. I imagine *Omega Quinn* would one day reach a similar skill level, if properly instructed. Can you describe her for me?"

"She looks like you," Kari whispered. "Dark eyes and dark hair. But paler. And smaller… much smaller."

He seemed satisfied with that description, his attention sliding to me once more. "When do you plan to attack Bariloche Sector?"

"Ander wants to go tomorrow," I replied, the information causing Kari to glance at me in surprise. I hadn't gotten to that part of the discussion yet. "We're planning to transport the Omegas back to Andorra Sector for medical evaluation," I added, assuming that was what he truly cared about. If Carlos really had a coveted V-Clan Omega in his midst, then Kieran would be very eager to retrieve her.

"What time tomorrow?" he pressed, making me frown.

"Likely late afternoon," I said slowly.

He nodded. "All right, I'll arrive in Andorra with two of my Elites around noon, and we'll shadow you across the pond."

"Elites?" I repeated.

But the line was already dead.

I gaped at my watch. "What the hell?" I hadn't given him the details to invite him to the party. Growling, I shot him a message saying as much.

To which he replied, *I don't require an invitation to do anything. See you tomorrow.*

"Shit." I forwarded the note to Ander, telling him to expect company from Blood Sector by noon. Then I turned my comm on silent because I didn't want to know his reply.

Instead, I focused on my mate and the worry carving lines across her pretty face. "Promise me you'll come back to me."

"Oh, I'll come back to you," I vowed. "And I'll bring your father's head with me as a gift."

Her lips parted on a gasp that I swallowed with my mouth.

She would worry about me as my mate. And just knowing that would send me back to her that much faster.

"I'm going to burn that sector to the ground," I whispered. "I'll ensure you feel every bit of that vengeance, too. Because I'm doing this for you, *my mate*, to demonstrate my worth to your wolf."

"You're already worthy of me and my wolf."

I smiled. "Yes, I know, but that doesn't mean I don't need to prove it, too."

My mouth silenced her protests.

Then my body soothed her aches and worries before my purr calmed her through the night.

By morning, she was sated and content. My perfect little wonder.

Everything I do, I do for you, I told her with a kiss. *Our future starts now.*

PART III

BARILOCHE SECTOR

CHAPTER THIRTY-FIVE

SVEN

An image flickered over my watch as Kari played with the comm I'd left for her. As much as I wished I could have brought her with me, I knew my wolf wouldn't have allowed it. She was my one weakness, the female I would give up my life for. So I needed her safe and protected in Andorra Sector.

Part of me felt it wasn't fair for her not to be part of this, since it was her I intended to avenge here. Which was why I'd left her behind with the communication device. I planned to show her the destruction when we finished here.

"No video-chatting while piloting," Kaz remarked from the copilot seat.

He'd shown up unannounced this morning, shortly before Kieran and his two "Elites" appeared in a stealth fighter jet. They'd slipped in through the dome opening that had been created for Kaz's entry, literally *appearing* out of thin air on the ground. No one had sensed or heard their approach, and I currently had no idea where they were in the sky nearby.

Fucking V-Clan wolves, I thought.

At least they were on our side today.

"Are you almost there?" Kari asked, her pretty face appearing above my wrist.

"About thirty minutes out from our dropping point," I told her, surveying the clouds around me. There were several jets making their way across the Argentinian airspace, all of us angled toward an old airport outside of Bariloche Sector.

Carlos would sense us soon, if he didn't already.

I expected him to fight.

Only, we'd sent a party gift ahead of us in the form of Enrique and Elias. They'd taken a stealth plane, similar to the one Kieran piloted, and had landed somewhere in the Andes Mountains to meet one of Enrique's allies—another Alpha who didn't appreciate Carlos's methods.

We'd received confirmation of their landing an hour ago.

Their latest correspondence informed us that the package had been delivered, which meant the counteragent to the hallucinogens was in the air. It was only a matter of time before the Alphas reacted, creating the distraction we needed to land.

Kari remained with us on our approach. I walked her through what I was doing, all the way down to engaging my landing gears. Kaz lounged beside me with a small smile the whole time, his amusement palpable. He kept joking about distractions while flying, but we both knew that I had this route handled.

"I need to go now, little wonder," I said as the plane touched down.

Already I could feel the battle in the air, my wolf itching to be set free. We all had our missions—mine was to find Carlos and kill the son of a bitch. Kaz had apparently felt left out of the game, hence his surprise arrival. So he was tagging along as my partner on the mission.

His job was to clear the way and kill anyone who stepped into our path.

Considering his penchant for blood, it seemed appropriate.

"I love you," Kari blurted out, the words ones she hadn't said to me before.

I smiled. "Repeat that to me when I get home, mate."

"Okay," she whispered. "And that's *me* okay, not *wolf* okay."

Kaz gave me a look, his eyebrow arching at the weird terms.

My grin only grew wider. "Speak soon, little wonder." I blew her a kiss and ended the call, then met Kaz's stare. "I don't want to hear it. Winter has you wrapped around her paw, too."

He shrugged. "I'm not denying it. But it's nice to see you so beautifully tamed by your *little wonder*."

I rolled my eyes. "I should have just dropped you in that nest in Buenos Aires on the way here."

"I'm not the rookie in training," he drawled. "That's you."

"Yeah, well, you ready to see what this *rookie* can do?" I countered.

His dark eyes lit up. "Time to put all my training to the test?"

"Something like that."

"Strike true, kill them all," he said, a smile in his tone. "Let's go make them bleed."

I unbuckled myself with a smirk and suited up.

The others had all landed throughout the airfield, and around us was a growing presence of Alpha wolves. But none of them were in animal form. I could sense their shifting energy, taste their gunpowder, and smell their aggression.

"They're feral," I growled.

"Indeed," Kaz agreed, his amusement long gone and his stance hypervigilant. "How do you want to play this, Mick?" he asked, using his preferred nickname for me. "Like Geneva?"

I considered that and shook my head. "Like Copenhagen."

His eyebrows lifted. "Yeah?"

"Yeah."

His lips curled into a savage smile. "Excellent. On three?"

"On two," I countered. "One."

I hit the door and leapt out of it first, then I rolled for the nearby tree cover that I'd purposely parked beside.

Gunshots rang through the air, whizzing past me, and Kaz returned fire from the plane, nailing the first set of assailants with perfect aim.

Just like Copenhagen, I mused.

"Oh, I like him," Kieran said, appearing beside me out of a shadowy mist. "Remind me to exchange contact details with him later."

"Sure, I'll get right on that," I deadpanned.

Kaz jumped out of the plane half a beat later, yelling my name. I immediately took aim, nailing the approaching Alphas with several quick shots that had Kieran whistling beside me.

"Are you here to spectate or do something?" I demanded.

"You want me to help?" he asked innocently. "Won't that take all the enjoyment out of it for you?"

"Yeah, you're right. I'd rather just sit around talking to you while shooting shit." I took aim at another Alpha in the tree line—this one opening fire on my brother's jet—as Kaz tucked and rolled to join us behind the trees.

He glanced at Kieran. "I thought V-Clan wolves liked blood, but you look awfully clean to me."

Kieran grinned. "Do I? I guess I'll have to fix that, hmm?" He disappeared into a whirl of black fog that dissipated on the wind.

Shrieks soon followed, causing my eyebrows to rise as I looked at Kaz. Never in my life had I heard an Alpha male make that kind of noise.

Blood splattered across the airfield, reflected in the low lighting of the setting sun.

Heads rolled in the wake of the shadows.

Then three ebony spires of steam formed in the middle before taking corporeal forms once more. Kieran had his hands tucked into his pockets and stood between his two *Elites*—beings that I now knew were his enforcer equivalents. "Is that better, Alpha Kazek?" Kieran called out conversationally. "Or would you like more blood?"

"Well, he's a joy killer," Kaz muttered.

I snorted. "He's certainly something."

Kieran merely grinned, clearly having heard us, and disappeared again.

"We'd better start running, or he'll kill everyone for us," Kaz said, irritation coloring his tone as he took off at a sprint.

"Is that the only reason you're here?" I asked as I chased after him. "To kill things?"

"Why the hell else would I choose to leave my mate?" he demanded, picking up speed.

"Because you missed me?" I suggested, easily keeping up with his pace.

"Yeah, I definitely miss babysitting you," he agreed. "I

mean, even now, I have to remind you to lead. You're the one with the path, right?"

"Remind me to lead," I repeated in a low grumble. "Prick."

I took over his pace, cutting sharply to the left as I recalled the way to Carlos's primary estate. Enrique and Elias were supposed to meet us outside. Their job was to head down into the prison system while I hunted Carlos.

Ander and Jonas were on Omega duty.

And who the fuck knew what the V-Clan wolves were doing? They had minds of their own and had no interest in planning with us.

Alana hadn't made the trip since she needed to act as Sector Alpha in Kaz's absence. Meanwhile, Ander had appointed Alpha Sam, whom Kat referred to as *Uncle Sammy* because of their familial relation, to lead Andorra in his absence. Normally, that would have gone to Elias, but he'd been tagged for the mission.

More of those shrieks rang out around us, causing Kaz to grumble, "Show-offs."

I almost agreed with him, but I figured we might as well welcome the help. "Remind me never to piss off a V-Clan Alpha," I told him.

"If I need to remind you of that, then you deserve the consequences of it," Kaz tossed back.

I chuckled and nodded. "Fair." I almost said something else, but an explosion rocked the earth, the unexpected impact sending me backward several paces and into a tree with an "Oomph."

Dots blinked in my vision, my ears ringing from the sound. *Land mine*, I vaguely recognized. *Shit.*

We hadn't picked those up on the drones because they were hidden in the earth.

Fucking hell. I landed on my side, my body paralyzed from the impact. I wasn't sure if I'd stepped on one or if Kaz had. I couldn't see or speak to find out.

Something warm touched my abdomen, the liquid pooling over my skin. *Blood.*

An ache stirred inside me, one born of pain and irritation.

Kaz was right to call me a rookie. I'd stepped right into a damn trap. *God damn it.*

I waited for my vision to clear and my ears to stop ringing. Hours seemed to pass. Then finally the trees overhead began to wave in and out before my eyes.

I still couldn't hear, my wolf furious inside me at the intrusion to one of my best senses. The scent of iron pooled beneath my nose, the source my own blood.

A wave of nausea swam over me, leaving me breathless and heaving.

"Get. Up." Kaz's voice in my ear sent a jolt down my spine. "Right fucking now, Mick. Get the fuck up."

I growled, his tone not one I needed or desired right now.

"There's an Infected pit right over there. I'll drop you in it if you don't start to move," he warned.

Your bedside manner is fantastic, I wanted to tell him, but my lips weren't moving.

"*Move*," he demanded, his Alpha energy shivering over me and commanding my spirit.

Only, my wolf snarled back at him, standing up for himself and telling him to fuck right off.

"See, I told you he was fine," Kaz drawled, making me blink.

"He's bleeding out," Elias replied.

"Yeah. He's had worse." Kaz didn't sound worried at all. "Besides, we have healers, yeah?"

I grunted.

Kaz whistled, the sound piercing my already bruised eardrums. "Prince Charming!" he shouted. "Need your medical expertise."

"Aww, you find me charming?" Kieran's familiar tones had me wanting to curl into a ball and die. "Wait until I meet your mate."

"You do not want to play that game with me," Kaz returned, lethality pouring off him. "Fix Mick so we can finish this mission."

"Pretty sure you've already spoiled your stealth approach with all the explosions and whistling," Kieran murmured, his palm settling on my shoulder.

I tried to flinch away from him, not at all keen on having his enchantments running through me, but as the healing essence touched my spirit, I couldn't help but breathe a sigh of relief.

Within seconds, my vision and hearing cleared completely, and I found surrounded by four of our men.

Kaz. Elias. Enrique. Kieran.

The latter kept his palm on me for another beat, then nodded. "Not completely healed, but it'll keep. Just don't step on another party favor, hmm?" He stood and disappeared into a whirl of smoke.

"Useful," Kaz decided out loud with a nod. "Very fucking useful."

"And creepy as fuck," Elias muttered.

Kaz just shrugged and held out his hand. "Ready to dance?"

CHAPTER THIRTY-SIX

KIERAN

The young Alpha and his lethal friend started off toward Carlos's estate again, this time at a steadier and more observant pace.

"Stay with them," I said to Cillian. "Ensure they survive."

"Yes, my liege," he replied with a low bow before dissolving into the shadows.

Lorcan stood on my other side, awaiting instruction.

We could destroy all of Bariloche Sector with a few sweeps of magic, but this conflict among the X-Clan wolves wasn't truly ours to fight. I'd really only come for one reason and one reason alone—*Quinnlynn*.

But to take her out safely, I needed the coast to be clear.

Hence, I'd helped handle a few of the Alphas along the way. Then I'd assisted the young Alpha purely because I liked him. From what I'd seen of Kari, he knew how to properly treat an Omega. Therefore, I'd rewarded him.

Of course, he would owe me a few favors now. And, well, those were always useful.

I slipped over the ground, my black shoes silent on the earth as I moved. Lorcan remained at my back, his insistence to protect me born out of his frustration that I hadn't allowed him to accompany me on my first trip to Andorra Sector.

I didn't need a guard to survive, something I'd proven time and again.

However, I indulged him on this trip, mostly because I wanted backup for my future queen. She was feisty and intelligent and had a knack for escaping me.

Not today, little trickster, I thought at her. *Today, I'm taking you home. Where you belong.*

She couldn't hear me because we hadn't mated yet. But I would be changing that as soon as I put my hands on her.

I allowed my nose to lead me, my instinct to destroy all in my path a playful amusement that taunted my mind. It would be so easy. One spell would send them all to the ground.

Oh, but I wouldn't risk my darling deviant. She thrived beneath chaos, able to escape into the wind without leaving any trace behind.

But I felt her now, her presence a beacon, which took me to a nearby tunnel that led underground.

Come out, come out, wherever you are, I mused, staying to the shadows and allowing my night vision to guide me. It was pitch black, just like my fur, but my eyes were all panther.

The damp coldness lit up like a flame, warning me of rocks and curves and poorly fused traps. Lorcan snorted at one, the trip wire nearly invisible to an untrained eye, but we both caught it well before we reached it. He phased in front of me, dismantling it so I wouldn't have to step over it.

Then we continued our trek, down deep underground where the Omegas were kept in cages, their conditions making my molars grind together. "Free them," I said on a whisper meant for Lorcan's ears alone. "Take them to safety above ground."

My silent companion nodded, going to work shadowing the females out to the airfield, where they would be put on planes destined for better sectors.

This was the pit of Carlos's depravity, the place he sent Omegas who were hurt to recover, which explained my Quinnlynn's presence here. As my destined mate, she had access to healing powers that were meant to be a gift to my betrothed. A family bloodline trait, one not many V-Clan wolves possessed.

I crept forward, following that trace of energy down the hall and to a room with a particularly battered Omega inside.

Quinnlynn glanced up from where she stood, her palm over the other Omega's heart. There wasn't an ounce of shock or surprise in her expression, just a note of resignation accompanied by a plea in her eyes.

"Help me," she begged. "Please help me heal her first."

"You felt my arrival," I murmured, realizing the cause for her lack of a reaction. She'd sensed my approaching energy just as I'd been able to trace her use of my power. It only worked when we were near each other, which was why it had taken me so long to track her down.

She nodded.

"You chose not to run," I added, taking in the scene before me. "You put her life before your own." Because we both knew she could have shadowed away from here the moment she felt my nearness.

Another nod.

"Admirable," I admitted, taking hold of her wrist and moving it away from the girl.

"Kieran, please," she whispered, her heart breaking before my eyes.

"It would be a suitable punishment to make you stand there while she dies," I told her, my voice velvety soft, my anger for this female rising with each passing second in her presence. "Fortunately for you, I'm not that cruel," I said, pressing my free palm to the female and mending the pieces of her broken soul.

Her energy signature warmed my being, whispering her name and history. The familiar pain made it impossible for me to leave her in this state.

"Hmm, you must be Kari's sister." I recognized the similarities in their genetic makeup. But unlike Kari before I'd healed her, this Omega had a mate. An Alpha. The twin of the other. I traced all the links with my mind, then focused on mending the broken one before me.

By the time Lorcan arrived to take her away, she was breathing steadily, the worst of her wounds closed and healing on their own.

"This one goes to Andorra Sector," I told him. "She needs more treatment."

He nodded, disappearing with her and leaving me alone with my errant little mate. "Hello, Quinnlynn. This game of hide-and-seek is growing tiresome, don't you think?"

She blew out a breath, causing the dark hair falling over her cheek to flutter in the breeze. "I don't know. It took you a few decades this round, so I think I'm getting better at it. Shall we go again for a century this time?"

I smiled. "No, little trickster. You hid and I caught you." I pulled her into my arms, my eyes holding her wary gaze. "Game over, princess. I win. Now it's time to go home. *Again.*"

CHAPTER THIRTY-SEVEN

ENRIQUE

Walking through the trees, I realized that this land no longer felt like my own. It was foreign. Abused. Soiled.

The stench of rot had overtaken the leaves, the Infected pits numerous and plentiful and grotesque in their upkeep.

This place was no longer home.

Which meant I was a wolf without a sector. I had no idea where I would go after this. My history hung a black cloud over my head, forbidding me from even asking for sanctuary in certain lands.

Kazek wouldn't accept me.

Ludvig wouldn't either.

Ander might, if I pled my case and performed admirably enough tonight. His Second seemed to like me all right. I'd already negotiated a safe haven for Savi and Joseph; maybe I could add my own name to the list.

A thought for later, I told myself. *Focus.*

The land mines outside Carlos's estate had proven tricky, with one of them already putting Sven on his ass. Fortunately, it was a residual hit. Kazek had seen it lurking a few steps before him and had shot at it with his gun before Sven could step on it.

Still did a number on the young Alpha. But Kieran's creepy voodoo fixed him.

I supposed the V-Clan wolves had their uses, but I absolutely would not be asking for sanctuary in Blood Sector. I'd rather be a lone wolf than surrounded by their crazy magic.

I shivered just thinking about it.

Then I focused on the task at hand, the estate within sight distance. Already we were farther into Carlos's lands than anyone else was allowed to be in Bariloche Sector. He had to know we were coming for him. But every Alpha he sent out to deal with us was taken down by well-trained assassins. It helped that the noncompliant Alphas—the ones previously controlled by narcotics—were fighting on our side, too. They were pissed, and rightfully so.

Your minutes are numbered, I thought at the Sector Alpha.

Two Betas ran out the front doors with weapons in their hands that they quickly tossed away as they made a break for it.

Kazek snorted. "That's what happens when you enslave your people. No loyalty."

"He'll be using the others as a meat shield," I warned him.

"You let me worry about that while you go find your brother," he replied, already moving toward the open door with his gun raised.

Sven moved right along with him, the two obviously trained for combat together.

Shouts and gunfire followed as they entered the house, and Elias leapt after them with his pistol ready. I entered last, not at all surprised to find the remains of several slaves who had probably refused to protect Carlos. Most of them were bleeding out from their throats, his teeth the clear weapon of choice.

"You think I'm going to give you a fair fight in wolf form?" Sven demanded, his focus on the wolf snarling in the corner. "Not a fucking chance."

I snorted. "Game's up, Carlos."

He growled back, clearly not at all pleased to see I'd been the Alpha to help the others attack him.

Fog ignited around us as Carlos deployed one of his safety mechanisms in the form of a toxic gas. But we'd all shot up full of the antivenom before leaving for Bariloche Sector. "It won't work," I called to my former leader. "I already prepared them for all of your tricks."

Elias pulled out two smoke bombs meant to diffuse the toxins, and let them go right next to the snarling wolf in the corner of the room.

They exploded, dissipating the fog and leaving us all unharmed. "Better luck next time," Elias drawled.

Then Sven took aim and put a bullet between the Alpha's eyes.

"Seriously?" Kazek demanded. "Just like that?"

"Yeah," Sven replied, shooting a glance at the other man. "My mentor always told me that I gain nothing by being cocky. Once you have the upper hand, you use it. Don't stall."

A slow smile spread over Kazek's lips. "Sounds like a smart mentor."

"He's the best," Sven countered.

"So fucking true," Kazek agreed, taking his own gun and firing two rounds into Carlos's chest as he finished shifting back to human form. "You still cutting off his head?"

Sven whipped out a knife in response. "Damn straight I am."

Kazek nodded, then glanced at me. "Go find your brother and the others."

I didn't wait, trusting them to safeguard the area while I hunted.

There was no guard at the prison door.

No wolves lurking in the halls.

Just a myriad of cells holding broken Alphas and Betas who had obviously angered Carlos at some point in time. I opened each of their doors, telling them they were free.

Some ran.

Some hobbled.

Most… didn't move.

Including the final cell that held my brother, his broken form held down by chains of silver. He looked starved to the bone, his body warped beneath all the weight of the metal.

"Joseph," I breathed, my heart breaking for him. "Oh… *fuck*."

He wasn't dead.

But he wasn't exactly alive.

He looked half-crazed, his eyes mad with starvation and reminding me of the Infected. I had no doubt he would lunge for me if I freed him, likely just to find something to sink his teeth into.

I wasn't sure how to move him. But he couldn't stay here. The others had already decided to burn this estate to the ground, in addition to several others.

"I'm here," I told him, not sure of how much that helped him. But I needed him to know that I'd finally found him. That I was going to save him. Somehow. Someway. I would *fix* this.

The others eventually found their way down to me, their objective to clear out the cells and help those who couldn't move on their own.

Elias showed up with a syringe meant to calm my brother, his snarls the thing of nightmares. I'd never been one for tears, but I felt them building in my eyes at my broken twin. "He just needs nourishment and his mate," Elias promised.

"He can't see Savi in this condition," I immediately replied. "He'll kill her."

"No, it'll require a very slow reintroduction," he said. "But we have the facilities for it."

I nodded, swallowing.

"And he'll have you there to guide him, too," he added sternly. "Right?"

"Of course he'll be there; he's his brother," Ander said as he came in to help handle my twin. As the strongest X-Clan Alpha among us—other than maybe Kazek—it made sense for him to do this part.

But Kazek showed up to help, the two of them wrestling my sedated, yet still feral, brother from the cage and slowly guided him upstairs. "Would be nice if Kieran hadn't fucked off without a word," Kazek muttered. "Could have used that magic touch right about now."

"We all knew he was here for the V-Clan Omega," Sven replied. "He obviously found her."

Kazek snorted, saying something in return, but my focus was on Joseph.

I'd finally done what I'd set out to do—I'd found my brother.

And now I had no idea what to do next. Heal him, clearly. But then what?

One day at a time, I told myself. *One day at a time.*

CHAPTER THIRTY-EIGHT

SVEN

My body ached as I entered the Andorra Sector dome, my exhaustion hitting me square in the chest. We'd spent the better part of two days cleaning up Bariloche Sector and dividing the refugees into different groups. Medical evacs had come and gone, the majority of them transporting wolves back to Andorra Sector to undergo significant treatment. Those who'd been in better shape had gone to Norse Sector and Winter Sector. And a handful had gone to other allies around the globe, including two Ash Wolves who'd gone to Shadowlands Sector.

The final plane had held a mixture of Omegas from various parts of the world. Enrique had offered to fly them home, saying it was the least he could do for our help in dissolving the situation. He'd return to Andorra Sector sometime next week. My brother had felt it was best because it would keep Enrique occupied while the Andorra physicians dealt with Joseph and Savi.

I flipped the landing gears with a sigh and relaxed into my seat.

"You did good," Kazek said, his tone uncharacteristically serious. "Real good."

My lips quirked up on one side. "So much better than Prague."

"Much better," he agreed. "You only had one minor setback with a bomb. And you didn't get bitten this time."

I snorted. "I didn't get bitten in Prague."

"Uh-huh."

"Teeth in the jeans don't count. He didn't break the skin."

Kazek considered it. "Yeah, all right. Only half a point deducted."

I rolled my eyes. "No points deducted unless they draw blood."

"Did I say that?"

"You did."

"Shit," he drawled. "Guess I need to rethink my rules."

"Why? You have another nest you want to drop me in?"

"Maybe not you, but Winter." He smiled then, his expression dreamy. "She wants to hunt zombies with me."

I chuckled. "That does sound like your kind of date."

"And what's yours?" he asked, unbuckling his seat belt to turn and look pointedly over at the head in a bag on the seat in the back.

"It's a token," I told him. "To prove I'm worthy."

"You don't need a token for that, Mick," he replied. "You're one of the worthiest Alphas I've ever known. Which is a good thing, because I'm not sure who would win a fight between us anymore."

"You," I answered without hesitation. "Because I'd take a knee."

"Yeah," he agreed. "Except I'd take that knee faster, and still win in the end."

I snorted and unfastened my seat belt, ready to get off the damn plane. But Kaz stopped me with a hand on my shoulder. "Winter said I can keep Alana on as my Second." He caught my gaze, that serious expression back. "I'm only accepting because you have a better opportunity in front of you. Otherwise, I'd demand you take the job."

I frowned. "Better opportunity?"

"Come on, Mick. You know your dad's been grooming you. With me and Alana gone, you're the natural choice as his Second in Norse Sector. And I wouldn't be surprised if he intends for you to succeed him someday, too."

I considered his statement and everything my father had set into motion around me. "He's always teaching, isn't he?"

"He really fucking is," Kaz muttered, but I caught the amusement in his gaze. "He called me as a professional courtesy to tell me about the Bariloche Sector plans, saying it only seemed fair since I told him about your call previously."

"Because he knew you'd fly right down to join us for the bloodbath."

"Yep." He grinned. "He knew I wouldn't let anything happen to you, either. But you proved you didn't really need me, apart from the land mine incident."

"And now you'll never let me live that down, will you?"

"Not for a long time, nope. I mean, you almost stepped right on it, kid. It was just three feet—"

"Yeah, yeah, yeah," I said, waving him off as I stood. "You saved my life again. Without you I'm lost. Yada, yada, yada."

He laughed. "I didn't go that far."

"Oh, but you will. Just like you'll never get over fucking Stockholm." I stalked over to grab the bagged head and shot a look over my shoulder. "You left me with a single pistol and stole my plane."

"I borrowed it."

I started toward the exit with him hot on my heels. "And then you chastised me for taking too long."

"Because you were slow," he replied.

"That happens when you're dropped into a damn nest with only six bullets."

"Not my fault you didn't use them wisely."

"Absolutely your fault since I had no warning," I replied, stepping outside as the door opened to populate the stairs.

"You had teeth as a backup," he offered. "And could have shifted to run faster."

I just shook my head. "You will never let me forget it."

"Nope," he drawled. "And now you gave me more to torment you about."

I sighed and started toward the building. Then I paused, thinking better of it, and decided to throw him off our little game. "Thanks for coming with me, Kaz." It was important to say, not just because I meant it, but because I felt like we were officially parting ways. Not for good. Just... walking down two new paths of life.

He studied me.

I studied him back.

Then he nodded. "I'm not going to hug you, Mick."

"Good. I don't like it when you touch me."

He stared at me.

I stared back.

And slowly he smiled. "Hmm, I approve." He clapped me on the shoulder and nodded his head. "Now go get your Omega."

He didn't need to tell me twice. My heart had been on pause for what felt like years without Kari around to revive me. I went straight to the elevator bay and up to our guest suite.

She was waiting for me in the entryway, her eyes filled with so much hope that my chest ached.

My female had grown into a new wolf, one who smiled and believed in a brighter future.

But as her gaze fell to the bag in my hand, I felt that hope melt away just a little. "You did it," she breathed.

"I did," I replied. "And I killed the two physicians who operated on you, too." I'd found her medical records in Carlos's study as we'd gone through all his files and effects prior to prioritizing the groupings for the refugees. "I took a video of them burning, if you want to see it," I told her.

She slowly nodded. "Yes."

I could almost hear Kazek somewhere approving of her need for blood. Perhaps I'd take her on a mission to hunt some Infected one day. It could be a double date with Kaz and Winter.

My lips almost twitched at the thought, but I had something more important to do right now.

I had to help Kari burn the past.

And that started with destroying Carlos's head.

EPILOGUE

KARI

Several Days Later

I stared at the door, studying its hinges and smooth wooden exterior.

Behind it lay a part of me I would never get back. A destroyed soul that had withered and died a painful death. One of my choosing.

Because I was no longer that female.

No longer broken. No longer a shattered fragment of existence. No longer an Omega slave.

But Kari Mickelson, mate to Sven Mickelson.

And we were finally headed home.

I pressed my palm to the wood, saying goodbye for the last time and leaving my old world behind. We'd burned my father's head in that room. I'd cried. Not for the loss, but for the pain he'd inflicted upon me, the destruction he'd wreaked upon my soul, and that dark part of me had perished along with him.

Because he couldn't hurt me anymore.

Sven did that. He saved me. He gave me hope. He

turned me into a new woman, one born of strength and *hope*.

He was the perfect mate, the other half of my soul, and as I turned to face him now, I realized he was my forever.

"I love you," I whispered, telling him the three words I'd held back since saying them to him over the video feed. I'd meant it then, but not like I did now. Part of me had been scared and worried about her mate. But now I knew he was healthy, alive, and very much mine. So I said them with purpose, meaning the heartfelt statement and showing him with my eyes how deep my love for him ran.

He reached for me, pulling me into his arms. "I love you, too," he murmured, his lips ghosting over mine. "Now let's go home."

I nodded.

Norse Sector was where my future lay, and while I still felt that tickle of unease, I chose to trust in my fate. To trust in Sven. To trust in myself and my inner wolf. She'd been there for me when I'd needed her most, and now, I would follow her instincts as well as my own.

"Yes," I said softly, taking his hand. "Let's go home."

With my mate.

With my love.

With my fully healed soul.

The future had never looked brighter. And now I had eternity on my side.

To fate, I thought, glancing one final time at the suite that had changed my life. *To life.*

Thank you for reading *Bariloche Sector,* the final story in the X-Clan series.

Sven and Kari were definitely different for me to write,

their relationship an emotional whirlwind that destroyed me at certain points, but their end was worth the pain and suffering. I hope you found the light in their happily-ever-after. And I hope you'll join me as I continue exploring this world with Kieran and Quinn's story in *Blood Sector*.

I'll also be revisiting this world in *Hunted: Sector World Captives*. Because Enrique's story isn't done. And that plane he just piloted didn't reach its final destination. I'll be joining *USA Today* and International Bestselling Authors Mila Young and Jennifer Thorn on a journey to the islands of the South Pacific where a plane of Omegas has just crash-landed in the heart of feral Alpha territory. The survivors are about to become the hunted...

Blood Sector
A V-Clan Novel

Quinn McNamara
Blood. Death. War.
A dynasty destroyed.
Leaving me as the ultimate prize.

I'm an unmated Omega wolf. A Princess. And destined to
rule. But the remaining Alpha Princes all want to claim
me, their brutal methods terrifying and cruel.

I've spent the last century running, hiding in places where
no one would think to look.
Only *he* found me. Prince Kieran, the most powerful shifter
of them all.

Our game of hide-and-seek has come to an end.
It's time for me to submit. Or to die fighting.

Kieran O'Callaghan

My little trickster escaped me once. She indulged in a dangerous game of chase throughout the sectors, but I've finally found my prize.

Poor little darling thought I valued chivalry and courting. I'm an Alpha Prince. I take what I want, when I want it, however I want it. And her sweet blood beckons the predator within me to destroy all her dreams of a happily-ever-after.

Let the Princes enjoy their Royal V-Wars.
As long as they bow to me as King of Blood Sector, I won't intervene.
Besides, I have a new pretty little Omega to tame. It's time to put a crown on her and make her my queen.

Author's Note: *This is a standalone dark shifter romance with Omegaverse themes. Kieran is an unapologetic Alpha Prince, and Quinn is a feisty Omega Princess. It's a match made in literal hell, where the antihero is the king.*

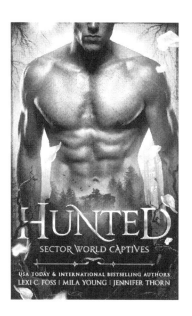

HUNTED
SECTOR WORLD CAPTIVES

Three standalone novels.
One world full of depravity and darkness.

Welcome to the South Islands, home to the most lethal Alphas on the planet.
These beings don't play nice with others. They've been banished.
And a plane full of Omegas just crash-landed in their isles.

We're being hunted.
Their feral growls follow us.
Their howls haunt us.
Their knots call to us.
And their savagery terrifies us.

Some will escape.
Some will be caught.
Three will be *claimed*.

This shared-world experience contains dark themes, Omegaverse vibes, unforgiving Alphas, and the Omegas who defy them.

LEXI C FOSS

USA Today Bestselling Author Lexi C. Foss loves to play in dark worlds, especially the ones that bite. She lives in Chapel Hill, North Carolina with her husband and their furry children. When not writing, she's busy crossing items off her travel bucket list, or chasing eclipses around the globe. She's quirky, consumes way too much coffee, and loves to swim.

Want access to the most up-to-date information for all of Lexi's books? Sign-up for her newsletter here.

Lexi also likes to hang out with readers on Facebook in her exclusive readers group - Join Here.

Where To Find Lexi:
www.LexiCFoss.com

Book One: Blood Laws

Book Two: Forbidden Bonds

Book Three: Blood Heart

Book Four: Blood Bonds

Book Five: Angel Bonds

Book Six: Blood Seeker

Book Seven: Wicked Bonds

Immortal Curse World - Short Stories & Bonus Fun

Elder Bonds

Blood Burden

Mershano Empire Series - Contemporary Romance

Book One: The Prince's Game

Book Two: The Charmer's Gambit

Book Three: The Rebel's Redemption

Midnight Fae Academy - Reverse Harem

Ella's Masquerade

Book One

Book Two

Book Three

Book Four

Noir Reformatory - Ménage Paranormal Romance

The Beginning

First Offense

Second Offense

Underworld Royals Series - Dark Paranormal Romance

Happily Ever Crowned

Happily Ever Bitten

X-Clan Series - Dystopian Paranormal

Andorra Sector

X-Clan: The Experiment

Winter's Arrow

Bariloche Sector

Hunted

V-Clan Series - Dystopian Paranormal

Blood Sector

Vampire Dynasty - Dark Paranormal

Violet Slays

Sapphire Slays

Crossed Fates

First Bite of Revenge

Other Books

Scarlet Mark - Standalone Romantic Suspense

Rotanev - Standalone Poseidon Tale

Carnage Island - Standalone Reverse Harem Romance

Printed in Great Britain
by Amazon